MOTHER'S DAY

T.J. EMERSON

Boldwood

First published in 2018. This edition published in Great Britain in 2023 by Boldwood Books Ltd.

Cover Design by Head Design Ltd

Cover Photography: Shutterstock and istock

A CIP catalogue record for this book is available from the British Library.

Paperback ISBN 978-1-78513-701-3

Large Print ISBN 978-1-78513-700-6

Hardback ISBN 978-1-78513-699-3

Ebook ISBN 978-1-78513-702-0

Kindle ISBN 978-1-78513-703-7

Audio CD ISBN 978-1-78513-694-8

MP3 CD ISBN 978-1-78513-695-5

Digital audio download ISBN 978-1-78513-698-6

Boldwood Books Ltd
23 Bowerdean Street
London SW6 3TN
www.boldwoodbooks.com

For Patricia

PART I

1

THEN

Friday 15 September, Royal Edinburgh Hospital

What would she say if she were with me? I imagine it sometimes – the two of us together. A reckless delusion, but I can't help myself. My image of her is never a clear one. How could it be? Sometimes she has my dark hair and brown eyes; sometimes she is a stranger.

In this fantasy, we are sitting together at a kitchen table. The heart of any home. In this fantasy, she is calm and willing to listen. I try to explain why I did what I did to her. I describe the circumstances, give her my reasons.

After a while, she holds up her hand. Her reproachful silence is a demand for truth. No more excuses.

I confess. I tell her that I had to survive. I say that in the end it was either her or me.

I chose me.

2

GRACE

September, twenty years later

I am abandoning her. Leaving her to the care of strangers. Leaving her here in this tiny room, the last space she will ever inhabit.

I have no choice. I have no choice and this is the best place for her. These are the facts, but the facts don't stop me feeling guilty.

She is sitting upright in the narrow single bed, held captive by the television fixed to the wall opposite. News 24 is on mute, white headlines tacking along the screen as soldiers in green uniforms dodge the smoking entrails of burnt-out cars.

'You've got a perfect view of the TV there,' I say.

She glances at me, bewildered.

'We're at Birch Grove Care Home,' I explain. 'You moved here from the hospital this morning.'

'I know, Grace. I know where I am.' Her wavering voice suggests otherwise. The effort of birthing the words leaves her wheezing, her tired lungs struggling to do what she once took for granted.

This woman is my mother, but sometimes I hardly recognise her. She no longer looks like an older version of herself; she just looks old. White wispy curls have replaced her black hair. Withered breasts hang defeated beneath her yellow nightgown. Only her dark brown eyes have remained unchanged. We still have those in common.

'I hope you like what I've done with the room,' I say. 'I wanted it to feel homely.' Mum's gaze doesn't budge from the screen. 'It's very cosy in here,' I add.

The ground-floor room is stifling. An overheated pharaoh's tomb, a stopgap between worlds, crammed with treasured possessions – family photographs, a collection of Neil Diamond CDs, a wooden crucifix hanging above the bed.

I rearrange the framed photographs on the sideboard. Mum and Dad's wedding portrait, my graduation picture, an assortment of holiday snaps of the three of us. I can barely recognise myself in my graduation picture. My face was much fuller then, and my hair reached down to my waist. A year later, I had it shorn into a pixie cut, a style I have kept ever since.

'Why aren't you at school?' Mum says. Is she in the present, asking why I'm not teaching, or does she think I'm a child again? She keeps travelling in time, random leaps that make me anxious. No telling where she might end up.

The TV claims her. I cross to the window and press my palms against the cool glass. Outside, the sky is a grey lid, sealed shut. Not long until the last of the evening light disappears. What time should I leave? A fast train from Brentham station will get me into London in half an hour. All I want to do is get back to the flat, pour myself a glass of red wine and drink it while soaking in a hot bath. All I want to do is climb into bed beside Mum, wrap her arms around me and beg her to never let me go.

* * *

Half an hour later, I'm sitting in the green armchair beside the bed. My head is muzzy, my legs leaden – Mum's energy taking hold of me. The room is slipping into darkness, but I cannot motivate myself to reach over and switch on the bedside lamp. Bored and petulant, I feel thirteen not forty-two, but the time for such childishness has passed.

Mum is my responsibility now; I've signed legal documents that say so.

I twist the silver puzzle ring on my right ring finger back and forth. An old habit. 'They've got loads of activities here, Mum,' I say, 'plenty for you to get involved in.'

'Don't think so, dear,' she replies, the dim light of the TV flickering across her face. She isn't stupid. She knows as well as I do that she has come here to die, and that it won't be long. A severe chest infection could finish her. The consultant at the hospital told me she probably wouldn't last the winter.

Screams erupt in the corridor, high-pitched and piercing. Panic flares beneath my ribcage. Outside the door, a few members of staff arrive and pacify the offending resident. *There, there, Mrs Palethorpe, let's get you back to your room.* My pulse thrums in my ears. I wait for it to settle before standing up and leaning over the bed. 'Bye for now.' Mum's cheek is warm against my lips. 'See you soon.' A rap on the door.

'Come in,' I say, as it swings open. The slight figure of a girl hovers in the corridor, her pale face luminous in the gloom. For a split second, I wonder if she is even real.

'Hiya, Mrs Walker.' The girl steps into the room and flicks on the overhead light, flooding us with brightness and life. 'I'm Emma. One of the care assistants here.'

Emma's dark, cropped hair frames a friendly, heart-shaped face. She wears a short-sleeved lilac tunic over black leggings. Lilac slouch socks spill over the top of her white trainers. Behind her in the corridor stands a trolley laden with large steel flasks and cartons of fruit juice. 'Lovely to meet you,' she says, pushing her fringe to one side.

'You too,' I reply, but she is looking at Mum.

'Anything to drink, Mrs Walker?' she asks.

Mum ignores her.

'Sorry,' I say. I can't help apologising for Mum. I want people to know she wasn't always this rude. That manners once mattered to her.

Emma smiles. 'That's all right. It's been a long day, hasn't it, Mrs Walker?'

'Please, call her Polly,' I say, 'and I'm Grace.' Emma asks me what

Mum likes to drink, and I advise strong tea with half a sugar. 'She's fussy about her tea, I'm afraid.'

'She's allowed to be fussy, aren't you, sweetheart?' Emma has the local Essex accent, the one my parents never let me acquire, even though my dad spoke with it. Her high, girlish voice suggests she isn't long out of school. Hard to say how old she is.

'So, Polly,' Emma says, 'strong tea with half a sugar?'

Mum remains silent. A protest perhaps at how small her world has become. A world in which the topic of tea can sustain a lengthy conversation.

'What about you, Grace?' Emma asks. 'Bet you could do with a drink?'

Her concerned tone undoes me. My throat is hot and tight, an omen of tears to come. Emma must sense them too because she pulls a tissue from her tunic pocket and hands it to me. I shove it in the back pocket of my jeans, determined not to need it.

'Moving day is well tough for the relatives,' she says, 'but remember you can come and see her as much as you like.'

'I'll only be coming on Saturdays for a while.' Why am I telling this to a stranger? 'The past few months... There's been all the hospital visits and social services to deal with, and I recently started a new job so—'

'You need a break, course you do. That's why I'm here, isn't it, Polly?'

Mum tears her gaze from the TV and looks at Emma for the first time. She watches as the girl hurries out to the tea trolley and returns with a white beaker.

'Let's try you without a straw first,' Emma says.

She places the beaker on the bedside table and rearranges Mum's sitting position. She is stronger than her petite frame suggests and has no trouble easing Mum forward as she rearranges the pillows. 'Right,' she says, picking up the beaker, 'let's see if my tea is up to your standards.'

Mum's expression is curious, thoughtful. 'Call me Grandma,' she says.

My stomach knots. Emma freezes, the beaker clutched in her hand. Poor girl looks lost for words, but just as I'm about to speak she giggles.

'I'm sure you'd be an awesome gran, but I'm going to call you Polly. Shame not to use such a lovely name.'

'Grandma.' Mum's face darkens.

'Mum, this is Emma.' My harsh delivery startles me. Mum, full of fury, jabs a finger in my direction.

'No,' she says. 'No.'

'How about a drink?' Emma says, but Mum's hand shoots out and knocks the beaker away. Tea cascades down the front of Emma's tunic. She gasps as Mum forms a fist and drives it against her chest.

'Mum. Stop it.' I step forward just as Emma backs away from the bed and stumbles over the chair. I catch her as she falls, her body light in my arms. 'I'm so sorry,' I say, helping her upright. 'Are you okay?'

'I'm fine.'

I keep hold of her arm, even though she is out of danger now. Her wide brown eyes gaze up at me. I sense a pull deep inside, a fish hook tugging at my guts. Without thinking, I reach out and brush her fringe away from her forehead.

'Sorry,' Mum gasps, 'I'm sorry.'

Emma breaks away from me and rushes over to the bed. 'It's all right, darlin'. I know, I know.'

'She didn't mean it,' I say. 'She'd never hurt anyone. Not physically.'

'It's not your fault, Polly,' Emma says. 'You've had a difficult day.'

Mum emits a pitiful sob, and I struggle to hold back my own tears.

'This is so hard,' I say.

'Bless your hearts,' Emma murmurs. 'The two of you must be very close?'

I hesitate, wondering if Mum might speak, but she is lost in her loud, ruinous tears.

'Yes,' I say, 'we are.'

We were close, many years ago, so this is not a total lie.

3

CASSIE

July

There she was. My mother. Sitting in the café at the heart of the Museum of Childhood in Bethnal Green. I'd found her. So many years apart, and finally there we were. Cassie Harrington and her mother, about to have lunch together. I could hardly believe it. She couldn't have chosen a more fitting place for us to visit. My second favourite tourist attraction in the whole of London.

She looked so out of place. A child-free woman, surrounded by tables packed with parents and their manic offspring. She glanced around her, seeming so lost and uncomfortable I almost felt sorry for her.

I'd hoped we might enjoy our lunch alone, but shortly after my mother arrived, her friend turned up. From the way they hugged and the frenzied tone of their greetings I could tell they hadn't seen each other for some time. I stayed in position at the table behind hers, sipping my Earl Grey tea, observing my mother as she chose her lunch at the café counter and carried it back to the table on a tray, unaware of me watching her.

The museum throbbed with the shrieking, squealing and laughter of the hyped-up children bouncing around it. The iron-frame structure soaring overhead kept the noise trapped beneath it. The two floors of galleries that rose up either side of us were packed. Visitors leaned on the railings, gazing down at us in the open-plan space below. Hordes of primary school kids waving worksheets pelted round the outskirts of the café before veering off to explore the glass display cabinets on the first floor. Every Saturday for the past nine weeks, I'd trailed the exhibits there, marvelling at the toys and games of the past as well as those of my own era. Imagining the other childhoods I might have had and the mother I might have spent them with.

The general din smothered most of the conversation at my mother's table, but I picked up the odd exchange. Her friend – a Californian woman called Zoe dressed in flowery yoga pants – explained that the museum was just round the corner from her brother's flat so she thought it would be an easy place to meet.

'It's fine,' my mother said. 'The food's pretty good.'

I pointed my phone in my mother's direction and took what I knew would be the first of many pictures. She looked good for her age. Tall, quite slim. Hadn't let herself go. I couldn't help making comparisons between us. She had short, dark hair, while mine fell in thick blonde waves past my shoulders. I felt betrayed by my bright blue eyes but reasoned that lots of daughters have different-coloured eyes than their mothers.

My mother and Zoe reminisced about Singapore. Sounded like they'd lived there at the same time.

'Honestly, Grace,' Zoe said, 'we haven't had half as much fun since you left.'

Grace. Such a beautiful name.

A man and a small, blond-haired boy occupied the table to my mother's left. The child, happy and boisterous, clapped his hands together and began to chant at full volume.

'Alfie the bear,' he said, 'Alfie the bear. Alfie, Alfie, Alfie the bear.'

The chanting continued. The boy's father, eyes fixed on his phone, made no attempt to quieten his son, an error that earned him black looks from my mother and her friend.

'This is my idea of hell,' my mother said in a stage whisper, and they both laughed.

I'd always wondered how she'd act around kids, and now I knew. Her flippant comment hurt me, and I began to wonder why I'd bothered. Why did I want to be with her anyway, after what she'd done to me?

The boy stood up on his chair. 'Alfie the bear,' he yelled, 'Alfie the bear.' His father looked up from his mobile and gave him a half-hearted order to sit down. 'Alfie,' the boy continued, 'Alfie, Alfie, Alfie the—'

His chair tipped backwards, sending him flying. His father reached out, but my mother got there first, catching the boy as he fell. I smiled, thrilled and relieved at this demonstration of her maternal instinct.

After my mother had lowered the boy to the ground and the father had stopped thanking her, she sat down again and rolled her eyes at Zoe. They continued the conversation as if nothing had happened, but I could tell the incident had unnerved her. She didn't finish her lunch, and she kept checking her watch when Zoe wasn't looking.

When they stood up and strolled towards the museum entrance, I joined them, pleased to overhear that Zoe's visit to the UK was only a flying one. As they said their goodbyes, my mother assured her friend they would see each other soon.

'Absolutely,' Zoe agreed. She walked away, stopping once to wave before she disappeared from our sight. My mother turned to go in the opposite direction and then hesitated. She glanced back at the museum entrance, and I could see how much she wanted to explore the place. How it had cast its spell on her.

Giving in to herself, she dashed inside. I waited, not wanting to follow too close. When I did enter the main building, she came storming towards me in a hurry, her face tight and angry. As if she couldn't cope with what the museum and its contents must have reminded her of. As if she had to get out of there as soon as she could.

***

Our first day out together didn't end there. After leaving the museum, we took the Tube from Bethnal Green. Two line changes later, we exited the Underground at Angel and turned left. At the end of Upper Street, we turned left again onto City Road. Unfamiliar with the area, I took pictures of the street signs for future reference.

We crossed over to Goswell Road and kept going, the traffic relentless at our side. She set a fast pace in her trainers, and I struggled to keep up in my wedge sandals. Trust me to have a mother who'd rather walk than catch the bus.

The late afternoon sun still had a sting, and before long my pink shift dress was sticking to my back and stomach. My mother marched on ahead, unruffled in grey linen trousers and a white T-shirt, her arms swinging at her sides.

We turned left into Lever Street and a few minutes later took another left towards a block of high-rise flats. After passing an Astroturf pitch surrounded by a wire fence, my mother headed for the front entrance of the grubby white block. Northfield Heights. I waited by a row of recycling bins while she entered a code into a keypad by the front door.

As soon as she disappeared inside, I hurried over to the area of patchy grass and trees in front of her block – the optimistically named North Green Park. I spotted a metal bench partly hidden by a droopy oak and got myself settled. To my right and left stood four-storey blocks of flats. Satellite dishes clung to their balconies, fighting for space with dead plants and racks of washing. Hardly the nicest of areas and not where I'd pictured my mother residing.

My eyes scanned her building, looking for a sign. Where was she? My body shook and a wave of nausea rolled through me. Fear or excitement? I was twenty years old, but felt reborn. As though my life had just begun.

A light flicked on and off again in one of the upper windows of the building. I counted upwards to the ninth floor. My mother? The usual emptiness hovered at my edges. I wrapped my arms around myself and tried to hug it away.

Then she appeared at the window.

I spy with my little eye. Something beginning with G.

I decided then and there to buy some binoculars. My mother stared out of the window for some time, off into the distance. She probably thought she was looking at the view, but I knew better. She was searching for something. She was searching for me.

4

GRACE

September

Where the hell is my front door key? It jangles as I search my handbag but won't give itself up.

'Oh, come on.' After a long day of teaching – two intermediate classes and one beginners – I'm desperate to get into the flat and unwind. My fingers locate the jagged outline of the key, which has slipped through a tear in the handbag's lining and now lies trapped behind the silky fabric. This keeps happening, but I never get round to repairing the offending hole. Removing the key will entail taking everything out of the bag.

I give up and turn to the potted rubber plant next to the front door. Hidden in the grey stones at the base of the plant is my key safe, a fake stone in a slightly darker grey than the rest. I take it out, open the compartment on the stone's flat base and remove the spare key hidden there for emergencies. With my track record, I make regular use of it.

The front door only opens halfway, hindered by the morning's post. Crouching down, I gather up the envelopes and takeaway leaflets, holding them against my chest as I traipse along the hallway, finally depositing them next to the tall vase of lilies on the breakfast bar that separates the narrow kitchen from the living room.

Dumping my leather jacket, backpack and handbag on the floor, I turn the living room radiator on to banish the early autumn chill. God knows how cold this place will be when winter kicks in. The gas boiler that powers the heating and water is ancient and fickle, but I tolerate it because the ex-council property is cheap and, as I keep reminding myself, temporary. After the short walk to Islington High Street, it's only another thirty minutes down Pentonville Road to the Capital School of English. Plenty of buses to catch en route if the weather's bad. The flat came furnished too. Handy, as I moved in with only a suitcase and rucksack. Two small boxes of books have arrived from Singapore since then but I've yet to open them.

I fetch a glass of water from the kitchen and sip it while sorting through the post – money requests from Oxfam and Greenpeace and a letter redirected from Mum's old address, enquiring if Mrs Polly Walker would like to renew her subscription to *Baking World* magazine.

My chest aches. No, she will not be renewing the subscription. Mrs Polly Walker is still alive, but Mrs Polly Walker's life is over. No more browsing through recipes for cupcakes and fruit tea loaf. No more baking the perfect Victoria sponge. I drop the letter onto the breakfast bar, resolving to deal with it later. Sometimes the more trivial demands of acting as Mum's power of attorney are the most upsetting. Right now I'd give anything for a brother or sister to talk to. Someone to call and share tearful laughter with about *Baking World* magazine. We could reminisce about Mum's culinary skills – safe territory. Yes, we would say, she was difficult sometimes, but her Victoria sponge was a winner.

There is no one to call. The memories of my mother, good and bad, are mine alone. Morbid questions creep up on me. Who will sort through my post when I die? Who will tie up my loose ends?

The sound of chirping crickets fills the room. Abandoning the post, I kneel down and rummage through my handbag for my mobile. My hands tremble as I pull it out. Always that flood of nerves, always the possibility of answering the phone to someone from Birch Grove and hearing that Mum's weary body has finally surrendered. The call both feared and hoped for.

My phone displays an unfamiliar number. 'Hello?' I say.

'It's me.'

I let a few seconds pass before saying, 'John?' As if I didn't recognise his voice straight away. 'You shouldn't be calling me.'

'You shouldn't have given me your number then.'

'No, I shouldn't have.'

In the pause that follows, I recall his hot breath in my ear.

His hoarse voice whispering my name.

'Guess where I'm calling from?' he asks. I guess but don't reply. 'My car,' he says.

The two of us squashed onto the back seat of his VW Golf, a jumble of limbs and half-discarded clothing, laughing at the windows steaming up around us.

'Look,' I say, 'that was fun—'

'It's not just that.' He is quiet now, sincere. 'I enjoyed talking to you.'

'I enjoyed talking to you, but that's not the point.' Or maybe it is. Maybe it wouldn't hurt to stay on the phone and talk to him again. Last night I spoke to a woman from an Indian call centre for ten minutes, just to pass the time. The woman's voice was warm and comforting, and to listen to it for longer I answered her marketing survey questions – I don't own a car, I use a MacBook Air, my mobile provider is Vodafone.

'You understand what I'm going through,' John says.

I sigh. 'Please don't call me again.'

'I'll see you soon though. We can hardly avoid each other.'

'Goodbye, John.'

I hang up and pour a glass of Merlot. The bottle is half empty, which is odd, as I rarely drink during the week. I thought I'd only had one glass out of it at the weekend but must have drunk more. Opening the door next to the kitchen sink, I step out onto the narrow balcony. A raw gust of wind attacks. I turn my face to it, take a sip of wine. Too weary to analyse my conversation with John, I decide that what happened between us was just a one-off. A mistake best forgotten.

I try to lose myself in the view. Tower blocks with golden windows and cranes studded with blinking lights litter the North London skyline. In the distance, illuminated, the dome of St Paul's. Stunning. Not quite as dramatic as the outlook from the twenty-first-storey flat I rented in Singapore, but at least I'm still high up. Out of reach.

I miss my old life. Humid evenings in Chinatown with the other teachers from the English Language Institute, washing down dim sum and chilli crab with bottles of Tiger Beer. Weekend trips to Malaysian islands and longer holidays exploring the parts of South East Asia I hadn't already visited or lived in. Hard to believe I've been back in the UK for five months. Five months in limbo. Unable to settle and unable to move on. Dad's death twenty-two years ago – a heart attack in his sleep – was swift and unexpected. Mum's demise is like waiting on a cold station platform for a slowly approaching train.

Screams, laughter and aggressive rap drift up from the park. Teenagers crowd round one of the benches, cigarette and spliff tips glowing. Seven years since my last cigarette, but I still suffer the occasional craving. Still linger on the balcony most nights in echo of an abandoned ritual, just to look at the view and let the day drain away.

* * *

Glass empty, I return indoors to get changed, swapping my work outfit of black jeans and a grey batwing top for grey tracksuit bottoms and a black sweatshirt. Grey Uggs replace my black ankle boots.

After putting a vegetable lasagne in the oven to heat up, I continue sorting through the post. When I lift up a brochure offering promotions from a nearby supermarket, a white A4 envelope falls onto the breakfast bar. I rip it open and pull out a card.

On the front, a heart made of pink roses. Beneath it a greeting in thick, pink letters.

HAPPY MOTHER'S DAY

I stare at the card, confused. Mother's Day is months away and besides, who would send me a Mother's Day card? I'm not a mother.

Inside, the card is blank. I examine the front of the envelope. My name and address printed on a label, the blurred postmark illegible.

My forehead begins to throb.

I carry the card and envelope to the hall cupboard. Junk mail, I tell myself, as I shove them into the red recycling box. Just junk.

5

CASSIE

July

The back of the silver picture frame slid into place with a click. I turned it over and gazed at the photo of my mother and me. My face took up most of the shot, but I could still see her, two seats behind me on the bus, oblivious.

The sound of light snoring drifted through from my bedroom. I placed the photograph inside the writing bureau and closed the lid. Wandering naked around the living room, I gathered up socks and boxer shorts, black skinny jeans and a blue-and-black-checked shirt. They all ended up in a heap on the brown leather lounge chair.

I paused for a moment in front of one of the sash windows and looked out into Highbury Fields. Joggers and dog walkers were out in force, even though it was almost 11 p.m.

'Hey.' Ryan appeared in the bedroom doorway, a towel round his waist and a shy grin on his face. 'Sorry about that. I don't usually fall asleep.'

'Well, you did give quite the performance,' I said with a smile.

He laughed. 'You were pretty good yourself,' he said in his Aussie drawl.

I'd given him the kind of sex he would remember. Offered myself in positions that would keep him coming back. 'What about this joint you promised me?' I said.

'Absolutely.' He spotted his clothes on the chair and retrieved a tobacco tin from the front pocket of his shirt. 'Is that an Eames?' he asked, nodding at the chair.

'An original.'

He whistled in appreciation.

I lay on the wide, white sofa and beckoned him to join me. 'This flat is amazing,' he said.

'It is.' Amazing because I could get to my mother's flat in half an hour on foot, less if I took the bus and less again if I went by taxi.

'I love Georgian architecture,' he said, gazing up at the high, corniced ceiling. 'Is this your place?'

'It's a rental. I've only been here a couple of weeks.'

He took in the rest of the room, commenting on its size and admiring the white marble fireplace opposite the sofa. 'The rent must cost you a ton?'

'It belongs to Quentin. My... my father.'

I rested my pale calves on Ryan's tanned thighs while he pieced together a joint of pungent grass with the same earnest attention he gave to his lattes and cappuccinos. Every now and then he touched the black feathered wings tattooed across his smooth chest, as if to check they hadn't flown away. Swirls of italic writing covered his arms, but I couldn't be bothered to read them.

This morning, I didn't even know Ryan's name. He was just a waiter in Aroma on Islington High Street, my mother's favourite café. A trendy place – exposed stone walls, mismatched china cups and saucers. My mother and I had visited it together on several occasions: she at a table by the window, me on the café's mezzanine level. I'd noticed Ryan straight away with his blond quiff, goatee beard and warm smile. My mother liked him too. Whenever he brought over her tea, they would chat for a while, and when she laughed, he laughed with her. My mother had a raucous, infectious laugh and a husky voice that commanded attention. Embarrassing, the two of them flirting like that, especially at her age.

This morning, as I'd watched Ryan show my mother one of his tattoos, I had no idea we would end up in bed together. I don't know why I gave him my phone number and made it obvious what he could expect if he called it. Maybe I wanted to be closer to my mother, to feel part of her life. After two weeks of surveillance, we'd only exchanged three sentences and touched once. I knew I had to be patient but couldn't help wanting more.

Ryan flipped open his gold Zippo and lit the joint. After a quick drag he passed it to me. 'Here you go.'

The grass soon had me giggling. I tried not to think about the promise I'd made Dr Costello – no drugs other than those he prescribed to me. Body buzzing, I handed the joint back to Ryan.

'You're bloody cute,' he said.

'Don't ever call me cute,' I replied and asked him a few questions about his life. He turned out to be quite the talker after a few tokes. I discovered he was twenty-three and a recent graduate in media and communications from the University of Sydney. His maternal grandfather came from Birmingham, and Ryan had always wanted to come to the UK. He'd arrived in London eight months ago and now lived in Finsbury Park with his friend and fellow Arsenal fan Nick. They were researching the idea of starting a coffee-roasting business together. Ryan said he considered making coffee an art form, and I blamed my laughter on the spliff.

'I love London,' he said. 'Reckon I could stay here for good.' He described the dull Sydney suburb he grew up in, talked fondly of his parents and his two older sisters. 'Where are your family from?' he asked.

I sat up, reached between his legs and took hold of him with a grip that made him groan. 'Oh Christ,' he said when I took him in my mouth. 'Oh fuck,' he gasped, as he emptied himself.

* * *

Afterwards, as Ryan dozed on the sofa, my phone buzzed from the top of the writing bureau. I checked it and found a text from Quentin:

Hope all well. Skype soon? Any probs with flat just ring agency.

I didn't reply.

Taking care not to make any noise, I reached into the bureau drawer and removed my scrapbook with its shiny silver cover. I wasn't in the mood for poring over my past, so I ignored the front of the scrapbook and opened it from the back instead. There I found the leaflet for the Museum of Childhood and, on the next page, a cinema ticket for the old film my mother and I had watched together a few days ago. That famous rom-com from the 1980s where the woman fakes an orgasm in a café. My mother hadn't struck me as the romantic type, but it takes time to get to know someone. Halfway through, she'd removed her scarf from around her shoulders and draped it on the back of her chair. It fell to the floor in front of me. Right onto my boots. I considered picking it up and holding it close but couldn't risk her turning round and catching me. Instead I let it lie there, a dark coiled thing, until the credits rolled and she stood up.

'You dropped your scarf,' I said, bending down to retrieve it. The scarf was deep red in colour and the soft, light fabric had to be cashmere. 'Here.'

'Thanks.' As she took it, the tips of my fingers touched her hand. First contact. Her clammy skin, the cool metal of her ring.

'You're welcome,' I said, but she had already reached the end of her row and was on her way out. I dropped back into my seat, savouring the delicious tingling in my fingertips until the lights came up and an impatient usher asked me to leave.

6

GRACE

September

'All tickets please.' The conductor rests a hand on the seat in front of me, displaying long nails painted like Union Jacks. I hold out my ticket, but she barely glances at it before moving on.

The 9.30 a.m. from Liverpool Street to Norwich will reach Brentham in fifteen minutes. Every Saturday I pray for a delay of some kind to cut short my visiting time, but it never happens.

I jump as a train clatters past in the opposite direction, packed with people heading for the capital. Further down the carriage, a baby wails. Reaching into my bag, I remove the white A4 envelope that arrived this morning.

Unease ripples through my bloodstream as I tear into it. Inside is a leaflet advertising the Museum of Childhood. My breath catches, but then I remember meeting Zoe there for lunch a few months ago. A fun reunion, but we could have picked a better venue. So much noise and then a little boy at the next table fell on me, leaving my shoulder bruised for a week. To top it all, I left my sunglasses in there. An expensive pair I'd saved for ages to afford. I rushed back to the café as soon as I realised, but someone must have taken them. I gave my contact details to the girl at reception in case the glasses turned up, but she must have put me on the mailing list instead.

Relieved, I slide the leaflet back in the envelope. Silly to get worked up over nothing.

* * *

Birch Grove is roughly a thirty-minute walk from Brentham station, but I take the longer route through the town centre. The high street is already crowded with shoppers enjoying the warm sun and fresh autumn breeze.

I walk past an Apple shop, formerly the Woolworths where I had my first Saturday job. Brentham's population must have tripled since those days. Housing developments for commuters have taken over former car parks and patches of wasteland. Factories that made ball bearings during the war are now luxury apartments. The engineering firm Dad worked for has survived, although it's now located miles away in some industrial estate.

WHSmith is still here too. Mum got a part-time job there when I started at the grammar school, went full-time when I began university and remained there until retirement.

Half an hour later, I reach an estate of 1970s houses. Streets and cul-de-sacs of identical detached homes in light brown brick. The house I grew up in is one of them, but instead of going there now, I carry on through the estate until I reach Birch Grove.

The care home is a two-storey, L-shaped building with a car park at the front and a small garden at the back. Ten years ago, during Birch Grove's construction, Mum declared the white concrete structure ugly and insisted it wouldn't weather well. The building's shabby façade has proved her right. Black streaks stain the concrete beneath the windows, like smudged mascara beneath teary eyes. But the interior of Birch Grove is clean and purpose-built and much better than the other places I looked at.

Hot, thick air assaults me when I step inside. Ammonia and floral air freshener battle for dominance. One of the cleaners, the ironically named Memory, is wiping down a high-backed chair in the reception area with a disinfectant spray. Wide-hipped and stoic, she rubs at a brown stain with a sigh.

I glance along the two corridors that lead in opposite directions away from reception, wondering if John might appear. He doesn't, and I'm not sure if I'm relieved or disappointed.

'Do you have an appointment?' Sitting at a desk by the front door is Brenda, who still thinks she's a receptionist for a stockbroking firm in the city. She scowls, impatient, her black hair standing on end. 'Have you got an appointment?'

'She does indeed.' Kegs, the manager, waves at me from his cluttered office, and I wave back. Short and stocky with a shaved head, Kegs looks nothing like the other managers I met while vetting care homes. Tattoos of parachutes decorate his forearms, inky reminders of his years as a paratrooper.

Last week he told me running an old folks' home was tougher than his tours of Northern Ireland and Iraq.

Brenda turns the pages of a non-existent diary. 'Mr Armstrong will see you now,' she says.

* * *

'We'll soon have you looking gorgeous.' Emma lifts the index finger of Mum's left hand and applies a coat of pearly pink varnish to the yellowing nail.

'I can't believe you persuaded her to put some proper clothes on,' I say. 'And to get up.' Mum, dressed in grey trousers, a white blouse and a pink jumper, is sitting in the armchair with Emma perched on a stool beside her.

'And we've had a shower, haven't we?' Emma says. Mum blinks, too engrossed in the news to answer Emma's question. What is it about old people and the news? Even before the dementia, she spent hours every day soaking up the doom, hate and violence. Maybe the closer the elderly get to death, the more they need to convince themselves the world isn't worth living in.

'Thanks for doing her nails too,' I say from my seat by the window. 'She always liked them neat.'

Emma shrugs. 'No probs. I do all the women in here.'

'It's very good of you.' Despite that first shaky encounter, Mum and Emma get on well. Mum seems calmer when Emma is around, and I'm always grateful for the distraction her cheery banter provides. 'I'm rubbish at anything beauty-related,' I say. 'I never do my own nails.'

'I thought about being a beautician once,' Emma says, 'but no way could I wax people's hairy bits. Gross.'

Over the past two weeks, I've discovered Emma is nineteen – older than I thought – and that after working in shops and cafés since leaving school, she's decided to get some experience in a care home. She hasn't been at Birch Grove long but says if she likes it, she might do a foundation course in Health and Social Care at Brentham College. She should; she's a natural with the elderly.

'Will you get a Saturday off soon?' I ask her. 'You've worked every weekend since I started visiting.'

Emma picks up Polly's ring finger. 'I like working Saturdays.'

'Must play havoc with your social life?'

'I don't have one.' Emma's head is bent over Mum's hand. I can't see her expression, can't tell if she's joking or not. I watch her delicate fingers wield the nail varnish brush. Her hands are tiny, as are her feet. My size-seven boots feel huge in comparison. I have Mum to thank for my large feet – a gift from her side of the family.

'Hello, my sweet.' Vera, one of the staff nurses, bustles into the room. 'Just need to take Mum's temperature,' she explains. 'It was a bit high this morning.'

Vera is all fleshy arms and greying, frizzy hair. Warm and efficient as always, she slips a thermometer into Mum's armpit. 'I'll try not to mess up your nails,' she says. The keys attached to her elasticated belt clank together as she moves. The ominous percussion makes me shiver.

'You all right, love?' Vera asks. 'I can turn the heating up if you're cold?'

I shake my head and smile. 'I'm fine.'

Vera removes the thermometer and declares Mum's temperature

satisfactory. After checking there are enough incontinence pads in the en suite, she hurries out of the room. 'Let's finish you off, shall we?' says Emma and resumes the manicure.

'Hello, Mr Erdoğan,' Mum says to the TV, greeting the Turkish president as if they are old friends.

'When I lived in Singapore, I had manicures all the time,' I tell Emma. 'They were so cheap.'

'I couldn't go anywhere like Singapore,' she says. 'Wouldn't like the food.'

'The food's incredible.'

'Don't like foreign stuff.' She dips the brush into the pink varnish and dabs it against the neck of the bottle as she pulls it out. 'You lived in loads of places, didn't you? South Korea, Thailand, Borneo. Somewhere else, hang on. Taiwon.'

'Taiwan. Mum told you all that?' This accurate recall unsettles me. Mum never showed much interest in where I was living and never offered to visit. She labelled my move abroad as 'typically selfish'. Never forgave me for choosing a life so different from hers.

'Yeah, she told me.' A surge of red in Emma's cheeks. 'We often chat about you, don't we, Polly?'

'Amen,' says Mum.

'She said you lived abroad for twenty years,' Emma adds. 'That's ages.'

'I suppose.'

She lifts Mum's little finger and coats the nail with three fast strokes. 'What made you decide to be an English teacher?'

'I'm not sure.' I twiddle my puzzle ring round and round. 'Just fell into it.'

'You went to university though?'

I nod. 'First person ever in our family to go.' Why do I feel the need to tell her this? It's as if I want to reassure her our backgrounds aren't that different.

'Did you do English?'

'No. I did a drama degree at the Northern Theatre School in Leeds.'

'Wow.' Emma straightens up. 'That's well cool. Were you an actress?'

I like the fact she's impressed. 'I did a few bits and pieces. Theatre stuff.'

'Bet you liked going to see Grace on stage, didn't you?' Emma says to Mum, who looks at her nails and declares them beautiful.

'She thought a drama degree was a waste of good A-level results,' I say. Mum tried to stop me going, but Dad intervened as usual and took my side. 'We argued about it for ages,' I add.

'I've never argued with my mother.' Emma looks sad, as if not arguing with your mother is a bad thing.

'Never?' I say, unable to keep the disbelief from my voice. I'm about to enquire if she still lives at home, but she interrupts and asks why I gave up acting.

'Don't really remember.' I twist the ring one way, then the other. 'Wasn't cut out for it, I guess.'

Emma looks disappointed at the explanation, but I have nothing else to say. Names and places, circumstances and reasons. They all fade over time. Emma will understand that one day. She will discover she cannot retrieve everything, even if she wants to.

7

CASSIE

August

No mother-and-daughter relationship is perfect. We all have bad days, and today was one of them.

I arrived at her block this morning, excited about spending a Saturday with her. As I took up my position behind the recycling skips, a trio of skateboarders rattled past, forcing me to jump out of the way, right into a pile of dog shit. I was so busy trying to wipe my Prada high-tops clean with a discarded copy of *The Sun*, that she left her building without me noticing. By the time I realised, she was already turning onto Goswell Road, and I had to run to keep up.

When we reached Islington, I crossed my fingers she wouldn't lead us into Angel Tube station and from there to Liverpool Street and to Brentham. The thought of another hospital visit didn't thrill me. Hours of waiting in the WRVS café in Brentham General with all the sick people and their depressed relatives, desperate for my mother to reappear so we could return to London.

Luckily she kept going along Upper Street. I kept my head down while passing Aroma, just in case Ryan was working. Shagging him was stupid, as it meant my mother and I couldn't have tea together in there any more. No chance of sitting quietly and observing her, not with him all over me. He'd called me loads over the past ten days, leaving a message each time. *Hey, Cass, how you going? Hey, Cass, been thinking about you. Hey, Cass, give me a call some time.* How dare he abbreviate me after just one night? I suspected he could be the clingy type, a bit obsessive. Not that I hadn't considered calling him back; he was sweet and good fun, and he didn't mind using a condom even though I was already on the pill. Can't be too careful, I told him and he agreed. What would be the point of calling him though? It wouldn't last – nothing ever does.

My mother turned off Upper Street and took us to the N1 shopping centre. We ended up in Sainsbury's, a new experience for a Marks and Spencer girl like me. Before getting started on the food, my mother picked up a bunch of white lilies and put them in her basket. She gets herself some every week.

We trawled the aisles. I decided to pick the same stuff as her, so I could imagine us having dinner together. A fun idea, but my mother turned out to be an irritating shopper. She examined every item she picked up for ages, reading all the labels. Sometimes she would put the item back on the shelf, only to return to it minutes later. Funny, the time she could take over decisions that didn't matter.

By the time we reached the checkout, my basket contained a jar of green curry paste, a tin of half-fat coconut milk, an organic chicken breast and a variety of vegetables.

'I'm making a Thai curry tonight,' I told the pudgy, fake-tanned woman at the checkout. Sandra, according to her name badge.

'Good for you,' Sandra said, her voice flat with disinterest.

Her lack of enthusiasm didn't dampen mine.

'My mother and I love Thai food,' I said. 'Family mealtimes are so important, don't you think?'

'Crucial,' deadpanned Sandra. 'Will you be needing any carrier bags today?'

When my mother and I left the supermarket, we lingered in the open-air precinct for a while, listening to a jazz trio that had set up in front of H&M. A lovely interlude, soon spoiled when my mother spotted a beggar outside Pret A Manger and hurried across to do her Good Samaritan routine.

The beggar was a girl about my age in a mud-streaked walking jacket, ripped jeans and battered hiking boots. Mousy dreadlocks hung around her pockmarked face. My mother crouched beside her and whatever she said made the girl smile. They spoke for a few minutes before my mother disappeared into Pret A Manger. She returned with a large paper cup of something hot. From the way the girl wrapped her filthy hands around it, I could tell she was grateful.

Jealousy gripped me as my mother squeezed the girl's shoulder in a comforting gesture. I'm only human. I wanted her hands on me; she owed me twenty years of touch and attention.

When my mother walked away, I didn't follow. Fuck her. Anger blazed inside me. Remembering a technique Dr Costello gave me to use in such moments, I visualised the anger as a ball of knotted golden thread, only I swallowed it, the reverse of the proper exercise, in which the knot of anger is unravelled and pulled out through the mouth in a long, golden line.

The beggar didn't see me coming. I waited until she put her drink on the ground and then marched past, making sure the toe of my left shoe found the cup and sent it flying across the concrete. Steaming tea spilled everywhere.

'Stupid bitch,' the girl screamed.

Back on Upper Street, remorse made me stop and take a few deep breaths. What if my mother had witnessed my cruelty? What would she think of me?

I returned to the precinct. The girl saw me coming and shrank back against the wall.

'I'm sorry,' I said, handing her a twenty-pound note. 'It was an accident.'

The girl snatched the money. 'Whatever.'

I felt like snatching it back but restrained myself. The girl had nothing, and I had everything. A mother I loved. A mother who would soon love me back.

8

GRACE

September

'What are the words for when you meet someone you like and over time you realise you are starting to like them more and more? We say you are...' I gaze out at the class, expectant. 'Three words. Third word is *someone*.'

'Fallen for someone.' Han from Korea the first to speak, capping his answer with his trademark cheeky grin.

I nod. 'Fallen?'

'Falling.' The correction comes as a chorus – Waleed, Bettina and Sophia.

'That's right,' I say, 'you fall for someone. And what kind of verb is this?'

'Phrasal verb,' says Waleed, fiddling with the zip of his red tracksuit top.

'And phrasal verbs are?'

'A verb plus a particle.' Nieve, nineteen and gloriously Spanish. Wide dark eyes, olive skin, long black hair twisted over one shoulder.

'Excellent.' I lift my marker to the whiteboard, where PowerPoint has projected the first part of the morning's lesson. My pen moves down the list of phrasal verbs on the board. Check out, ask out, go out. Turn down, let down, get on, split up. Phrasal verbs connected with relationships: the focus of the morning's lesson.

I stride to my desk in the corner of the room. Before class, I pushed the students' desks together to make a rectangular conference table in the middle of the room, a hub designed to promote the idea they are learning from each other, not from me. I never sit, preferring instead to keep on the move, to keep the energy as high as possible in the classroom.

'Okay.' I hit return on my laptop keyboard, moving the lesson on to the next stage. The students laugh as images of a man and a woman appear on the whiteboard, a comic strip depicting the beginning and end of an ill-fated romance. 'Split yourselves into two threes and a pair,' I say. The group subdivides with minimal fuss. 'Discuss what you think is happening in this story. Three minutes.'

Good-humoured chatter fills the room as the students confer in their groups. A sound I still love to hear after all my years of teaching. I walk over to the second-floor window and gaze at the traffic crawling along King's Cross Road in the rain. The grimy glass rattles in its frame. The three-storey office building the school occupies could do with renovations, but the organisation doesn't have the money for that.

'Sorry to disturb you.'

I swing round to find Linda, the school's director of studies, smiling at me from the open door.

'Can you pop by my office when you're finished?' Linda says. 'I need a quick word with you.'

I nod as she pulls the door shut. My stomach clenches at the thought of my overdue background check. Has it come through? Stupid to worry, but I can't help myself. The same anxiety surfaces each time I start a new job.

'One more minute, everyone,' I announce to the class. Returning to my desk, I sort out the next set of worksheets. The task calms me down and helps me focus. This Tuesday morning advanced group is one of my favourites. An interesting mix of Spanish, Italian, Korean and Nigerian students; all of them hard workers. Over the years, I've grown to respect my students and the effort they put into learning a language I take for granted. Many students I teach want to attend British universities, and to do so they endure years of graft before their degrees even start.

When the last minute is up, I hand out the worksheets. Each shows a printed version of the comic strip, as well as a list of ten sentences. 'Match each sentence below to one of the pictures,' I say. 'Five minutes.'

I hurry back to my laptop and click on my music library. 'Here's something to help you along. It's a song about a phrasal verb.'

Immediate recognition and laughter from the students. 'The Beatles,' says Bettina, the bright beads in her braided hair clacking together as she sways from side to side. 'Don't let me down,' she sings, raw and throaty. 'Don't let me down.' The others applaud her and then join in, one hearty burst, before returning their heads to their worksheets.

* * *

Linda is attacking the keyboard of her computer when I step into her office.

'Grab a pew,' she says.

I pull a chair up to her desk, silently admiring its organised appearance. Every sheet of paper corralled in a wire tray, no stray pens on the run from the penholder. Linda lost her marketing career to the recession and recovered from the blow by retraining as a business English teacher. It didn't take her long to power through and become a director of studies. She still wears the skirt suits and stilettos that belong to her former career, and her black, bobbed hair is always straight and shiny. Whilst mascara and muted pink lipstick form the extent of my daytime make-up regime, Linda is never seen without red lips and a flawless, powdered complexion. I think she's a few years older than me, but it's hard to tell.

'Sorry.' Linda frowns at her computer. 'Won't be a minute.'

My stomach tenses again. What is she looking at on her screen? Something to do with me?

'Screw this.' Linda pushes her keyboard away. 'Sorting out next term's timetables is a logistical nightmare.'

I force a smile. 'I can imagine.'

She leans back in her chair. 'I wanted to have a word with you in private. It's a confidential matter.'

The background check? My throat is dry, my heart pumping fast. I tell myself to relax. It's not as if I have a police record.

'There's an assistant director of studies post coming up at the Capital School's Hampstead branch,' she says. 'I thought you might like to apply.'

'Oh.'

'It hasn't been advertised yet and it's a permanent position.' Linda lowers her voice even though no one can overhear us. 'They've got a new DOS there and he's keen to get the post filled. You'd be in with an excellent chance, and I'd certainly put in a good word for you.'

My stomach unwinds, my shoulders drop. 'Thanks for thinking of me, but I'm happy here.'

'You know permanent positions don't come up that often.'

I nod. 'With things as they are, I can't really commit to permanent.' Nor do I want to. Temporary contracts have always suited me just fine.

'How is your mum?' Linda asks.

'Up and down – you know how it is.'

'I certainly do.' Linda has told me before about losing her mother to Parkinson's three years ago. 'That's why I would urge you not to put your life on hold for her,' she says. 'Harsh as that sounds.'

'It's not only because of her. I'd just rather teach than manage.'

'There are days I think you might be right.' Linda sighs. 'I feel like a fraud supervising someone with your experience. Should be you behind this desk, not me.'

'You've got the better outfit for it,' I say, and Linda laughs.

We chat for a few minutes – I update her on how my classes are going; she insists we need a staff night out soon.

'Yes, let's do that,' I say, getting up.

'Oh, hang on.' Linda's words stop me as I reach for the door handle. 'I meant to say that your background check came through.'

When I turn round she is already typing at speed, lost in whatever is on her screen.

I clear my throat. 'Is everything okay?'

Linda looks up, confused.

'With the check,' I add.

'Of course. I'm satisfied I haven't hired a master criminal.' She smiles. 'Either that or whatever you did, you got away with it.'

9

CASSIE

August

'Hello, darling.' Quentin's lined face loomed out from my laptop screen.

'Hello,' I replied. Harsh, white sunlight lit up the luxurious apartment he sat in. Bright blue sky filled the balcony doors behind him. 'How's Dubai?' I asked.

'Good.'

Both of us displayed wide, fixed smiles, but the distance between us wasn't only geographical.

'How are you?' I asked.

'Well. Very well.' His gaunt widower's cheeks contradicted him. His once thick silver hair looked thin and unkempt, his beard a matching straggle.

'Are you sure?'

'I'm fine,' he insisted. 'Just busy.'

'How's the... the project?' I'd never paid much attention to Quentin's work.

'It's going well. You wouldn't think Dubai had room for another hotel, but there you are.'

Quentin was an architect and the director of his own successful firm, a business he'd set up with his substantial inheritance. He'd told me his family history many times, but I remembered only that the money originally came from timber. Cutting it down, moving it around. Something like that.

'We're running ahead of schedule,' he said, 'which is a miracle and probably won't last.'

Better not, I thought. He was supposed to be away until March.

'I doubt I'll be coming back for Christmas,' he said.

'No worries.'

'I thought you could come over here for the holidays?'

'We'll see.'

He sighed, and I knew what was coming. 'It won't be the same without her,' he said. 'Can you believe it's been almost seven months?'

It never took him long to mention Isobel. He rubbed his wedding ring, a habit he'd acquired since her death. Three rubs, as if summoning magic, as if the action might make his wife reappear.

'I think about my mother too,' I said, which was true. I thought about Grace every day. Isobel I'd managed to push aside, but now she barged back in, bringing guilt along with her. I pictured her as she was in healthier days, her plump body contained in one of her black, wrap-around dresses. Her wavy, ash-blonde hair clipped up, exposing long earrings of beaten silver.

'She only ever wanted you to be happy,' said Quentin.

She'd wanted much more than that. She'd wanted me to love her in a way I never could.

'Yeah, well,' I said, 'sorry to be such a disappointment.'

I waited for Quentin to declare me no such thing, but instead he said, 'Are you keeping busy?' His sharp tone unnerved me. For a moment, I feared he knew what I'd been up to.

'Very busy.'

'Have you signed up for your A-level retakes yet?' I shook my head, and Quentin sighed again. He still believed I could achieve the four A grades predicted for me in my teens. Pity I wasn't in a fit state to pass the exams at the time. 'You are keeping up your therapy?' he asked. 'That's very important.'

'I am... Jesus... Get off my back.' I wanted to remind him that none of this was my fault. My mother was to blame for my behaviour, not me.

He looked so haggard with disappointment I couldn't stand it. 'I've got a boyfriend,' I announced.

'Really?' His surprised tone shouldn't have offended me. After all, I'd never had a boyfriend before.

'He's called Ryan and he's from Sydney. He works in hospitality.'

I expected Quentin to interrogate me, to show concern about my choice of company, but instead a relieved smile lit up his face.

'It's wonderful you're connecting with people,' he said. 'Your mother would be proud.'

Isobel would be amazed. *No one will like you if you don't like yourself, Cassie.* That's what she used to say when my brief flings with the opposite sex ended. The ones she knew about anyway.

Quentin's mobile rang in the background.

'Don't let me keep you,' I said. He clearly didn't care what was going on in my life as long as I stayed out of trouble.

'It can wait.' He asked if I was managing on my allowance. Did I need any more? Maybe he meant it in a nice way, but I felt he wanted to remind me of everything I owed him. As if I could forget. He and Isobel had adopted me when I was eight months old. After my first birthday, they moved to a village in Surrey, to the large white house I grew up in. Each summer they took me to another large white house near Aix-en-Provence. They gave me cats and dogs in place of siblings. Offered me riding, cello and ballet lessons, but they couldn't give me what I needed most – my mother.

'Have you settled into the flat okay?' Quentin said. 'Any problems?'

'It's fine.' Number 33 Highbury Terrace was one of many London properties Isobel had owned and which now belonged to Quentin. Years ago, when Quentin set up his architecture firm, she'd started a rental agency to make use of all the flats and houses her father had left her.

'What was wrong with the Notting Hill place?' he asked.

'The location wasn't right.' Too far from my mother. Much too far.

'Highbury Terrace was one of Isobel's favourites.' Quentin's bloodshot eyes filled with tears. 'We lived in that flat for a year when we first got married.'

'Yes, you told me.' I didn't feel unsympathetic for his loss, just aware that loss was nothing new to me. I'd lived without my mother since the age of seven, when Isobel and Quentin told me I was adopted.

'I've got to go,' I said.

'Sorry.' He blew his nose. 'I'm struggling a bit today.'

His grief stirred nothing in me. Isobel's death had left me numb and, besides, I had my mother to focus on now.

'Bye, Quentin,' I said and banished him with a click of my mouse.

In the silence of the flat, memories of Isobel gathered around me. I thought of the notes she would leave on my pillow after our frequent arguments.

I love you, darling girl. Nothing will change that.

You may not see me as your real mother, but I will love you until my dying breath, as any mother would.

Emptiness filled me. I grabbed my phone and called Fastlane Chauffeurs. Quentin had set up an account for me there, supposedly only for night-time travel or emergencies.

'I need a driver, please,' I said when I got through. 'Selfridges,' I said when they requested a destination.

* * *

Four hours later, I sat on the soft, beige carpet in my living room. Five Selfridges bags surrounded me, bulging with purchases. My latest binge had cost MasterCard over two thousand pounds. Quentin wouldn't be happy when he got the bill, but I didn't care. This lapse had only happened because of him.

I thought shopping might rid me of Isobel, but she'd hounded me into the changing rooms, insisting that the black shift dress by Chloé did nothing for my pale complexion and that I had no chance of filling the Calvin Klein push-up bra I'd set my sights on. Ignoring her advice, I'd bought both.

Death had made Isobel much easier to disregard. She'd never believed I would find my real mother. In the past, she'd discouraged me from trying. Said I'd only bring myself more pain.

As I surveyed the bags, the emptiness returned, even stronger than before. Only one thing to do. I called Ryan, who answered on the third ring.

'Hey, Cass,' he said, trying to sound casual. As if he hadn't rung again at lunchtime and left another message.

'I'm sorry, mate,' I said in a parody of his accent, 'I've been crook. Sick as a bloody dog. That's how come I didn't call you back.'

He burst out laughing. 'That's not a bad impression.'

I wanted to hang up, but the thought of Quentin stopped me. He hadn't asked about Ryan because he'd assumed it wouldn't last. I thought about my mother too, about us meeting and her asking me questions, sussing me out. She would ask if I had a boyfriend and I'd say, of course. We've been together a while now.

'You still there, Cass?' Ryan asked.

'How soon can you come over?' I said.

10

GRACE

October

Aroma is packed. I rushed here after my Sunday morning yoga class and managed to grab the last table. All around me, the bleary-eyed and hung-over sip coffees and smoothies. Some read newspapers, while others stare at phones and laptops. Modern jazz plinks away beneath the whirr of the juicer and the hiss of the coffee machine.

'Hi there.' Ryan appears with my order. 'How you going?'

'Good, thanks.'

He lays a mismatched china cup and saucer and a glass teapot on the table. 'Here's your Sencha green tea,' he says in a flat, tired voice.

'How are you?' I ask.

He shrugs. 'Been better.'

'Late night?' The dark pouches beneath his eyes hint at one.

'Nah. Girlfriend trouble.'

'That's easily solved. Whatever happened was your fault and you should apologise.'

'Funny. I reckon she'd agree with you though.' He smiles. 'She's a high-maintenance girl, that's for sure.'

The way he says this suggests he's not ready to give up maintaining this girl yet. He's sweet, Ryan. Seems like the kind of boy who likes being in a relationship. The kind of boy I dismissed in my youth as not exciting enough.

'Bet you wish you were back in Singapore today?' He nods at the window and the damp, dismal morning beyond it.

'Not half.' My navy trench coat hangs on the back of my seat. I bought it yesterday in preparation for the winter ahead. We talk for a bit longer, about Sydney mostly. I know the city well from numerous visits there and always enjoy reminiscing about it.

'Cool nails by the way,' Ryan says before heading back to the counter.

I spread out my fingers and admire Emma's handiwork. She insisted the aqua blue varnish would suit me, and she was right. She spent ages yesterday on the manicure, dismissing my concerns about keeping her from her duties. Any excuse for a skive, she joked. With Mum busy tutting at a news special about the migrant crisis, Emma and I chatted away like we were in a beauty salon. Emma asked if I had a boyfriend, and I told her no. She shook her head when I asked her the same question. Said she used to have one, but he was too needy. Got on her nerves.

I pour my first cup of tea. As I sip the hot, fragrant brew, I cringe at the memory of asking Emma if she still lived with her parents.

'I lost my mum a long time ago,' she said, which made sense of why she'd never argued with her. 'I was very young so I never knew her.'

I apologised for my tactlessness and then made it worse by asking if she lived with her dad.

'He died last year,' Emma said. 'It's fine though,' she added, bright and defensive. I wanted to place an arm around her narrow shoulders. Reassure her she wasn't alone.

After I empty the last of the tea into my cup, a tingling starts at the base of my neck. It spreads out across my shoulders and down my spine. The sensation of being watched.

Outside, low dark clouds bruise the sky. I scan the faces of the people strolling past the window. Looking for what?

Twisting in my seat, I spy a baby strapped into a buggy a few tables away. The baby's dark, solemn eyes observe me without pity and refuse to blink when I stare back.

In the end, I look away first.

* * *

I return to the flat on edge, restless. Wishing I could shove some clothes in my rucksack and take off for a break somewhere exotic, like I used to do on a regular basis. Instead I have to settle for housework as a distraction. Just as I'm wrestling the hoover out of the hall cupboard, the doorbell rings.

'All right?' Trish, the woman who lives in the flat opposite, is lurking next to the rubber plant. A small, hunched woman, Trish is probably not much older than me, but her worn face suggests otherwise.

'Hi,' I say, my stomach lurching at the sight of the white envelope in her hands.

'That postman's a cock,' Trish says. 'He delivered me your stuff yesterday, only I didn't notice at first and then you wasn't in so I thought I'd better hold on to it and then I was babysitting for my Shelley last night and I stayed over, so…' She holds out the envelope.

That familiar tremor at my core.

'He's always messin' up my post,' she says. 'I don't see why he should get away with it.' Trish, who will tell anyone willing to listen about her violent drunk of an ex-husband, doesn't put up with any man's failings. As she rants on about bringing up the postman's incompetence at the next block committee meeting, I grab the envelope and rip it open.

'And if Wendy from number four comes to the meeting, I'll be telling her to get her kids in line,' adds Trish, who doesn't tolerate many women either. 'They leave their toys all over the bloody place. I nearly fell over Buzz Lightyear on the stairs the other day.'

Another card. Cluster of pink balloons on the front and a message in thick silver letters.

BEST MUM EVER

Inside, the card is blank.

'Are you going to the next committee meeting?' she asks.

'Have you had anything like this in the post?' I hold up the card, gripped by an irrational fear that it might not be real and that Trish will insist she can't see it.

'Nope,' she says. 'Not had nothing like that.'

'You're sure?'

'It's not Mother's Day, darlin'.' She shrugs. 'Probably a bloody marketing thing. I spoke to one of those call centre people one time and got tons of crap in the post afterwards.'

I remember the Indian woman with the warm voice and the extensive list of questions. 'You're right,' I say. 'Just a marketing thing.'

When Trish leaves, I lock the door. My hands shake as I add the card to its predecessor in the recycling box, smothering them both with a copy of *Red* magazine and an empty soya milk carton.

* * *

Later, after hoovering the entire flat, I settle on a stool at the breakfast bar with my laptop, determined to catch up with overdue emails. I reply to one from Zoe and another from Rosabelle, a former student from Taiwan now studying at Cambridge. I also send light-hearted, newsy messages to several friends from Singapore. It feels good to remember who I am and the life I have lived. The life I will return to one day.

Emails done, I indulge in some random surfing – the weather forecast for Singapore, the screening timetable at the Soho Curzon, the website for the Capital School of English.

My name is listed on the staff page along with everyone else, and a recent picture accompanies my short biography. I hate having my details out there, where anyone can find them. I tried to get out of it. Surely temporary staff shouldn't feature, I said to Linda, but she insisted. Up until now I've avoided any Internet presence. Networking sites hold no appeal for me. I've no desire to get in touch with anyone from school or university. No desire to relive the past.

I exit the site and distract myself with the state of various celebrities' marriages.

Dan Thorne

I'm not aware of having typed his name, but I must have done. There it is, in the search engine, daring me to hit return.

I've never looked him up. Not once. My index finger jabs at the keyboard.

Dan Thorne Dan Thor Dan Th Dan D

All gone.

The new lilies in the vase next to me are all closed apart from one. Armed with a piece of kitchen towel, I delve into the open bloom and rip off the stamens, the rusty pollen staining the white paper like an exotic powdered paint.

* * *

At night in bed, black words float behind my eyes.

BEST MUM EVER

The words hover there, demanding attention. Surely if ignored long enough, they will go away and let me sleep?

No such luck.

I get out of bed and pad across the cold floorboards to the hallway. Opening the cupboard, I retrieve the cards. After tearing them up, I push the shreds to the bottom of the red box.

Back to bed, but sleep keeps its distance. The ever-present soundtrack of traffic rises up from the streets below. Tonight, the police sirens sound louder than usual. They sound as though they are coming for me.

Tossing and turning. Imagining the shredded cards sticking themselves back together.

BEST MUM EVER

Up again. Tracksuit over my pyjamas. Boots and jacket on, dragging the recycling box from the cupboard.

'You're being ridiculous,' I whisper, as I take the box in the lift to the ground floor and then outside to the row of coloured recycling skips at the left of the building.

My breath condenses in clouds around me. Paper already trails from the red skip, but I shove the contents of the recycling box into it, force-feeding the container's bristly mouth until no evidence remains.

11

CASSIE

August

To be fair, the old women at the WRVS café made pretty good coffee. I told one of them so, as she handed over my cappuccino. We'd become quite familiar over the past few weeks, these cheery volunteers and I.

I picked my usual spot at one of the café's outer tables. It faced the hospital's reception area, giving me a clear view of the double doors that led to the main wards. My mother couldn't enter or exit without me seeing her.

Apart from the café, the dreary foyer contained a newsagents and a pharmacy. In front of the newsagents stood one of those children's rides popular at supermarkets. A green plane with big black eyes, a propeller for a nose and two bucked teeth. As a child it would have terrified me. As a child most things terrified me.

My phone buzzed with a text from Ryan, asking how my day was going. He was thoughtful like that. He seemed to live by the motto tattooed on his right shoulder: *You get what you give*.

I texted him back:

OK. Visiting sick relative

I added a row of sad, yellow faces.

Bummer

He replied.

I sent him a picture of my frothy coffee with its sprinkle of Cadbury's drinking chocolate on top, and he countered with a snap of one his signature creations: a latte with a decorative leaf of raw cacao.

Beat that!

For once, I looked like other people, smiling at a message meant just for me. For once, I was someone with a boyfriend and a mother. A grandmother too.

The bouquet of pink and white roses I'd bought for Grandma sat in a hessian bag on the chair beside me. I'd dressed up too – the black Chloé dress with black wedge sandals. Slightly formal for a summer's day, but this was a big occasion.

A bald, emaciated man in grey pyjamas and a burgundy dressing gown sat down at the table behind me with a groan. The wheels of his intravenous stand rattled as he pulled it close. His weak voice called out an order of hot milk and a toasted teacake.

Last week, my mother had occupied his table. The café was so crowded she'd had to share it with another woman about her age. The two of them ended up exchanging stories and that's when I'd learned what had brought my grandmother to hospital. A long list of conditions, but as soon as I heard dementia, I knew it would be safe for her and I to meet. She probably wouldn't say anything to my mother about the visit, nothing credible anyway. I didn't want her to spoil the surprise.

My mother appeared in the foyer before I'd finished my coffee, dabbing at her eyes with a tissue, her visit over. She didn't come to the café for a drink. She couldn't get out of the hospital fast enough.

After reapplying my lipstick, I set off across the foyer and passed through the double doors. A long corridor lined with amateur artwork greeted me on the other side. I followed the blue arrows on the signs above my head and took the lift to the fourth floor.

I waited outside Ward 8 for a while, too nervous to go in. What if my grandmother didn't like me? Quentin's parents had died before I turned five, as had Isobel's father. Isobel's mother, Beatrice, couldn't stand me. One morning, aged nine, I overheard her and Isobel discussing me in the kitchen. Beatrice declared me 'not right' and 'strange' and 'nothing but trouble'.

'We don't know what kind of stock the girl comes from,' she added.

'I know, Mother,' Isobel had said. 'That worries me sometimes.'

The hot, muggy air hit me first when I entered the ward. Then came the smell – disinfectant, overcooked vegetables and an unmistakable base note of shit. I pressed my silk scarf against my nose and inhaled faint traces of Chanel Mademoiselle.

I waited for someone to stop me, but nobody did. I sailed past the gossiping nurses at the reception desk and found myself in a long, blue room lined with beds on both sides.

What a sight. Half-dead people moaning and writhing beneath their sheets. A woman screeching. A pot-bellied man shuffled the length of the ward, hairy arse hanging out the back of his hospital gown.

Where were all the nurses? I scanned the ward but couldn't see any. Not that I blamed them for hiding at reception.

A young male nurse appeared and tried to skulk past me. 'Excuse me,' I said, 'I'm looking for Mrs Walker.'

He scratched his freckled nose. 'Polly's over there,' he said. 'Bed twelve I think.'

Polly. Great name for a grandmother. Old-fashioned and sweet.

To my relief, I found her sitting up against her pillows, a serene expression on her face. Someone, my mother perhaps, had brushed her hair and moistened her lips with pink gloss. 'Hello, Grandma,' I said. My heart raced as her sad eyes examined me. Would she approve of what she saw?

A shaky smile spread across her face. 'Hello, pet.'

Instant recognition, instant acceptance. I couldn't have asked for more. Did she know about me, I wondered, or had instinct told her the connection between us?

'I've brought you these.' I lifted the flowers from the bag and held them close to her face. She edged her nose inside one of the pink roses.

'Lovely,' she said.

Another scent overpowered the flowers. Something meaty and rotten.

'My ulcer,' wailed the ghost-faced woman in the next bed. My stomach heaved. A blue curtain hung next to my grandmother's bed, and I pulled it all the way round, sealing us off from the rest of the ward.

'That's better,' I said. Unable to locate a vase, I placed the flowers on the narrow table at the foot of the bed. My grandmother's right ankle stuck out from the covers, swathed in a plaster cast. I really wanted to sign it but managed to resist.

'Pretty little thing, aren't you?' she croaked. My cheeks flushed with pride.

'Thanks.' I dragged a heavy beige armchair closer to the bed. The seat's plastic cover squeaked when I sat down.

'You from the church?' my grandmother said.

'No. I'm Cassie.'

'Did Father Francis send you?'

I sighed. Her dementia was both a blessing and a curse. I had so much to ask her, so much I needed to know, but it appeared she would be little use.

The blue curtain swished open, revealing a stocky nurse in blue overalls.

'What is going on here?' she asked, her accent Eastern European. Polish, I decided, after reading Agata on her name badge.

'We're trying to get some privacy,' I said.

Agata's broad, open face left no hiding place for her annoyance. 'Polly has not been good this morning,' she said. 'Please leave the curtain open so we can see her.'

'She looks fine to me.'

Agata didn't reply, but her flared nostrils spoke for her.

'Could you find me a vase for those, please?' I said, pointing to the flowers.

'No flowers allowed on the ward.'

'What?'

'Hospital policy. No flowers on any wards.'

'That's ridiculous.'

'You don't think we have better things to do than care for flowers?'

'Private hospitals allow them.'

'Oh, well.' Agata folded her arms. 'I wouldn't know about that.'

'No.' I fixed her with a cool stare. 'I don't suppose you would.'

She flounced off, muttering in Polish. My grandmother gazed after her and then her eyelids drooped. Great. All the effort I'd made, and she was about to fall asleep.

'It's me,' I said, 'your granddaughter.'

Her eyes jolted open. 'Grace?' she said. 'Only trying to help.'

I wanted her to pay attention to me, not ramble on about my mother, but what could I do? She looked so out of it, so weak.

'Grace?' she repeated, louder this time.

Agata was watching me from the other end of the ward.

No doubt waiting for me to upset her patient in some way. 'I'll let you rest.' I stood up and reclaimed the unwelcome flowers. 'I'm so glad I met you, Grandma.' I suspected she wouldn't be alive much longer. What if I never got to see her again?

She gestured for me to come closer. When I bent over the bed, one of her soft, warm hands guided my left ear to her mouth.

'Grace is a sinner,' she said.

12

GRACE

October

In Mum's kitchen, cardboard boxes cluster round me, their lids wide open. Where to start? I open the cupboards of the imitation pine dresser and survey the three dinner services Mum insisted on having – everyday, better and best. The crockery will have to wait until I get some old newspaper to wrap it in, as will the glasses that line the dresser's shelves.

Raindrops pelt against the window. A miserable Saturday morning. After making a start on the house, I'll brave the weather and go to Birch Grove.

I open the tall pantry next to the oven and stare at the stash of tinned food inside, still reluctant to clear out Mum's possessions. The act of doing so feels disrespectful, but it's necessary. Her savings have covered the extra care costs so far, but the money will soon run out, and what if Mum lives longer than predicted? The house has to be sold.

I work my way through the tins. Those with a good expiration date go in the box marked CHURCH. Everything else goes in the bin.

The estate agent who came this morning urged me to get the place ready for viewing as soon as possible. A cheery, overweight man in his early thirties, Mike couldn't hide his joy at the prospect of a quick sale.

'This is prime commuter property,' he said. 'We'll have no problem shifting it.' He assured me no renovations were needed. 'Whoever buys this'll gut the place and start from scratch.'

My heart snagged at his words, a surprising reaction. From my teenage years onwards, I'd looked down on my parents' suburban house as soulless and unimaginative, and I haven't thought of it as home for a long time. I didn't even consider staying here after returning from Singapore. Yet as Mike tapped the house details into his iPad, I realised it was all I had left. My own ancestral pile. It hurt to think of strangers stripping the place bare, carrying my history piece by piece to a skip in the driveway, until I am the only proof that Frank and Polly Walker ever existed.

The pantry is soon empty, exposing dusty shelves. I search around the sink for a cloth, all the time aware of Mum's statue of the Virgin Mary gazing at me from the windowsill, blue-robed arms spread wide. Getting rid of that will be a pleasure. 'What are you looking at?' I ask her, crouching down to open the cupboard under the sink. While rummaging among the cleaning products for a J-cloth, a wave of dizziness forces me to sit on the cold beige tiles. I haven't slept well since the second card arrived, waking every night at 3 a.m., disturbed by a dream I cannot remember. Each time I try it flits away, like a butterfly eluding a net.

Hauling myself up, I turn on the hot tap. Before wetting the cloth, I rip it in half, one of Mum's money-saving tips. Two cloths for the price of one. Wiping the pantry shelves, I wonder what else of her will live on in me.

Shelves done, I ponder what to tackle next. Disheartened by the amount to do in the kitchen, I contemplate going upstairs. The large box I left in my bedroom twenty years ago is still there, unopened. I should really find out what's in it but can't face doing so today.

I wander into the living room, half expecting to see Mum in the brown recliner, staring at an unfinished crossword.

Everything has remained untouched since she had the fall and went into hospital – Zimmer frame next to the chair, a copy of the *Daily Mail* on the coffee table. It makes me sad to think of her here alone, to think she might have been scared. I did my best over the past few years, returning to the UK more frequently when I realised her forgetfulness had a cause more sinister than old age. I fought for a diagnosis of dementia from her uninterested GP, and I organised carers so Mum could stay in her own home for as long as possible. She'd insisted on that.

The living room is more cluttered than the kitchen. So much stuff. It'll take me weeks to sort through it all, to decide what to keep and what to give away. And what of all the heirlooms? My nan's collection of crystal animals that passed to Mum and which now should pass to me. But I have nowhere to keep them and no one to keep them for.

* * *

I arrive at Birch Grove to find a tense atmosphere in reception. Kegs is ushering a weeping man into his office.

'I know, mate,' Kegs says, 'I know.' He closes the office door behind him. There must have been a death today.

Brenda is sitting at her desk, her hair even more dishevelled than usual.

'We're all prisoners here,' she chants, 'we're all prisoners here.'

My stomach leaps into an anxious flutter. My eyes flick to the front door with its electronic keypad. I know the code. I can leave any time I want.

As I pass the TV lounge, a shrill scream makes me freeze in the doorway. A skeletal woman with long silver hair sways in front of the television, wielding a dinner knife. Vera hovers nearby, and next to her stands John.

'Come on now, love,' says Vera, 'why don't you let me have that?'

'Let it go, Mum,' John says. I can't take my eyes off him. Tall and rugged in his jeans and grey sweatshirt, he radiates vitality amongst all the weakness and demise.

'Stay away,' his mother shouts. A blank-eyed man in the armchair nearest to her starts to cry.

'That's enough,' John says, stepping forward and grabbing his mother's wrist. 'Please.'

She drops the knife and lashes out at his face, catching him on his chin. 'Get off me, you little cunt.' Then she stops, as if her batteries have run out, and falls to her knees. Opening her mouth wide, she wails like a frustrated child.

'It's all right. I've got you.' John reaches down and scoops her up. I step aside as he carries his mother out of the room, accompanied by Vera's longing sigh. A warped version of the famous scene from *An Officer and a Gentleman.*

He strides away down the corridor. His mother batters his skull with her fists, but he doesn't say a word.

* * *

Mum is in bed today, her face ashen. Her eyes open when I kiss her forehead.

'Grace,' she says, breath rattling in her chest. 'Only trying.' *Only trying to help.* A pet phrase of Mum's, one I heard often while growing up. A phrase usually delivered in a tone of wounded martyrdom.

'How are you feeling today?' I ask, even though the answer is obvious. I drag a chair to the side of the bed. Mum's tattered Bible lies open on the bedside cabinet. I close it and put it away in the drawer.

'Emma?' Mum says.

I sit down. 'Emma's not in today.' On my way to Mum's room, I passed the tea trolley, only to find a different care assistant in charge of the drinks round. 'Surinder told me she's off sick.'

The minutes pass. Neither of us speaks. Without Emma's chatter the room is dangerously quiet.

Mum holds out her left hand. When I clasp it, she surprises me with a reassuring squeeze. A once-familiar action, unaltered by her knotty knuckles and paper-thin skin. Tears fill my eyes as I sense all the years of touch in Mum's fingers. How many times have these hands held, caressed and comforted me? Stroked my eyelids closed when I couldn't sleep. *Curtains down. Off to beddy-byes.*

'Don't,' Mum whispers, tightening her grip on my hand.

'It's okay.'

Her face twists with rage. 'Don't,' she says, louder this time, her neat pink nails digging into my skin.

'That's enough.' I try to break free, but Mum's nails drive deeper. How can someone so frail be so strong? 'Stop it.'

'Don't do it. I'm warning you.'

'Please, Mum. Let go.'

* * *

I escape into the corridor and head for the visitors' kitchen, in need of a cup of tea and some respite.

Don't do it. I'm warning you.

Angry red crescents on the back of my hand. Mum has lashed out at me before, but it always comes as a shock.

In the kitchen, I find John slumped at the yellow Formica table, his head in his hands. He looks up and gives me a defeated smile. This is where we first met last month, only to find ourselves having sex in his car an hour later.

Unsure what to do, I ask if he wants a drink. He nods and soon we are sitting at the table together – black coffee for him, peppermint tea for me. I glance at his wedding finger and the thick gold band there.

'Is your wife here?' I ask.

He shakes his head. 'Mum and Debbie fell out years ago. My wife is a champion grudge holder so she hardly visits.'

Now I know three facts about him – his wife's name is Debbie, he has two daughters and he works as a premier account manager for the Brentham branch of Lloyds. I don't want to know any more.

'It's nice to see you,' he says.

I don't feel good about what happened between us last time, but in our situation the rules don't seem to apply. We are cut off from our real lives, from the people we would normally be.

'Sorry about the TV room,' he adds. 'Mum's having a terrible day.'

'Isn't it weird how we feel obliged to apologise for them?' I place my hand on the table, putting my raw, red marks on display. 'Mine's not having a great day either.'

'Christ.' John peers at the damage. 'Good job euthanasia isn't legal. It'd be bloody tempting.'

Neither of us laughs at the joke. His hand seeks mine on the cold Formica and our fingers interlock. His thumb finds the centre of my palm and treats my flesh to a gentle massage. Our eyes meet in a silent, mutual acknowledgement of what we are about to do.

'Come on,' he says.

He drops my hand when we step out into the corridor. I expect him to head for the main door and go out to the car park, but he turns in the opposite direction.

'Where are we going?' I ask. He walks ahead without answering, but I follow anyway. Memory lumbers past with a mop and bucket in her hand. She gives me one of her long, knowing looks.

John leads me along the corridor to the back stairwell. His hand rests on my shoulder as he hurries me down to basement level. He peers through the glass panel on the fire door before steering me into a corridor with blue walls and a low ceiling. He opens the first door on the left and sticks his head inside before beckoning me on.

The laundry room. Warm, cottony air envelops me as soon as I step inside. Machines whir and rattle mid-cycle. The door of one of the tumble dryers hangs open, a tussle of pale blue sheets half delivered into the waiting basket.

John locks the door. My body hums with anticipation, the thrill of just-about-to.

It happens fast. Frantic, painful kissing. His hands fumble with my belt as I unbutton and unzip him. He pushes me backwards towards the sink unit until the hard edge of the draining board digs into my lower back.

'Turn around,' he says.

The ridged metal is cool against my left cheek and smells of bleachy lemons. I shut my eyes and concentrate on the rhythm of him. I groan and urge him on, urge him to fuck everything out of me. Everything everything everything, until nothing but peace remains.

13

CASSIE

August

The key I got cut from my mother's spare worked perfectly. I'd watched her pick up that ridiculous fake stone and take out her emergency key loads of times when she couldn't find her normal one.

Once inside, I locked her front door behind me. The flat was stuffy and still and silent. I couldn't move, too overcome at being in her home for the first time. It felt like Christmas, when Isobel and Quentin would buy me far too many gifts and I never knew what to open first.

I began by exploring the hall cupboard, discovering towels and bed linen, a hoover and a rusty boiler trailing copper pipes. Next to the hoover, a red plastic box overflowed with magazines and flattened soya milk cartons.

Bathroom next. I inspected everything. Her toothpaste claimed to be whitening, and her moisturiser promised to plump tired skin and erase fine lines. She didn't have many toiletries, and her washbag sat open on the ledge next to the sink, as if she wanted to be ready to pack up and go at any moment. That would change once she knew about me.

In the bathroom cabinet, I found tampons, sanitary towels and ibuprofen. It made me feel sick to think she could still get pregnant, but then I found several packets of contraceptive pills and the nausea vanished. Whatever my mother had done to me, at least I didn't have brothers and sisters to contend with. The first few days I'd followed her, my nerves were all over the place in case it turned out she'd had another child.

I spotted several dark hairs plastered to the white tiles above the bath and gathered them up in a piece of toilet roll. Flipping up the lid of the small pedal bin, I squatted down for a look, coming away with a used cotton wool pad and two waxy ear buds. I added them to the hairs, folded up the toilet paper and stashed it in my Prada tote bag. To finish, I sprayed my wrists with her perfume – Dark Amber and Ginger Lily by Jo Malone.

A narrow counter divided her kitchen and living room. As I dumped my bag on it, I noticed a black sweatshirt draped over one of the stools. I couldn't resist pulling a couple of stamens off the pungent lilies in the big vase and rubbing the pollen into the soft material.

In the kitchen, I found the cupboards almost empty apart from two packets of brown rice and three tins of baked beans. Isobel had always kept her kitchen well stocked and permanently infused with the scent of something baking or simmering. Looking around me, I realised the entire flat would fit into Isobel's kitchen. I'm sure my mother thought the Harringtons could give me a better life, but that's not the point. I was meant to be with her.

In the fridge, I discovered a bar of dark chocolate and broke a chunk off to nibble on. A half-empty bottle of Pinot Noir sat beside the microwave, and I poured myself a glass. No need to rush. I'd trailed my mother on the Underground to Liverpool Street earlier this morning, which meant she'd be in Brentham dealing with my grandmother for ages.

Grace is a sinner.

What my mother did to me was a crime, not a sin. However, my grandmother could have been referring to other offences of my mother's that I knew nothing about. It was also possible my grandmother knew nothing about me. Perhaps she'd never even known her daughter was pregnant.

Sinners could be forgiven. Sometimes I wasn't so sure about my mother.

On the work surface sat a chrome block full of knives. I slid each one out, then in again. Contemplated hiding in the flat until her return and giving her a proper surprise.

I drained the wine and proceeded to the bedroom. The white walls matched the linen on her low double bed. The duvet lay tangled in the centre of the mattress. I threw myself onto it and inhaled her musty sleep scent. Rolling onto my back, I lowered my head to her pillow, into the dip carved by the weight of her skull. Eyes closed, I wafted my hands through the air, as if to catch any traces of her dreams that might linger there.

After a few minutes, I got up and turned my attention to the two cardboard boxes behind the bedroom door. The stickers plastered all over them showed they'd come from Singapore. They contained books – historical fiction and travel stories. No photo albums or cards or letters. No glimpses into my mother's past. I felt disappointed, like an archaeologist whose dig has failed to uncover hoped-for evidence.

I did find an old photograph of my mother and her parents on top of her chest of drawers. She looked about six or seven years old and had on a pair of flared denim dungarees. My grandfather – who I'd guessed must be dead – had a thick black moustache, bushy eyebrows and a warm smile. I couldn't believe the tall, attractive woman beside him was the grandmother I'd seen in Brentham General. Old age sucked. I wouldn't visit her in hospital again; the place was just too depressing. If Grandma did die soon, what would my mother do? Where might she go?

On the opposite side of the room, the mirrored doors of the built-in wardrobe beckoned. I accepted their invitation to investigate and eyed up the items on the rail inside. I had nothing from my mother, no memento of any kind. Why shouldn't I take something? Didn't daughters always borrow clothes from their mothers' wardrobes?

Hangers clattered against the rail as I rifled through her sparse collection of jeans, trousers and tops. I wanted something special but nothing leapt out at me. For fun, I tried on the one dress my mother owned, a mauve silk thing from AllSaints. It swamped me, the hem low on my shins, the shoulders sliding down my arms. I slipped my feet into her lone pair of stilettos. Her feet were three sizes bigger than mine, and I laughed at the sight of myself in the mirror. The laughter continued as I clip-clopped along the hall like a kid who'd raided the dressing-up box.

Back in the kitchen, I poured some more wine and carried the glass into the living room. English language textbooks lay strewn across the floor. I'd discovered my mother's profession a few days ago, after trailing her to several English language schools. She'd looked smart and nervous, so I'd assumed she was attending interviews. I couldn't bear to think of all those students getting her guidance and nurturing. Then I realised she'd only turned to teaching to fill the void I'd left. Her students were a substitute for me.

I sat at the counter and sipped my wine, imagining us there together, me perplexed by A-level homework and her helping me with it, patient and wise. An official white envelope propped against the vase distracted me from my fantasy. My mother had already opened it so I removed the letter inside and had a look. It was from a company called the Beaumont Care Group.

We are writing in response to your recent visit to the Birch Grove Care Home in Brentham.

The letter confirmed my grandmother's place on their waiting list and stated a room would become available for her soon.

Interesting.

I finished my wine and took the glass over to the sink. As I rinsed it in warm water, I looked out over the park. The day was hot and close, the blue sky blemished by dull clouds. My bench was empty, waiting for me and my binoculars to take up our usual position.

I returned the glass to the draining rack where I'd found it and stood with my hands dripping into the sink. Birch Grove Care Home. Grandma wasn't going anywhere soon and neither was my mother. We'd have plenty of time to get to know one another. I gazed up at the gloomy sky for some time, mesmerised by the frail tips of two clouds kissing.

14

GRACE

October

Lunchtime. Alone in the strip-lit staffroom of the Capital School of English, I search through the damp jackets on the coat hooks behind the door. No sign of my cashmere scarf. Did I have it when I left Aroma? I remember rushing out of the café and then a downpour forced me onto a bus. Perhaps I left it on there? Losing things is becoming a habit. Two months ago, I lost my phone and had to replace it. Since then small things have gone missing on a regular basis. Last week my electric toothbrush disappeared, and I still haven't found it. Did I throw it away by mistake? At times I feel Mum's dementia might be catching.

Max saunters in. 'Hi there.'

'Hi.'

Max, twenty-six and from Camden, is blessed with cheek and charm. With his short black hair and dark stubble, he is a favourite among the female students, a position he never exploits, managing their crushes with tact and kindness.

'How was your class?' he asks, commandeering one of the four desks at the centre of the cramped room.

'Fun. They're a great group.' I give up on the scarf, annoyed with myself for being so careless. I bought it years ago in Goa, and it has seen me through all seasons.

The staffroom door opens again. Theresa hurries in, already wrapped up in her red velvet coat.

'Shouldn't you be at your tutorial?' Max asks.

'I'm running late. My beginners group is a fucking nightmare.' Theresa, a slender Chinese girl with a strong Belfast accent, is a champion swearer. She rushes over to Max and gives him a kiss. 'Just wanted to say goodbye.'

Max and Theresa have been together since their first week at university. Both work at the school part-time and both are studying for a Master's in Applied Linguistics at UCL. After that they plan to get married, teach in Saudi Arabia and save up enough to put a deposit on a house so they can have kids. I'm not sure whether to be impressed or terrified at their level of planning.

Theresa hurries out again just as Barney, the school's teacher of business English, marches in. Barney's short, wiry frame is decked out in Lycra cycling gear. He lifts his fluorescent jacket from one of the coat hooks, says a quick hello and dashes out again.

'Don't tell me he's training for another triathlon,' Max says. 'I'm sick of sponsoring him.'

'All for a good cause, I'm sure.' I claim the desk opposite Max and remove my lunch from my backpack. Cheese salad sandwich and a banana already turning brown. I nibble at the sandwich while Max leafs through a thick textbook on linguistics. At his age, I had none of his dedication to my career. Back then, teaching served as a way for me to travel and live abroad. A means of escape.

After finishing my lunch, I take my phone from my bag and reread the text John sent this morning.

I get hard just thinking about you.

My cheeks flush. Neither of us made any promises as we parted ways outside the laundry room four days ago. We gave each other what we needed at that moment, nothing more, and our sporadic texts are merely a distraction. A game to lose ourselves in.

I type a quick reply:

What exactly are you thinking?

Our encounter on Saturday left me loose-limbed and drained and resulted in my first night of uninterrupted sleep for a week. Since then I've felt calmer, able to see that the stress of Mum's decline has affected me more than I realised. I must remember that, if anxiety takes hold again.

Another text from John:

Will call you later and tell you?

I'd like that

I reply.

My phone rings. Is this him calling now? I glance at the screen and see the number for Birch Grove.

'Hello.' Heart stuttering, I rush out into the corridor, phone pressed to my ear. Is this it? Is it over?

'Hiya, love, it's Kegs.'

I'm not ready. Not ready for Mum to go, and I should have been there.

'Nothing urgent,' he says, 'but your mum had a bit of a fall this morning.'

'Is she okay? She's not hurt, is she?'

'Bit shaken up and bruised but she's fine. The doctor's coming after lunch to give her the once-over. Just to be on the safe side.'

'What happened?'

'We think she must have tried to get out of bed on her own. Emma found her when she came round with breakfast. She did a brilliant job of keeping your mum calm.'

My throat closes up at the thought of Mum confused and in pain. I cough to clear it.

'Thank God Emma was there,' I say.

* * *

I leave work just after four-thirty and decide to walk home, despite the return of the morning's rain. Umbrella up, I stride along Pentonville Road. I cannot get Mum's weak and frightened voice out of my head. Kegs called again mid-afternoon to tell me the doctor had examined Mum and found no sign of any fractures. I spoke to her then and explained I'd taken time off work to come down tomorrow afternoon.

'Only trying,' Mum whispered.

Up until today, the reality of her impending death has kept its distance. I've always assumed there would be plenty of warning, followed by a long, drawn-out passing. What if Mum had died today, without me there? That thought is unbearable, surprisingly so. As is the thought of spending every day at Birch Grove, keeping a bedside vigil.

Cold air encircles my throat, reminding me I need another scarf. In Islington, I head to the shopping centre and nip into H&M. I select a long scarf in grey wool and make for the till. As I pass the racks of jewellery, I consider buying something for Emma. A small thank-you gift for being so kind to Mum. Why not? Her wages are probably pitiful, and it would be a nice gesture.

I stare at the rows of earrings, necklaces and bracelets for some time. What to buy a nineteen-year-old girl? What would Emma like? Uncertain what to choose, I decide to get a voucher.

I leave the store with the scarf around my neck and a gift card for twenty pounds in my handbag. Upper Street is busy, buses pulling up and expelling passengers onto the already crowded pavement. As I wait for the lights to change at a crossing, I notice a small, dark-haired girl marching along on the opposite side of the road. Emma? I call her name but a passing bus drowns me out. By the time it has moved on, the girl is further away. Even from this distance, my mistake is obvious. The girl I'm staring at wears a smart, tailored coat and high-heeled boots. An expensive-looking bag hangs from her right shoulder. She is nothing like Emma.

* * *

In the lobby of my block, the lift takes ages to clank and groan to the ground floor. Once the doors open, I have to step over a green plastic water gun and a pink bucket to get inside. I nudge the toys out of the lift with my foot, certain that Wendy or one of her kids will be on the hunt for them later.

When I reach my floor and step out onto the landing, the white light on the wall beside me flickers on and off, as if sending a Morse code message. SOS.

The sensor light outside my flat comes on when I am still a few metres away. That's when I see her, sitting upright not far from the front door. A chunky doll in a pink gingham dress and yellow cardigan. One eye is shut, but the other is open and looking right at me. As if she knows who I am, as if she has been waiting.

My thigh muscles soften. My jaw clenches. The doll's chestnut brown hair gleams beneath the light. Reason tells me this toy is a random deposit by one of Wendy's feral brood, but biology has pushed me into panic mode.

I run towards my front door, skirting the doll, one hand in my bag searching for my key. For once I find it right away and ram it into the lock.

The door swings open, but the doll stops me from entering. I sense her behind me, lonely in the dark. I walk back to her and crouch down. Short sharp breaths stick in my throat.

She is so light when I pick her up. Nothing like the soft, dense weight of the real thing. I lift up her left eyelid, but it drops shut as soon as I release it. Her body is bare beneath the dress, her plastic legs sculpted into replica rolls of fat. There are deep creases on the palms of her hands. I do not touch them.

The yellow cardigan hangs open, so I do the buttons up one by one.

I lick the tip of my right index finger and rub away streaks of dirt from her cheeks and forehead. Once she is presentable, I hurry back to the landing and place her beside the lift. Then I return to the flat, close the door and seal myself in with lock and chain.

15

CASSIE

August

'Feta and courgette or quinoa and kale?' Ryan asked, holding out two Tupperware containers.

'Both,' I said.

'Is the right answer.' He scooped several spoonfuls of each salad onto a paper plate and handed it to me. As well as preparing homemade food for the picnic, he'd brought cutlery and white cloth napkins from his flat.

Hyde Park on a Friday lunchtime was full of people soaking up the sun. Picnickers like us sprawled on the grass, while in the shade of the nearby chestnut trees, a group of men and women endured an exercise boot camp – press-ups, sit-ups and lunges.

'I love London park life.' Ryan split a miniature bottle of Prosecco between two plastic champagne flutes. 'Cheers.' We'd agreed to take turns showing each other our favourite city activities. Ryan loved picnics in the park – any excuse to be out in the sun. His tanned body looked good in the grey board shorts and white T-shirt I'd bought him.

'So, did you tell your mate about me?' he asked, stabbing an olive with his fork. Thanks to my white lie, he thought I'd spent the morning with an old school friend. In reality, I had an appointment in Harley Street with Dr Costello.

'Of course,' I said, 'we spoke about you loads.'

'Glad to hear it.' He asked a few questions about my 'friend' – what was her name, what did she do, where did she live? I pointed to my full mouth and mumbled that the food deserved our undivided attention. 'Can't argue with that,' he said.

Between us we devoured the salads, following them up with a piece of sweet, sticky baklava. After I'd finished, Ryan brushed a stray flake of pastry from my chin. 'Your shoulders are a bit pink,' he said.

Over my navy cropped trousers, I wore a white vest top of my mother's that I'd borrowed during my last foray into her flat. Far too baggy, it required a camisole underneath for decency's sake, but wearing it made me feel close to her.

Ryan produced a tube of sun cream from his backpack and insisted on applying it for me. When he lifted the vest straps to reach the skin beneath, I ordered him to stop. I didn't want him touching anything belonging to my mother.

I took her mobile and headphones from my handbag and told Ryan I needed to lie down. 'My friend was exhausting,' I said. 'Always analysing everything. Never stops talking.'

'Whatever you want, babe.'

We lay down, him on his back, me with my head on his stomach. I entered the code for my mother's phone, one I'd watched her use many times. Clicking on her music, I scrolled through the playlist I'd made of all her most relevant songs – 'Mother' by Tori Amos, 'Three Babies' by Sinéad O'Connor, 'Mother's Ruin' by Kirsty MacColl. I chose 'Mama' by the Sugarcubes. All these mother-related songs were a sign. Did my own mother realise how many she had and what they meant? Did she know she was longing for me?

Getting hold of the phone was easy. She left her bag hanging on the back of her chair in the WRVS café two days ago, and when she returned to the counter to buy another green tea, I made my move.

Ryan's fingers wound themselves into my hair. He liked playing with my hair. A few nights ago, he'd asked about my family again. I didn't feel ready to tell him about the adoption, so I let him believe the Harringtons were my parents. I did tell him about Isobel's death though, and afterwards he'd held me close for a long time.

As the sun made kaleidoscopes of my eyelids and Björk wailed in my ears, I thought about Dr Costello.

'Good for you, Cassie,' he'd said when I walked into the room and announced my first ever relationship. I sat in one of the black leather recliners by the window and waffled on about Ryan while Costello lowered his towering, bulky body into the chair opposite me. He listened with an encouraging smile until my cheeks got hot and I went silent.

'So you're settling in to your new life?' he said, unbuttoning his waistcoat. He dressed like a snooker player – grey waistcoat, grey trousers, black shirt. A dense mass of man, his own planet.

'I suppose.' I rearranged the straps of my vest. Flaunting my mother's top in front of him gave me a thrill.

He asked how Quentin was getting on.

'He's still pretty miserable,' I said.

Costello nodded. 'He needs more time to come to terms with what happened.'

'It's nearly eight months since Isobel left.'

'Left?'

'What?'

'You said Isobel left.'

'So?'

'Do you find it hard to say she died?' He leaned forward, pulling me into his gravitational field. I wanted to resist, but I couldn't.

'She still left me,' I said, 'it's the same thing.'

'Is it?'

'Everyone always leaves me.'

He frowned. I knew he was about to declare my statement an example of incorrect thinking and suggest we work through it together, so I derailed him by announcing my intention to get a job.

'A job?' He sounded wary. 'I see.'

'Just part-time to start with.'

'What sort of job?'

'One where I can give something back.' A smile tugged at my lips, but I didn't let it loose. 'I want to help people in need.'

'That's very commendable, Cassie,' he said.

'I know,' I replied.

* * *

After the picnic, Ryan and I caught the Tube back to Highbury and Islington. I told him I had a quick errand to do, and he followed me along the High Street to Toni & Guy.

'I'd like an appointment with one of your colourists,' I said to the magenta-haired receptionist.

'What you wanting done?' she asked.

'I fancy something different. A permanent colour.'

Her long black nails pecked at the keyboard in front of her. 'Just a colour?'

'A cut as well, please.'

Ryan stroked the back of my hair. 'You won't take too much off, will you?'

I shrugged. 'We'll see.'

16

GRACE

October

For the first time in weeks, I venture up the stairs of my childhood home and enter Mum's deserted bedroom. The brass carriage clock she has been asking for sits mute on the bedside table. I pick it up, turn it over and twist the wind-up mechanism until a loud ticking erupts. I set the clock to the right time – almost noon. I'm running late for today's visit to the care home.

This morning I woke again at 3 a.m., shaking in the aftermath of the fugitive dream. Only at the first hint of dawn did I drift off again, waking just before ten. The clock has left a clean, rectangular space in the dust on the bedside table. I should be packing Mum's stuff away, but instead I fetch a duster and polish from the kitchen and wipe the bedside table down. Then I dust the bottles of perfume on the dressing table and return them to their exact positions. I polish every surface in the room before changing the yellow linen on the bed for a crisp, white set.

My efforts exhaust me. Unable to resist the freshly made bed, I take refuge beneath the duvet and lie down, staring up at the stiff peaks and swirls of the Artex ceiling. I can't rest for long. Have to get to Birch Grove before Emma finishes at one so I can give her the voucher and thank her in person. Reaching my arms back, I press my palms against the smooth walnut headboard. Although my parents replaced their mattress many times over the years, the bed itself was given to them as a wedding present. As a child, I would climb into it every Sunday morning and snuggle between their warm bodies.

The bed has a special history. Mum spent the last ten weeks of her pregnancy confined to it. Placenta praevia. During this time, she returned to the Catholic faith she'd abandoned in her teens. She prayed in this bed, day and night, for the life of her much-wanted, much-tried-for child. A child conceived after years of failed attempts and two miscarriages. Convinced God's grace had spared her child, she named it in his honour. Then she set about repaying Him with her devotion – church every Sunday her weekly instalment. Dad and I were left behind to amuse ourselves while she did so. I soon worked out Dad resented God's intrusion into his marriage. A second child might have helped, but although I survived the birth, Mum's womb did not.

I yawn. The skin beneath my eyes feels stretched and thin, as if I could pierce it with my finger and find nothing beyond. I remember the doll – her droopy eyelid, her plump, plastic hands. Later that night, I returned to the lift in search of her, but she was gone.

* * *

It is almost one o'clock when I leave the house, a chilly breeze gathering momentum around me. I pull up the collar of my trench coat and tie the wide belt in a tighter knot.

A lone figure waits in the car park of the care home.

Emma. She waves as I approach.

'Hiya,' she says, 'where were you this morning? Your mum and me were waiting for you.'

'I got held up.' I've never seen her out of uniform before. Blue jeggings cling to her skinny legs. Her green Parka is zipped up tight, but her white plimsolls are far too flimsy for the weather. She pulls a packet of Marlboro Lights from her coat pocket, takes one out and lights it with a pink lighter. She looks too young to smoke, and I long to warn her of its dangers. Watching her inhale, a familiar craving resurfaces. I remember how soothing that first drag can feel, how the worries of the day can be exhaled along with it.

'Could I pinch one of those?' I say.

'You smoke?' Emma asks, incredulous.

'Not normally.'

'Sure.' She holds out the packet. 'Stressed are you?'

'A little.' I take a cigarette and welcome it between my lips. It tastes harsh and synthetic, alien and familiar.

Emma sparks up her lighter and I lean in, my chin brushing the hand she holds cupped around the flame. I suck in the bitter smoke and wait to cough or get dizzy but, after seven years, it's as if I've never given up. Deep inhale and exhale. Jaunty flick of the ash. 'Thanks.'

'There's something I've been meaning to ask you,' Emma says, her expression serious.

I feel light-headed. A delayed nicotine rush? 'Go ahead.' I feel oddly nervous of what she might want.

She tells me she's decided to apply for the Foundation in Health and Social Care course at Brentham College but is having trouble with the forms. 'They want me to do a personal statement thing, but I'm crap at that sort of stuff. If I write something down would you have a read of it and help me?'

'I'd be happy to.'

'Cool.' She blows a series of immaculate smoke rings that take me by surprise. The trick seems out of place on her, too sophisticated. Then she chucks her cigarette butt to the ground and crushes it with her plimsoll.

'Cheers,' she says, 'better get going.' She smiles before scurrying away. It is only when she turns left at the end of the street and disappears that I realise I forgot to give her the voucher.

'Emma,' I call, setting off after her. The breeze has upgraded to a blustery wind, whipping the ash from the tip of my cigarette. I put it out and drop it in a bin, appalled at the rancid taste in my mouth.

Turning onto Layer Road, I spot Emma walking ahead of me. I call out again but she is too far away to hear. The fish hook dances in my guts and an invisible line spools out between us, drawing me on.

I should return to Birch Grove, but instead I trail a safe distance behind Emma, letting her lead me to the centre of town and along the High Street. Fascinating, to see her out of the care home environment. To glimpse another side of her. She walks with an unexpected confidence, hips swaying, head held high. The walk of someone used to being looked at.

I bargain with myself – if Emma goes into a shop, I'll stop this and leave her alone. She doesn't. Instead she takes us away from the town centre towards the Chelmsford roundabout. Upon reaching it, she descends into the underpass. Only when she emerges from the other side do I follow.

With the underpass behind us, we walk up Priory Road, past the entrance to the bus station and into one of Brentham's rougher areas. Despite our proximity to the town centre, the narrow, terraced houses here are run-down and in need of repair.

Emma darts across the road and enters a street with a sex shop on one corner and a pub called The Fat Cat on the other. She waves at a bald hulk of a man swigging a pint at the pub's lone outside table. By the time I cross over, she is turning left down the side of a building and is soon out of sight.

I hesitate. What am I doing here? I should leave now.

My legs have their own agenda. Edging forward to the spot where Emma disappeared, I find a narrow passageway between a tall, three-storey house and a high wall. The passageway is dim and dank and empty. My heart picks up pace as I enter it. Set into the side wall of the house is a white door. The panel of buzzers next to it shows the building is divided into flats. None of the buzzers have names beside them.

Litter all over the passageway. Crushed cans of beer, cigarette butts, torn magazines. Stepping away from the door, I kick an empty wine bottle. It spins and clinks. My heart races round my chest as I look for the emergency exit. My throat constricts. Where has all the air gone? I feel like I'm breathing through a straw. I turn back but the entrance to the passageway recedes before me. So far away, how will I ever reach it?

My heart beats faster still until I'm certain it will burst through my ribs. Am I having a heart attack?

With one hand on the side of the house and the other on the wall, I grope my way towards the distant exit. My whole body shakes as I inch forwards. Upon reaching the street, I glance up at the building and see a light in the top-floor window and the silhouette of Emma, standing with her back to the glass.

Biology takes over, a fast walk first and then, at the end of the road, I run.

PART II

17

CASSIE

October

Emma was kind and selfless. Emma was caring, compassionate and full of empathy. Emma was nothing like me. Sometimes I hated her for that, as well as for her terrible clothes, her lack of intelligence and that truly dreadful accent.

I hated how much I needed her.

When Emma met my mother for the first time, she was so nervous she almost blew it. She stood for ages in the doorway of my grandmother's room with an idiotic look on her face. I wanted to say, *hello, Mum, it's me, Cassie,* but instead Emma said, *hiya, Mrs Walker,* in that common voice of hers. I'd imagined my first conversation with my mother so many times but never thought we would talk about tea. Emma handled that quite well, I must admit. She talked about tea as if it mattered, as if she really wanted to make Polly Walker the perfect cuppa. She said things like 'sweetheart' and 'my love' and 'bless your heart' – phrases she'd heard the other care workers using.

She couldn't help offering my mother a drink. I enjoyed that. A small kindness, one a daughter might do for her mother on a daily basis. The offer almost had my mother in tears, but Emma came to the rescue with a tissue. When my mother made excuses about not visiting, I was furious. *Trust you to avoid your responsibilities,* I wanted to say, but instead Emma dished out chirpy reassurances. Good old Emma. Bless her heart.

When Polly asked Emma to call her Grandma, I didn't know what to do. Surely she couldn't have recognised me from the hospital, not with my hair cut short and dyed? Not with brown contact lenses in? It seemed I'd underestimated the bond between us. She would have recognised me in any disguise.

Perhaps that's why her attack on me came as such a shock. Kegs had warned Emma during her induction that some of the residents could be violent, but still. When my grandmother punched me in the chest, I felt spurned. For a moment, I forgot how ill she was and wanted to hit her back. Luckily I fell, and what a landing. Right into my

mother's arms. She was there, waiting to catch me. I couldn't let her go, even after she put me back on my feet. My hand on her arm, her eyes staring into mine. Did she recognise me? Up close I could see the faint creases at the corners of her eyes and the tiny grooves at the sides of her mouth that marked her smile's parameters.

Then Grandma started weeping, and Emma had to go and fuss over her and be all patient and understanding. Good old Emma. Bless her heart.

* * *

Good old Emma was tired. She'd covered an early Sunday shift today to help out a desperate Kegs. She'd hummed her way through seven hours of arse wiping, bed changing and tea making, still high from the conversation with her mother the previous week. *Would you help me with my application?*

Yes, of course I will.

Emma had found a way in.

I had found a way in. Emma and I were so close now; it was easy to merge into her. Especially when living in her cold, damp bedsit, surrounded by her things.

I switched on the two halogen fires, filling the poky room with a bright tangerine glow. The bedsit had no central heating, so after moving in I went to Argos for the first time ever and bought the heaters. Argos was fun – flicking through the catalogue, marking up the slip of paper with the cheap biro. Sort of how I imagined Bingo might be.

With one room to live and sleep in and a tiny bathroom, my new second home was a big step down from the Harringtons' French holiday villa. After Kegs had rung to offer me the part-time job at Birch Grove, I'd considered commuting to Brentham for my three shifts a week but the 7 a.m. starts made that impossible. Besides, I intended to do the role of Emma justice. I trawled through Gumtree until I found a place that sounded fitting for her and offered the landlord six months' rent up front. Two days later, I had the keys in my hand.

'I'll get something done about the door,' the landlord had promised before legging it down the stairs and roaring off in his white transit van, but he still hadn't repaired the splintered door frame or replaced the flimsy chain. Every night I jammed a chair under the door handle. Just in case.

After turning both fires to maximum, I climbed into the made-up sofa bed. I'd given up folding it back into a sofa in the mornings. Emma wouldn't bother. My duvet, also from Argos, had a cerise cover decorated with a white slogan instructing me to keep calm and go to sleep. The bedsit had basic furniture, but I'd bought all the extras myself – pink and blue plastic tumblers, cheap cheery plates covered in red polka dots with mugs and bowls to match. Thanks again Argos. Bingo!

Shopping as Emma was fun but time-consuming. Having to get into character, to think about what Emma would like, what Emma would buy. Her limited budget horrified me, but I managed. Sure I had to get taxis back and forth from Argos to the bedsit and yes, I paid the taxi driver extra to help me carry everything up the three flights of stairs, but apart from that my portrayal radiated authenticity.

My mother's acting genes had not gone to waste. My character research was well underway before I made that first phone call to the care home. I watched a few old episodes of *TOWIE* and hung around Brentham High Street, listening to people in shops and eavesdropping on teenagers in Starbucks. Mimicry had always come easily to me. By the age of five I could spook Isobel with my impression of her. *Don't be naughty, darling.*

After plenty of rehearsal, I called Birch Grove. *Hiya. Are you looking for any care workers at the moment?*

18

GRACE

October

The email arrives just after 8 p.m. on Monday evening. EmsBabe@yahoo.com. The subject line reads: *Forms n Stuff.* Hands trembling, I open it.

> Hiya sorry too hassel u. Hope its OK to e? Got your add from the office. Was gonna print out my application stuff and give it too u at the wknd but you didn't turn up. Hope u r OK? Attached my statement thing but no probs if u r to busy too look. Cheers if u do. See u soon? Ems

The warm laptop hums against my thighs. I shift to the edge of the sofa and resettle it on my knees before reading the email again.

> Hope it's OK to e?

Not really, but I suppose all the staff have access to my contact details.

See U soon? Ems

Sweat coats the back of my neck. Over the past eight days, I've managed to put what happened in the passageway to the back of my mind. Now this email has sabotaged my efforts. I don't know what's worse, the memory of having a panic attack or the fact I followed a girl I hardly know back to her home for no reason.

I could put off answering the message, but that wouldn't be fair. Emma's a decent girl and deserves the help I promised. The application must be important for her to contact me.

Hi, Emma. Thanks for your email. Good you've made a start with the forms. I'm happy to take a look. I won't be in to visit Mum this weekend so I can either email my thoughts to you or we can speak when I come to Birch Grove the weekend after next. Hope all is good with you. Best wishes, Grace

After hitting send, I sit in silence for a while before placing the laptop on the coffee table. I get up and switch on the overhead lights, flushing the darkness from all corners of the room.

My mobile rings. Hesitant, I pick it up from the breakfast bar and see John's name on the caller display.

'Hi, gorgeous,' he says when I answer.

'Didn't expect to hear from you today.'

'Just been to the gym. Thought I'd call before I head home.'

Home to eat dinner with his wife. Home to play with his kids. I should hang up but don't want to be alone with my thoughts.

'Grace? You there?'

'Sorry. Yes.' He will be calling from his car as usual. I don't ask where he's parked. A quiet side street maybe, a lay-by, a secluded corner of the gym car park.

'I've been thinking about you all day,' he says.

'Really?' I can't help smiling. 'Shouldn't you have been finding devious ways to move rich people's money around?'

'I did a bit of that too. Seriously though, I've been thinking about our last phone call. That was quite something.'

'I aim to please.'

He laughs. 'Satisfying as these calls are, I hope I'm going to see you in person this weekend?'

'Sorry. I'm not planning to come down.'

'What kind of daughter doesn't visit her mother two weeks in a row?' he says, mock serious.

'The kind whose mother is driving her nuts.' My reply sounds light-hearted, but I mean it. The stress of dealing with Mum has finally got to me. Why else would I do something as bizarre as following Emma? 'I'm just having a bad few days,' I say.

A fine line glitters. Will John cross it? Will he insist I tell him more and let me make emotional demands not covered by our arrangement?

'What are you wearing?' he asks. His question is my fault. That day in the laundry room, I ordered him not to climax inside me. Confused, he asked if I was on the pill. Yes, I told him, but we had to have boundaries. He understood right away. Our sex had to be different from the sex he had with his wife. We couldn't get too involved.

'I'm wearing tracksuit bottoms,' I say, 'with an old sweatshirt and very warm socks.'

'Sexy.'

'That's me.'

'You'd look good in anything.' His voice is deep and breathy; I can tell he is raring to go. Probably has his zip undone already, tissues at hand to remove the evidence. 'Tell me a story,' he says.

I'm not in the mood but don't want the call to end. 'Once upon a time.' I return to the sofa and lie down.

'Once upon a time, what?' he says.

I make up a fantasy, the two of us meeting as strangers in a park on a hot summer's day. Me in a floaty dress without underwear. Sitting on his lap under the shade of a leafy tree. His fingers inside me.

John groans with pleasure as he touches himself. I usually enjoy my inventiveness, the variety of settings, characters and positions that pour out of me, but tonight I need to talk about other things. I need to tell him I don't feel right, that I haven't felt right for some time. I need to talk about Mum and my fears for the future, but instead I gasp and moan and pretend to be touching myself too.

***

After John hangs up, I fish my Marlboro Lights from my handbag, slip on my coat and step out onto the balcony. My cigarette is lit within seconds, the old habit back in my life as if I'd never escaped it. I exhale the first drag into the raw, damp air, at one with the teenagers in the park below. By the time the cigarette runs out, I've resolved to put the past couple of weeks behind me and pull myself together.

I return inside and take my laptop to the breakfast bar, determined to read through Emma's application and get it out of the way.

> What I think will be the best about the foundations in Health and social Care is I will get too learn about what I luv. I have not been a worker with the eldarly for very long but it really is fun and I think im pretty good at it!!!!!! I wood like one day too maybe manage a care home or train as a nurse.

I stop reading. Emma's statement will take more than a few tweaks to get it right. Some of my intermediate-level students have a better grasp of English. I open a blank document, intending to jot down a few suggestions, but instead I stare at the empty screen, fingers quivering over the keys.

A tremor in my guts as the buried fault line shifts and cracks. I see myself crouching on smooth, cool flagstones, surrounded by fag butts, greasy chip paper and empty Carlsberg bottles. The bottles clink as I press myself against the rough stone wall of the passageway. I shiver in the darkness. I hear wheels rumbling over the cobblestones of the street nearby. Hiding is pointless. She will find me. She always finds me.

The image erases itself. My fingers stab at the laptop keyboard.

My name is Grace Walker. It is 9.16 p.m. I am wearing grey tracksuit bottoms and a black sweatshirt. I am in my living room.

I stare at what I have written. Then I delete it all.

19

THEN

Tuesday 5 September, Royal Edinburgh Hospital

My name is Grace Walker. It is 5.19 p.m. I am in my room on Simpson Ward.

I know who I am. I know where I am. That's something. The flashbacks come and go. One minute the past and the present are in their proper place, the next they are trying to trick me.

My name is Grace Walker. It is 5.20 p.m. I am wearing jeans and a navy T-shirt. Writing down simple facts seems to help. Makes me feel grounded.

This morning I had a flashback to the passageway. Saw myself on the ground like an animal, back against the wall. Eyes squeezed shut, hoping that would protect me from her. She called my name as she got closer. That sweet, high voice only I could hear. I told her this couldn't go on; this behaviour had to stop. She replied with her hands, her small, soft hands on my thighs, on my belly, at my throat. Where did all the air go? I'm safe from her in here. That's something. Must remember this at nights when terrified I will never get out.

She and I are done. It's over.

Simon (Dr Jamieson) gave me this notebook and pen this morning. He told me to keep a diary, write stuff down, get things out of my head. Said some patients find this useful. I asked if I had to let him read the diary, and he smiled and said no. Said this was a hospital not a prison. He also reminded me

I came here voluntarily. Thank God they kept me at the police station long enough for me to calm down. Long enough for me to understand that if I didn't agree to go with them to the hospital, I would be admitted under section.

Simon is young and has a kind face, and I believe what he says. He has a soft, well-spoken voice. He wears beige chinos with a blue-and-white-striped shirt and brown deck shoes. The room we met in had bare blue walls, a desk and two swivel chairs. He doesn't know much about why I'm here. When the police dropped me off, they handed me over to a stern nurse in her fifties, who took me to a room and asked me to get undressed. Once naked, I crossed my arms over my stomach, scared she might examine me, but she handed me a gown and then weighed me and took my blood pressure. She seemed in a rush.

Simon described what happened to me as an episode. A brief psychotic episode. I asked if it would happen again. What if I kept losing myself? He said he hoped it was an isolated incident, but he couldn't guarantee it. He said it would help to have some idea of what had triggered the episode.

'Maybe you could write down what you remember?' he said. 'Try and establish a narrative of events.'

'Like a confession?' I said.

He removed his round, wire-framed glasses, leaned towards me and said, 'Do you consider yourself a criminal, Grace?'

20

CASSIE

November

Black, thunderous clouds crowded the sky outside my grandmother's window, but we didn't care. We had News 24 on with no volume and Neil Diamond singing 'Forever in Blue Jeans' full blast – a song about how being with the people you love is much more important than money.

'Well true, Neil,' I said, 'well true.' I always kept up Emma's accent, even when it was just me and Grandma. Better to be on the safe side and, besides, she liked Emma. Everyone liked Emma.

My grandmother hummed along, a totally different tune to the one blaring from the CD player, but she seemed happy enough. She didn't protest as I rubbed off the remains of her latest manicure with nail varnish remover. The pearly pink had begun to chip, and I didn't want her looking scruffy.

'Why was Grace a sinner?' I asked, trying to catch her off guard. Every now and then I threw in a question like this, to try and discover how much she knew. As always she responded with a vacant look. Poor woman. Even if she had known anything, she'd probably forgotten it by now.

My phone buzzed in my tunic pocket. Carrying our mobiles around with us on duty was forbidden, but everyone did it.

Hey! How's ur gran? Tell her to get well soon so I can see more of u!! xxx

'Have I shown you a picture of my boyfriend?' I asked Grandma.

She pointed at the TV. 'Lorraine Kelly's lost a bit of weight.'

I held up a selfie of Ryan and I standing next to Kylie Minogue's statue in Madame Tussauds. 'Ryan said he'd always wanted to be in a threesome with Kylie, so we took this picture.' I explained our thing of going to each other's favourite places. 'Tussauds was his choice, not mine,' I said. 'I've never been before, but it was actually quite fun.'

My grandmother paid no attention.

'Honestly,' I said, 'you could at least look. It's not easy me coming down here all the time.' I put my phone away. 'Ryan's not happy about it, you know.'

A bit of an exaggeration, but when I'd told Ryan that my gran in Brentham was out of hospital but in need of my help a few days a week, he did ask questions. How come I had to do it? Shouldn't my gran have proper carers or other relatives to assist her? Did I want him to come with me one time? I insisted that helping my gran was no problem; after all, I'd wanted to do something worthwhile. He thought my nights away were spent in my grandmother's house.

I fetched her hairbrush and moved it gently through her sparse hair.

'Grace?' she moaned.

Irritation flashed through me. 'You won't be seeing her for a while,' I said for the tenth time that morning. 'She's not coming this weekend.'

The arrival of my mother's email in my inbox last week had left me euphoric. My first ever written communication from her. I was a bit disappointed when she said she'd be missing another visit, but at least she promised we'd see each other soon. Then, yesterday, I got another email from her, saying she wasn't coming this weekend either. Maybe not even next weekend. She needed a break, she said. She did offer again to send me her comments on my application, but I said I'd rather we spoke in person.

I have to admit my anger kicked in then. A break? Was I supposed to just wait until she deigned to show up again? I would of course be able to keep an eye on her in London, but that wasn't the same as hanging out with her as Emma.

'Grace?' said my grandmother.

'Shut up.' I was sick of hearing my absent mother's name. She was never there when I needed her. Grandma squealed as I dragged the brush hard against her scalp. 'I'm sorry,' I said, dropping the brush on the bed. 'Sorry.'

'Only trying,' she whispered.

'You can be...' I pinched her cheek so she'd know I was joking. She could be infuriating at times, but I never stayed mad with her for long. Wasn't that always the way with family? 'I suppose my mother does deserve a break,' I said. 'She was so stressed when I saw her; she cadged a fag off me.' My grandmother was lost to the TV. Just as well. I didn't mean to grass my mother up for smoking. 'Maybe I'll send her a gift to cheer her up. Her job must be proper draining with all those students sucking her dry.'

Grandma shifted position and ended up slumped across her pillows. 'Don't want you falling out again,' I said, straightening her up. Finding her on the floor last time had upset me. Seeing her lying there, fragile and helpless like a wounded bird. I'd stayed with her, reading out quotes from her Bible to calm her down. I picked the ones she'd underlined, and despite not being a fan of the Good Book I appreciated her choices. One of the proverbs stayed with me. *The crown of the aged is their grandchildren.*

Afterwards, all the staff praised me for helping her. Kegs said I had a gift for caring. I enjoyed the attention, even if was meant for Emma and not me. The gift voucher my mother sent here for me showed I'd gone up in her estimation.

After the fall, Vera had instructed us to pull up the safety rails at either side of Grandma's bed whenever she was alone. As I settled my grandmother back into her pillows, I considered leaving the railings down and hanging around in case she fell again, and lo and behold there I'd be like a guardian angel. Or, a more merciful option, I could help her out of bed, ease her down to the floor and pretend she'd fallen. Kegs would ring my mother again, and maybe she'd come down sooner.

I yanked up the safety rails. 'See you later, Grandma.' I kissed her soft, warm cheek. 'I could never hurt you. We're family.'

* * *

I headed for the kitchen. Morning tea break approached, and I needed to get the trolley ready. My Birch Grove keys clinked in my pocket as I walked. A noise that made me feel important and responsible. Like I belonged.

In the corridor, I met Surinder. 'Hiya, babes,' she said.

'Hiya, babes,' I said back. A typical Emma–Surinder exchange.

'Oh my God,' she gushed, 'I love your leggings.'

'I know, they're well lush. H&M.' I longed to boast about the gift card from my mother, but I'd already told everyone at Birch Grove my mum was dead.

'The purple swirly bits totally match your tunic.' Surinder tucked her long black hair behind her ears and pointed to the gold studs that decorated them. 'You like?'

'Well nice.'

'Arun got me them. He's in my good books now.' I liked Surinder. She was only two years older than me but had two sons already. She and her husband, Arun, didn't have much money but they loved their kids. That was all that mattered.

'Sure you can't come to the fireworks tomorrow?' she said.

'Nah, sorry.' She'd invited me to a Bonfire Night event with Arun and the boys, but I'd pretended to be attending one in Colchester with some old school friends. I'd also refused Ryan's invitation to join him and his mates for the fireworks in Hackney, claiming I'd be with my grandmother. So many excuses to keep track of.

'Fag later?' Surinder called out as she carried on down the corridor.

'Totes.'

On my way past the TV room, I spotted Mrs Palethorpe doing her slack puppet impression in one of the armchairs. I called most residents by their first names, but Mrs Palethorpe didn't invite that sort of intimacy. She could be scary when she was on one, but today she appeared to have the whole of Birch Grove's medicine cabinet inside her. Drool sparkled on her chin and her vacant eyes gazed at the wall. Poor old thing. Being pumped full of sedatives was no fun. I should know.

In reception, Brenda and Memory were having their usual argument – Memory wanting to wipe down the desk and Brenda telling her she didn't have any record in the diary of cleaners coming into the office. I admired Brenda, messing with Memory like that; I wouldn't have dared. Memory always looked at me like she knew what I was up to.

The door to Kegs's office opened, and Kegs showed out Mrs Palethorpe's son, John. Vera once described John as dishy, but I didn't think he was anything special.

'Cheers, mate,' John said to Kegs as he left, 'we appreciate everything you're doing.'

'Emma,' Kegs said when he saw me, 'have you got a minute?'

My heart stuttered. 'I was just off to get the tea trolley sorted.'

'Won't take long.' Kegs returned to his office. I followed him and waited in the doorway, legs trembling. What if he was on to me?

'Don't look so worried,' he said. 'I just want a quick chat.' A quick chat about what? My references? I closed the door behind me and claimed the only chair not covered with cardboard boxes.

'Sorry about the mess,' Kegs said. 'Some of the Christmas decorations arrived this morning.'

'Already?'

'Christmas lasts forever here, darlin'.'

'Sounds fun,' I said with a fake, Emma smile. 'Is everything okay?'

'Fine.' Kegs opened the box of Celebrations on his desk and offered me one.

'No, thanks.' Relatives liked to buy us chocolates when their loved ones died. Celebrations seemed a bit inappropriate though.

Kegs weaselled out a mini Bounty with his hairy fingers and popped it in his mouth.

'Is something wrong with my references?' I regretted the question straight away, but I needed to know. 'If they haven't arrived yet I can give the people a ring or something.'

He shook his head, jaws busy with the Bounty. 'Nope,' he said after he'd swallowed it, 'meant to say they came through a couple of days ago.'

I knew they had; I'd sent them. One from a café in Clacton, the other from a shoe shop in Colchester, neither of which I'd worked in. Easy really. I'd set up fake email addresses and written myself two positive but not unrealistic references when the requests came in.

It appeared Kegs had believed them and why wouldn't he, with his staffing issues? At my interview, he'd asked for my passport to confirm my ID, which wasn't a problem as my first name is Emma. I may have lied about my age to my mother, but I'm using my real name. From the moment the Harringtons had revealed the full story of my adoption, I'd insisted on being addressed by my middle name: Cassie. A name my mother might recognise if she came looking for me. While checking my passport, Kegs had joked that Cassie was a bit of a posh name, and I'd laughed and agreed.

Satisfied my ID was in order, he'd said I could start before my background check and references had come through. I'm not implying he was remiss. He cared about Birch Grove, but he needed more staff to run the place properly. He did give me a full induction day with safety and fire training.

'Now then,' Kegs said, taking a swig from the World's Greatest Boss mug on his desk, 'you seem to be enjoying it here?'

'I love it.' Emma was the cheery sort who didn't mind emptying shitty bedpans and wiping up vomit for scandalously low pay. Even I didn't mind it as much as I'd feared. The job had made me stronger, given me muscles in my arms that even Ryan had noticed. And I slept well after a shift – bone-deep and dreamless.

'There's more hours going if you want them,' Kegs said. 'We always need the help.'

'Thanks. I'll have a think about it.' No need to go overboard. Extra hours would make it impossible to run my two lives, and I still needed my London existence. With my mother only at Birch Grove one day a week, I still liked to see her in London too, although I had to be careful now she and Emma had met. When following her in the city, I wore a blonde wig, a black beanie and sunglasses, even on cloudy days.

On the office wall hung a black-and-white photo of Kegs in his army uniform. At my interview, I'd asked where his name came from and he'd told me that as an eighteen-year-old corporal, he'd stolen four kegs of beer from the officers' mess, an escapade that earned him a spell in military jail and a nickname that has stuck with him for over thirty years.

'Did you ever spy on anyone when you were a soldier?' I asked.

Kegs nodded. 'We used to go out on surveillance all the time in Northern Ireland.' He told me that on one mission he'd hidden in a ditch for four days, just to get a picture of an IRA suspect.

'Patience,' he said. 'Patience will always get you your man.'

'What about going undercover? Did you ever do that?'

'No, thank God.' He shook his head. 'Hardcore stuff that. Not everyone's got the guts for it.'

'I can imagine.'

'Consequences were pretty grim if the other side got hold of you.'

I smiled. 'Guess the trick is not to get caught then?'

21

THEN

Tuesday 5 September, Royal Edinburgh Hospital

After he gave me the notebook, Simon asked what had happened in the hours before my arrest. Most of that day is a blank, I told him. I remember leaving my flat, and I remember the police hauling me out of the dark, dank passageway, but the bits in between are gone.

'Short-term memory loss is not uncommon after a psychotic episode,' he said. I hoped that meant he'd stop questioning me, but instead he asked what I thought had triggered the episode.

Her. Always her. Demanding my attention, begging me to notice her.

He asked what had been happening in my life. What stress had I been under? No stress really, I said. Nothing out of the ordinary.

Not sure if he knew I was lying, but he went on for ages then about how our memories can store our traumatic experiences just out of reach until we can deal with them. A protective measure.

I thought he meant our minds could edit the bad stuff out and get rid of it for good, but he said no, not for good. The memories still exist somewhere.

Pity. I have a lot I want to forget.

'I would describe it as knowing and not knowing at the same time,' he said.

I said not knowing would be bliss, and he looked at me for a long time, as if deciding something. Then he said I seemed like an intelligent young woman so he'd level with me. He said I was only one of many emergencies he had to deal with, that the system was flawed, that he never had enough time to treat his patients properly. Or information – he doesn't have instant access to my medical records, which I was relieved to hear.

He urged me to make the most of the short time we have together. To try and make sense of what happened so I'd have a better chance of recovery. He said otherwise all he could do was patch me up with medication and send me back out into the world again.

'Talk to me, Grace,' he said, 'and I'll do my very best to help you.' He looked so kind, so sincere that I almost considered it.

She and I are done. It's over. I'm going to write our story down, start to finish, and get her out of my head for good. Then I won't be tempted to talk about her. Then I might just get away without anyone else knowing.

22

GRACE

November

Gritty-eyed and irritable, I lean against the wall of the classroom. The students in my Thursday morning IELTS group are still half asleep. They stare blankly at the photocopied exercise in front of them. The dull, repetitive work required to pass the IELTS exam and gain entry to a British university never kindles much enthusiasm from these students, even the keen ones from my favourite advanced group. I usually seek ways to liven up the material but am too tired for the challenge today.

'Look again at the text,' I say, 'and decide if the statements below it are true, false, or not given.' The students avoid me by subjecting their worksheets to further lethargic scrutiny. 'Do the statements agree with the text?' I ask, my frustration mounting.

No one answers. My eyes travel around the desks, seeking some sign of comprehension. 'Waleed?' I say. Waleed is normally quick to participate, but even he responds with a shrug. After so many years of teaching, I've grown comfortable with long pauses in class and can usually ride them out until a student offers something. On this occasion, I can't bear the silence.

'How many possibilities are there for each statement?' I ask.

'Anybody?'

Nieve raises her head. 'Three.'

'At last. Thank you, Nieve. And they are?'

Nieve rakes her fingers through her long, black hair. 'True, false or not given.'

'Brilliant.' My exaggerated sigh of relief raises a few laughs. 'Spilt yourselves into pairs and work through the rest of the exercise with your partner.'

The room fills with sighs and the rustling of paper. I wander over to the window. The sun is a pale yolk in a white sky. I turn my back on the group so they don't see me yawn.

My forehead has been throbbing for two days now. As though something is trying to drill through it. Each night, the unremembered dream chases me awake, and I sense it getting closer. I feel as if I'm treading water by the drop-off shelf of some vast ocean – warm shallows at my back and treacherous currents ahead.

I close my eyes. The chatter of the class builds behind me. I drift into a limbo, aware of the sounds in the room but distant from them.

Grace? A voice calls to me. *Grace?* A girl's voice, sweet and high. A voice only I can hear.

'Grace?' It is Nieve's voice. I jerk away from the window, stumbling as I turn round. All eyes are on me.

'We've finished,' says Nieve, a bemused look on her face.

'Great,' I reply. They are waiting for me to take control. To guide and help them. I want to run from the room, to escape their expectant expressions. I swallow. 'Let's check your answers. Nieve, you start us off.'

* * *

I enter the staffroom to find Max kneeling in front of the photocopier, sliding a wad of A4 into the paper tray.

'Jeez,' he says, 'you look rough.'

I dump my backpack on one of the desks. 'Thanks.'

He slams the paper tray shut and springs to his feet. 'Hangover?'

'Wish I had that excuse.' I trail over to the kettle, find it half full and flick it on.

'White, two sugars,' Max says with a grin.

My pounding head makes finding a witty reply impossible. After washing up two mugs in the grubby sink, I put a green tea bag in one of them and a bag of Tetley in the other.

'Bloody thing.' Max jabs at the photocopier's control panel as if playing pinball. Each buzz and beep of the machine ricochets between my temples.

'Grace, there you are.' Mandy, the school's receptionist, pops into the room, vivid in her lime green jumper. A warm, motherly woman in her early fifties, Mandy claims her bright clothing keeps her cheerful. 'This came for you in the morning post,' she says, holding out a small, square box.

I take the parcel from her.

'See you later.' Mandy lets the door slam as she goes. The kettle comes to a zealous boil. The photocopier is in full flow now – a throaty whir as it scans, a staccato buzz as it spits out paper.

I remove the Sellotape from the lid of the box and open it. 'Anything exciting?' Max asks.

Nestled in the foam packaging inside is a mug. I pull it out. The mug is white with pink lettering.

WORLD'S GREATEST MUM

Nausea swells inside me and pushes up my throat. I spin round, lean over the sink and let out a stream of hot, watery vomit.

***

I sit on the sofa, knees hugged to my chest. I've been sitting here since returning from work. How long ago was that? Outside my window, the last dregs of light are draining from the sky.

Leaving work early proved easy. Max assumed I had a bug of some kind and ordered me to go home. He offered to cover my afternoon class and said he'd pass on my apologies to Linda.

The mug sits on the coffee table. Perhaps my work details had found their way onto the same database as my home address? Possible, but I also know anyone can find me from the school's website.

Bile rises up my throat. I see myself in a green hospital gown on a narrow hospital bed. I've been waiting ages. Is it time? My hands grip the sides of the bed, resisting the urge to touch my belly. If I connect with what has grown inside me, I might not be able to give it up.

I shut the memory down. Can't stop shivering. Need to think.

Either I am losing myself again, or someone is sending me reminders of the past.

My laptop is soon out of my backpack and coming to life on the coffee table. Once it warms up, I go to Google and begin to type.

Dan Thorne.

I hit return and the Dan Thornes of the world appear in a list. Dan Thorne, accountant. Dan Thorne, baseball player. Dan Thorne, motor mechanic. Dan after Dan, but I cannot find him. I bring up the image results instead and trawl through the thumbnail portraits.

Bright green eyes stare out from the centre of the screen. I click on the image, follow the link to the original website and find myself on the staff profile for Dan Thorne, drama tutor at Brighton Central College.

His face looks just as I remember it. A few lines on his forehead perhaps, but his bone structure is as striking as ever. His hair is short now, receding a little at the temples. I find a link to his biography – *don't follow it, quit now.* Too late.

I live in Brighton with my wife, Stella, and our two beautiful children.

Images bombard me: Dan, beaming with pride, his hands caressing Stella's swollen belly. Those same hands scooping bathwater over a baby's delicate shoulders. Chubby infant fingers entwined in his slender ones.

I close my eyes, but that doesn't stop me seeing.

23

THEN

Wednesday 6 September, Royal Edinburgh Hospital

The story starts with Dan. I first kissed him in the Three Tuns, the pub in Headingley where everyone from the Northern Theatre School hung out. We were supposed to be working on the final acting project of our degree – an adaptation of a famous book, to be performed by a cast of four. My group, which included Dan, had picked Jean Cocteau's Les Enfants Terribles. When the other two cast members didn't show up to rehearsals one afternoon, Dan suggested we go to the pub to rewrite the final section of the script.

During my three years at uni, I'd never acted with Dan. Our year of drama students had been split in half, and Dan was in the other group to me. I'd heard he was difficult to work with, and he rarely socialised with the other students. The girls he slept with spread the word that Dan might be good-looking, but he was cold and mean and moody. The course tutors had decided to mix the students together for this project, so I just had to get on with it.

After three pints apiece, I forgot about the script. I also forgot about Dan's reputation. He turned out to be fun and easy to get on with. We chain-smoked roll-ups, slagged off some of our tutors, confessed our crushes on others. Dan told me he wanted to act in films.

He had the looks: sharp cheekbones, green eyes, shoulder-length blond hair. As we talked, I noticed a gaggle of first-year girls at the bar glancing over at him with lust and me with envy. When he went to buy us another pint, one of the girls – petite with milky skin and wild red curls – tried to chat him up. He crushed her efforts with a disinterested glance. He looked like a centuries-old vampire weary of humanity; I couldn't keep my eyes off him.

When he returned and sat down beside me, I felt like I'd won something. As if he'd chosen me over everyone else in the room. As our fourth pint disappeared, he asked me loads of questions about myself. He even asked how I was coping after my dad's death.

Dad, already cooling when Mum dragged me in to look at him. Is he dead? she kept screaming. Is he dead?

I'd never even realised Dan knew about my loss. I told him I was doing okay. Still found it hard at times.

He gave me a sympathetic smile and rubbed the tight muscles between my shoulder blades. His hands felt warm to me and not at all mean. I picked up my copy of the script and suggested we work on the tricky final scene, but he said he had a much better idea.

'What?' I asked, as he pulled me to him. His insistent tongue was as warm as his hands.

'I'm not shagging you just like that,' I said when we came up for air.

Dan grinned as he worked a hand between my thighs, but I said I was serious. I made it clear I wasn't that easy.

He told me to kiss him again and I did.

24

CASSIE

November

I dreamt of Isobel. Sick Isobel, scrawny and yellow, a Hermès scarf covering her bristly scalp. I was trying to get away from her, but her skinny fingers closed around my wrists.

'Your mother didn't want you,' she said.

I shot up in bed, hot and shivery – 1.16 a.m., according to my digital clock. Ryan lay beside me on his stomach, face squashed against the pillow, his breathing heavy. I rarely slept when he stayed over, preferring instead to doze and keep an eye on him. Last week, I caught him sneaking out of bed in the night. *Go on then,* I'd told him, *leave. I know you want to.* He'd called me a drama queen and said he was only going to the toilet. Upon returning to bed, he'd reached out and pulled me to him.

The mattress creaked as I slid off it, but Ryan didn't stir. In the faint light coming from the hallway, I unhooked my mother's white vest from the back of the door and slipped it on. It hung loose around me as I padded barefoot along the hall.

In the living room, I switched on the fire and turned it up until the flames flared from the fake coals. A half-smoked joint lay abandoned in the ashtray on the coffee table. I resuscitated it with Ryan's Zippo and took a deep, greedy drag before flopping onto the sofa and sinking into the welcoming cushions. As much as I enjoyed the role of Emma, coming back to my own flat was always a relief. Emma had taught me to appreciate my efficient central heating and comforting fire. She'd taught me gratitude for my deep bath, my power shower and my warm, fluffy towels.

Good old Emma.

The joint soon fizzled out, but my tingly lips and heavy limbs proved it had worked. I gazed up at the ceiling, stroking the soft fabric of my mother's vest. On the nights Ryan didn't stay over I slept in it, hoping to entice her into my dreams. No luck so far; Isobel kept showing up instead.

I pulled off the vest and spread it across the cushions at the other end of the sofa. I did this sometimes, when my mother and I needed to talk. One day we would converse for real, so it made sense to rehearse. Some of our chats had been lovely. Once, for example, we spoke about my conception. I'm not naïve; I know many children are impulses, whims, accidents. Urges fulfilled in the backs of cars, against walls, on sofas during advert breaks. As it turned out, my conception occurred on the Greek island of Santorini, in a hotel room with a queen-size bed and white linen curtains that billowed in a sea breeze. My mother spared me the embarrassing details but did reassure me I'd been conceived in love.

Tonight's conversation would not be so pleasant.

'I don't think you realise how much pain you've caused,' I said. She sat still, said nothing. 'Not just to me. There's Isobel and Quentin… and plenty of others.'

The Mrs Lockhead incident came to mind. I told my mother about William Lockhead joining my class at the village primary school when I was nine and how, one morning, during dropping-off time in the playground, I'd noticed his mother kissing him goodbye at the gate. One of the other mums called her name, and she looked up and responded with the most beautiful smile I'd ever seen. I noticed she had the same colour eyes as me and wondered if she might be my mother too. Why not? My real mother was out there somewhere. Scared and excited, I approached her and introduced myself. She laughed when I flung my arms around her waist. A nervous laugh. Her red fingernails dug into me as she tried to free herself.

'That was just the start of it,' I said to my mother, who offered no apology in return and showed no sign of remorse. These rehearsals had shown me our future conversations could prove challenging. What else did I expect with our difficult history? At least Emma could have fun with my mother and get to know her slowly, so that when the time came our reunion would stand a better chance. The thought of dropping Emma and showing myself to my mother terrified me. She'd rejected me once, why not again?

Your mother didn't want you.

Isobel had flung this insult at me during our last ever conversation, her face all hollow fury. I'd never seen her like that before. Quentin had warned me that the sprawling tumour on her brain would alter her behaviour, but I never thought she'd hurt me like that. At that moment I'd hated her. I'd wanted her to die.

Ryan touched my shoulder, making me jump. 'Come back to bed,' he mumbled.

'Can't sleep.'

'I'll help you sleep.'

The emptiness swirled inside me. 'You snore.'

'I don't,' he said, indignant.

'I'll sleep on the sofa.'

'Christ, Cass. Might as well be in bed at home on my own.'

'Off you go then.'

'What?'

'If you'd rather be at home, why don't you just leave?'

'I didn't say—'

'Get your stuff and get out of my house.'

His hurt expression didn't fool me. He stormed off into the bedroom and returned minutes later, fully dressed and clutching his cycle helmet. He couldn't have been that upset because he remembered to snatch up his dope tin from the coffee table.

'I'm so sick of this shit,' he said, as he opened the front door.

'You're the one who's leaving,' I shouted after him.

I watched him cycle away into the night.

'Loser,' I whispered, but a strange ache blossomed in my chest. Returning to bed, I lay awake, restless, missing his warmth. Traces of the Calvin Klein aftershave I'd bought him rose up from his pillow to haunt me.

I ventured into the kitchen in search of something to help me sleep. The cupboard beside the steel Smeg fridge contained my medicine box. A clear plastic tub full of the anti-anxiety tablets and anti-depressants prescribed by Dr Costello. My chemical pick-and-mix. He'd also given me sleeping tablets. I broke one in half and swallowed it with a gulp of water.

The chalky bitterness of the pill on my tongue took me back three years to the Five Oaks private hospital. Flat on my back, insides pumped clear of paracetamol, fluid from an intravenous drip seeping into me. Resting, rehydrating, replenishing. Dr Costello at my bedside for our first meeting. His manner comforting but firm.

'Cassie,' he said, 'if you're honest with me, I can help you. Will you be honest with me?'

I nodded.

'We'll need to talk about your mother,' he said. 'How do you feel about that?'

I'd summoned as much of a shrug as the tubes trailing out of me would allow. 'It's complicated.'

25

THEN

Wednesday 6 September, Royal Edinburgh Hospital

I did shag Dan just like that. Took him from the pub to the poky terraced house I lived in and fucked him on the stairs. Jeans round our ankles, carpet rubbing the base of my spine raw. He grabbed my long hair and pulled my head back, gazing into my eyes in wonder. 'You're something else,' he said.

I told him I wasn't on the pill. He said not to worry; he came from Irish Catholic stock so the withdrawal method was in his blood. When I offered to get a condom, he paused mid-thrust and looked at me with disappointment. He said he didn't wear condoms. Said they ruined sex for him, and I wanted him to look at me with wonder again so I said, 'Okay, just be careful,' and he laughed and pushed himself in deep.

'Trust me,' he whispered, 'last thing I want is a kid.'

Trust him I did and spent the next few days sticky with him – his residue on my back, my stomach, my chest. My housemate, Marcie, hammered several times on my bedroom door over the weekend to tell us to keep the noise down, but we didn't care.

He stayed for a week. Then he brought clothes to keep in my drawers and left a razor in the bathroom. When Marcie moved out because she couldn't stand him, Dan moved in. My friends stopped visiting, but I hardly noticed.

He wouldn't relent on the condom issue, so I went on the pill. Thought it was the responsible thing to do. 'Your call,' he said when I told him. The pill had never agreed with me, and after a few weeks of taking it I started to gain weight.

Sometimes I'd catch Dan looking at my new, curvier shape with distaste. 'Pity you can't keep the tits but get rid of this,' he would say, pinching my stomach tight between his fingers. University finished. We graduated, me with a first-class honours, Dan with a 2:1. We made the most of the long, hot summer, filling our days with sex, cheap wine and slightly more expensive drugs. We told ourselves we deserved a break before our busy careers began. We signed on the dole and applied for as many credit cards as we could. I had £7,000 of Dad's life insurance money lying untouched in a bank account. Money earmarked for paying off student debts and helping me get on my feet. I didn't tell Dan about it. Deep down, I must have known I'd stretched lust into domesticity with someone I shouldn't have.

Summer ended. We auditioned without success for theatre companies in Yorkshire and London and had to take part-time, cash-in-hand bar work at the Three Tuns. Serving students in the pub where we'd first kissed, students who gave us pitying looks.

Dan got the first break. At the end of September, he signed a six-month contract with Agitate, a theatre company started by Stella Piselli, a girl who'd graduated from NTS the year before us. Stella with the long black hair who drove a white VW Beetle and had a Victorian town house in Headingley, courtesy of her rich French father. Bilingual Stella, fresh from a Fringe First at the Edinburgh Festival and flaunting a year of Arts Council funding for her latest project. Dan never stopped talking about her. 'Stella thinks we might tour the show internationally.' 'Stella's folks said we could use their place near Nice to rehearse.' 'Stella's met this guy from the Royal Court who loves her ideas.' Stella this, Stella that. Stella fucking Stella.

26

GRACE

November

From inside the bus shelter, I have a clear view of the entrance to Brighton Central College. A few students pass in and out of the doors of the squat, ugly building. I take my phone from my coat pocket and check the time – 12.23 p.m. When I called the college yesterday, the perky receptionist confirmed that Friday morning classes finished at 1 p.m. and that yes, Dan Thorne would be teaching.

When he comes out at lunchtime, I'll follow him.

A wild burst of wind pummels the plastic walls of the shelter. Overhead, bulky clouds move across the sky like a carnival parade. I fiddle with my puzzle ring, twisting it round. Why would Dan contact me now, after all this time? An attack of conscience? I'm not sure, but he's a possibility I have to rule out.

What if he called in sick this morning like I did? What if he eats his lunch in the canteen or his office? I could find his office and confront him there but would rather we met in a neutral, public place.

Resigned to waiting, I light a cigarette and wonder if Dan is leading a workshop today. I remember the excitement of arriving in an empty theatre space, a morning's exploration ahead, not knowing where it would take me and what I would discover about myself.

After years spent touring the world with our award-winning theatre company, Agitate, Stella and I returned to the UK to settle down and start a family.

As well as reading Dan's staff profile, I looked up Agitate and read about their innovative two-handed shows that had played at UK and international theatre festivals. Not quite the film stardom Dan dreamed of, but he's done more with his training than I have. He always swore he'd never teach, but at least he's only doing it part-time.

I'm also currently pursuing an MA in Screenwriting.

Stella's dad must still be funding her lifestyle if her husband can afford to study.

I also investigated Stella's sleek and stylish website, which details her flourishing second career as a writer.

As a bilingual poet, I write and am published in both French and English.

Bien fucking *sûr*.

What if the two of them meet for lunch? The thought of seeing them together rouses an ancient jealousy that should be extinct. Yesterday, I visited a beauty salon and had my eyebrows and upper lip threaded, an effort I knew was for Dan. Looking my best would give me the confidence to approach him, I thought. Nothing wrong with that. This morning, I made rare use of all the contents of my make-up bag. As I applied a swish of blusher, I recognised the urge to please him, the familiar craving for his approval. The old me encased in the new, a sleeper self, suddenly activated.

* * *

At five past one, a throng of students surges through the main doors. Animated conversations fill the street, conducted at after-class volume. I spot the drama students straight away. They are louder than the rest, their hand gestures flamboyant – *look at me, look at me, look at me.* As they pass, I recognise the glow that follows a good workshop or rehearsal. The buzz of the shared creative process.

The exodus dies down. Just as I consider giving up, the doors open and there he is. Hands in the pockets of a double-breasted black coat, a brown leather satchel over one shoulder. He moves fast, forcing me to speed-walk to catch up. He looks fit and lean – no sign of middle-aged spread.

At the crossing, he doesn't wait for the green man. He never did. I dart between oncoming cars, wishing as I used to twenty years ago that he wasn't so reckless.

He leads me down a series of narrow streets I remember from childhood visits to Brighton with my parents. Streets now lined with cafés, delis and boutique shops selling clothes, furniture and kitchenware. I imagine Dan and Stella shopping here at the weekends, purchasing expensive wines and cheeses and gadgets to use in the kitchen of their beautiful home. Maybe they live in one of the coloured houses overlooking the city. Or maybe they have a flat in one of those white Regency buildings by the beach.

We pass a sign for the promenade and moments later the horizon is all water. Grey and restless, but not dramatic enough to reflect the state of my nerves. I need giant, foaming waves. A shipwreck sea.

Dan enters a beachfront café. While he removes his coat and seats himself at the window counter, I slip inside and claim a table nearby. I leave my coat on.

'What can I get you?' the waitress in the tight black vest asks me. I point to green tea on the menu as if mute, not wanting Dan to hear my voice. The waitress nods and slinks over to him.

'Flat white and smoked salmon bagel?' she asks.

'Perfect,' he says, watching her walk away. He takes his phone from his satchel, taps the screen and presses it to his ear. 'Hey, it's me,' he murmurs, 'got your message and that's no problem. I'll pick Holly up when I've finished. Love you.'

I was once pregnant with this man's child. I don't want to think about it, but his presence is activating all sorts of memories. They hum inside me, as if I'm a tuning fork vibrating to his frequency.

The pregnancy came to light on a wet January morning. The instructions on the back of the test read one blue line negative, two blue lines positive. As the second blue line appeared, I heard Dan burst into the house, banging the front door behind him. I pelted down the stairs, brandishing the piss-sodden test stick.

'I'm pregnant,' I said, at exactly the same moment he announced he was leaving me for Stella.

With perfect timing, we released a simultaneous 'oh.'

The colour drained from Dan's face. He pushed past me and stamped up the stairs. I followed and found him in the bedroom, gathering clothes in a frenzy and stuffing them in his rucksack, as if terrified I would give birth there and then and he would never get away.

The waitress brings my tea. I feel like throwing up in the cup. Coming here was a mistake. My instinct warns me to leave now, to leave the past unprovoked, but anger propels me out of my seat and over to the window counter.

'Hello,' I say. He turns and fixes his bright green eyes on me. I stare back, mesmerised. 'Dan?' I ask, as if not totally sure.

'Yeah, I'm Dan.' A beat of awkward silence passes. 'Sorry to be rude, but I honestly can't place you.'

He can't either – I can tell. He was never that good an actor. He has erased me and what happened between us from his mind, and it seems ridiculous now to think he could have sent the cards and the mug.

'I'm truly awful at remembering people,' he says.

I have my answer. Time to go. *Go.*

But I don't move.

'You really don't recognise me, do you?' I say.

He responds with his slow, sexy trap of a smile.

'Do you work at the college?' he asks.

I cannot speak. All I can do is hold his gaze until I dawn on him.

It takes a moment. He frowns first and then his eyes grow wide.

'Grace?'

The waitress appears with his order. 'Here you go, Dan,' she says. 'Enjoy.'

Still stunned, he forgets to thank her, and she stalks off looking surly.

'Jesus,' he says finally. 'I didn't... Your hair's totally different... Sorry... I wasn't expecting to see you here... obviously.'

'Obviously.'

He stirs his coffee round and round. An actor relying on a prop. Buying time while he gathers his thoughts, hunts for that lost line. When he lays the spoon down on the saucer, I know he has found his place and is ready to go on with the scene.

'What are you doing here, Grace?' he asks in a low voice. 'Why do you want to see me?'

'I don't. I was sitting here having a cup of tea and you walked in.'

He pales. 'You live in Brighton?'

'Just here for the day.'

His face relaxes then. He thinks he is out of the woods, that this meeting is just a coincidence. 'Great,' he says, lifting his cup from the saucer. 'I mean, it's a great place for a day trip. Have you been to the Royal Pavilion? It's really worth seeing.'

Small talk? Seriously? 'You've got children,' I say, incredulous. 'Two of them.'

He places his cup back on his saucer with staged precision. 'Been looking me up online, have you?'

I shrug. 'Who doesn't look up their exes?'

His disdainful expression confirms he has never searched for me.

'Did you follow me here?' he asks.

'No.' A craving for a cigarette comes over me. 'Of course not.'

He steeples his fingers together and brings them to his lips, as if contemplating how to reprimand a difficult student. 'Listen,' he says eventually, 'I'm sorry about what happened back then, but we did the right thing.'

'I don't recall you doing anything.'

He leans closer. 'You would have been arrested if it wasn't for me. Or have you forgotten that?'

I am standing in a bedroom, a pillow clutched to my chest. Feathers pool around my feet. I hear Dan on the other side of the door. *Sorry you got called out. It's nothing; we'll sort it between ourselves.*

'Grace?' he says.

'What?'

'If you're feeling guilty, you shouldn't. You did what you had to do.'

'Luckily for you.'

He lays a hand on my shoulder. To an onlooker his gesture might appear one of comfort, but I can sense the silent warning his flesh transmits to mine. *Stay away from me. Stay away from my family.*

'What's done is done,' he says, 'you need to move on.'

'So you can enjoy fatherhood in peace?' I shake his hand free and march out of the café, tears stinging my eyes. Outside, the wind's squally temper threatens to knock me off course, but I keep on walking. I don't look back.

27

CASSIE

November

I found a dead body today. Mr Reeves in the room next to my grandmother. At first, I didn't notice, too busy opening his curtains and chatting away about the mild November weather and the strong winds forecast for the next few days.

Then I heard the birds, their singing louder and more vivid than usual. A choir of individual voices rather than a mass of chirping. I realised the room was cold, despite the moderate temperature outside and the heat from the radiator.

'Mr Reeves?' I said, but I already knew.

He lay curled on his side, his knees almost touching his chin, like that game where you try to make yourself as small as possible. His eyes and mouth were wide open and his mottled hands had contracted into claws.

I found Vera two doors down. She hurried back to room five with me and pressed her fingers against Mr Reeves's neck. 'I haven't touched him,' I said, 'and I haven't disturbed anything in the room.'

'It's not a crime scene, love,' she said with a chuckle. 'Have you seen a dead body before?'

I nodded. Isobel's bulging eyes came back to me. Death was not serene, as I'd always been led to believe. It wasn't pretty.

Vera opened the windows. 'Off you go, Dennis,' she said, talking not to the body but to the empty air above it. 'No point you hanging round here.' She walked over to the door. 'Come on, Emma. Let's leave his spirit to float out of here in peace.'

We went to the office and told Kegs about the death. A little while later, the undertakers arrived, armed with a wooden coffin. Once they'd placed Mr Reeves inside, they carried it along the corridor and past the dining room where most of the residents were eating breakfast. Some waved, one person clapped and another wailed. It reminded me of a contestant being evicted from the *Big Brother* house. I whispered this to Surinder as we walked behind the coffin and she giggled. Vera, Kegs, Memory and a few of the other care assistants appeared at reception, and we all stepped outside to watch the undertakers load the coffin into the back of a black van. Kegs stood parade-ground straight. I kept expecting him to salute.

When the van drove away, Surinder and I stayed outside to have a fag.

'You must have got a right shock, babes,' Surinder said.

'Oh my God, totally.'

'It still freaks me out when I see a dead body. I should be used to it by now.'

I wondered what Mr Reeves's last breath had sounded like. Isobel had made a sort of choking sound.

A red Golf pulled up in the car park. John Palethorpe behind the wheel, his wife in the passenger seat.

'Vera totally fancies him,' said Surinder as John stepped out of the car. We both snorted with laughter. He opened the passenger door for his wife and helped her out. She didn't bother to thank him. Her glossy dark hair glinted with copper highlights. She wore a stylish faux-fur jacket, black skinny jeans and her knee-length boots had a thin stiletto heel. As she got closer, I could see she was one of those women who would look younger from the back than the front.

'Hello, girls,' John said, as they passed us. The sour-faced wife said nothing. After they'd gone inside, Surinder informed me that Mrs Palethorpe owned the beauty salon on Waldon Lane.

'She looks like a right miserable cow,' I said.

'She is. Hardly ever visits.'

Back inside Birch Grove, the atmosphere felt weird. A post-death aura hung over the place. I wanted to go and see my grandmother right away, but I had the tea trolley to prepare. The routine task soothed me. Emma loved routine. She liked fetching the steel flasks down from the shelf and counting out teabags and measuring out spoonfuls of instant coffee. She always wiped down the trolley with antiseptic spray first, even when it didn't need it. She took pride in these simple tasks. She enjoyed counting out cups, saucers and beakers and stacking them in the bottom half of the trolley.

I enjoyed these tasks too. More than I could have thought possible. Who knew menial work could be so rewarding? Such a healthy way to lose oneself. Isobel had never imposed any chores on me, but now I wish she had. Sometimes, while stripping and making beds, or folding up hot sheets straight from the tumble dryer, I would find myself in a trance. I'd told Dr Costello this in my last session, when he'd asked how my new job was going. He agreed domestic chores could be very therapeutic. I told him that in these trances I didn't think about the past. Or about my mother. He sat up then and asked if I'd been thinking of my mother again recently. I said no, not really, but I'm not sure he believed me. Luckily, a fib about my working hours meant we agreed to limit our sessions to once a month for a while. 'Seeing as you're doing so well with the job,' he'd said.

* * *

By the time I wheeled the tea trolley to my grandmother's room, she had a visitor. A plump woman with wiry grey hair had wedged herself into the armchair next to the bed, her wooden walking stick resting against her thigh.

'I'm Margaret,' she said, 'one of Polly's friends from church.'

Margaret accepted my offer of tea with enthusiasm and called me an angel when I passed her the steaming cup. While she slurped away, I perched on the side of Grandma's bed and helped her drink her tea. In between sips she kept coughing, which worried me. What if she was coming down with something? She refused the biscuit I offered her. Wouldn't take a bite.

'Where's the coffin?' she asked, pointing to the door. 'Where's it gone?'

Margaret sighed. 'She's been saying that since I got here, poor thing. She's so confused.'

'The coffin's gone now, sweetheart,' I said and relayed the morning's drama to Margaret.

With teary eyes, she reached out and patted my grandmother's hand.

'I'm so sorry,' she said. 'I didn't understand.'

Grandma squeezed Margaret's hand in return. 'Not your fault. I'm mad as bats.'

We all laughed. How amazing to have my grandmother fully present in the room, the TV forgotten for once.

'Have you and my... you and Polly known each other long?' I asked Margaret.

'Gosh, yes.' Margaret got nostalgic then, filling me in on all the fun stuff she and my grandmother had done over the years. Baking for church fundraisers – apparently Grandma made award-winning Victoria sponges in her day – singing at funerals, arranging the church flowers. They'd played bridge together too and, along with a few other friends, went on holiday once a year. 'We went to Rome to see the Vatican,' she said. 'We flirted something rotten with the Italian waiters, didn't we, Polly?'

My grandmother giggled.

I could have listened to Margaret's stories all day, but after a while, my grandmother strayed back to the TV, and Margaret said she should be getting on.

After she'd said goodbye to Grandma, I guided her into the corridor. 'You must know Polly's daughter?' I said.

'Grace?' Margaret couldn't hide her disdain. 'Not really. She never came to church, apart from the occasional Mother's Day service.'

'She doesn't seem the religious type.' I knew I should stop talking but couldn't help myself. 'She's supposed to visit once a week, but to be honest she hasn't been for ages.'

'That doesn't surprise me,' Margaret said, 'they weren't close. They hardly saw each other for twenty years. I think they had a falling-out, but Polly never said what about.'

* * *

When I returned to my grandmother's room, I found her weeping.

'Bless your heart,' I said, grabbing a tissue from her bedside table. 'What's all this?' I dabbed her eyes and wiped her cheeks.

'I'll be in a coffin soon,' she whispered.

'No, you won't.' I held the tissue against her nose and she blew into it. 'Good girl.'

'Grace?' she said.

'Not today. Next week, if you're lucky.' I thought about what Margaret had told me in the corridor. 'You fell out with Grace because of me, didn't you?'

My grandmother moaned and sank back into her pillows, spent and meek. No way would I get anything lucid out of her now. I checked my watch.

'I've got to get back to work soon,' I said, 'but I can read to you for a bit first.' Picking up her Bible, I sat beside her on the bed. I quoted some stuff from Luke, including a good bit about Jesus bringing a girl back from the dead. After that, I read out a brilliant line from Matthew 10:26. 'Whatever is now covered up will be uncovered, and every secret will be made known.'

My grandmother's hands reached for my face, and her cold fingers smoothed my eyelids shut, the way people do to the dead. The way Vera did to Mr Reeves earlier. Neither of us moved, and in the stillness, I noticed the comforting ticking of the carriage clock. A nice moment, I thought, one I would always remember.

'Grace is a sinner,' she whispered, and the moment evaporated.

I opened my eyes. 'So you've said.'

She pulled me close and only when my ear touched her lips did she speak again.

'Grace killed her baby.'

28

THEN

Wednesday 6 September, Royal Edinburgh Hospital

I only stopped taking the pill because of Stella. Early October, a week into Agitate's rehearsal period, she held a party at her town house. She swanned around her minimalist living room in a tight black dress that showed off her concave stomach and long, tanned legs. I spent the whole evening feeling fat and self-conscious in a vintage pencil skirt.

The next morning, hung-over in our drab, messy bedroom, I announced I was coming off the pill. Dan said it was my call, too busy getting dressed for his rehearsal to care. The cast were going out for the day in character, an exercise they did on a regular basis. Stella couldn't get enough of improvisation it seemed. According to Dan, she could remain immersed in character in any situation. 'Nothing throws her,' he kept saying. 'She's fearless.'

I said I'd give the coil a try, and he said to do whatever felt best.

That afternoon, I visited the family planning clinic and picked up a leaflet about the coil. It didn't seem worth making an appointment right away. In three weeks' time, the first leg of Agitate's nationwide tour would begin, taking Dan away from home four nights of every week until Christmas. I decided to get the coil fitted in the New Year, certain we could manage our own precautions until then.

As soon as I stopped taking the pill, the pounds began to drop from my body, but Dan didn't notice. Keeping his attention was becoming a struggle. When we were in bed together, I was sure he wasn't thinking of me.

At the start of November, the morning of the day Dan had to leave on tour, a man from the electricity board arrived to fit a new token meter in our cellar. We sat at the kitchen table eating our breakfast as the man hammered and drilled beneath our feet.

Dan dared me to shag him right there and then. Challenged me to some role-play.

'That's your husband in the cellar,' he said, 'and I'm his best friend you're desperate to sleep with.'

I recognised his dare as a test. The kind of test he thought Stella would pass and I would fail. Seconds later, I was on my knees in front of him, proving I could be fearless too. As soon as he got hard, I straddled him and told him to hurry before my husband caught us.

Surprise flashed in his eyes, just for a second, and I caught him glancing at the open door that led to the cellar. His hesitation made me feel powerful.

'Is someone too scared to do the job?' I said.

He grabbed my waist and soon had me moving at a rhythm that suited him. He whispered that I was a dirty little slut. We speeded up, the slap of skin on skin echoing round the kitchen. He said he was going to come inside me. Said that's what dirty little sluts liked. Then he smirked, clearly expecting me to surrender and order his withdrawal, but I said nothing, just gripped him tight with my thighs.

Seconds later came the hot stream of his ejaculation. I had to put my hand over his mouth to stop him crying out.

He left two hours later, and I spent the rest of the day weeping at his absence, torturing myself with thoughts of him and Stella together. In the midst of my pain and self-pity, it didn't occur to me to take the morning-after pill. Two days later, my period started. Only light bleeding, but as stopping the pill had sent my cycle haywire, I never suspected anything. After Christmas, I noticed myself carrying extra weight again. Festive excess, I thought. That and the comfort eating I'd indulged in for weeks to suppress my suspicions about Dan and Stella. After the tour started, Dan had shown little interest in me. We hardly ever had sex.

Two days after New Year, during a rare fit of housework, I came across the leaflet from the family planning clinic. As I browsed through it, one line in particular jumped out: Before making an appointment to have a coil fitted, please ensure there is no chance you could be pregnant.

That was when my tender breasts and weight gain took on a new significance. That was when I looked back over the past eight weeks and tried to remember if I'd had a proper period. That's when I started to panic.

29

GRACE

November

Dr Lucy Anderson GP – please, call me Lucy – is short with bobbed red hair and doesn't look old enough to be a university graduate let alone a partner in a private practice and what am I doing here anyway?

'You were telling me what you felt during this first incident,' she says.

'Sorry. Yes.' The incident. I describe my racing heart, blurred vision, and the sensation of the world receding from me. I omit that the symptoms occurred after I stalked someone.

Lucy covers a lined A4 pad with vigorous scrawls. The scratch of pen on paper is the only sound in the tidy, sterile consulting room. Euston Street is only minutes away, but the din of the traffic doesn't penetrate here.

'Okay.' She finishes her notes with an emphatic full stop. 'You're quite right; you did have a panic attack.' She removes her rimless glasses and lets them dangle from her hand. The action looks rehearsed, as though she is still experimenting with the role of doctor.

'Have you had panic attacks before?' she asks.

'No.'

'Suffered from anxiety in the past?'

'Not really.' As a private doctor, Lucy won't have access to my medical records. 'No more than anyone else.' I came here seeking a prescription for something to calm me down and help me sleep, but Lucy is intent on a thorough consultation first.

'And you've had another attack since?' she says.

'Sort of.' A week ago today, after my visit to Brighton, I started drinking red wine at 5 p.m. I woke just after four the next morning, head thumping as fragments of the previous day assembled themselves.

'And you experienced the same symptoms as the previous attack?' Lucy asks, still scribbling away.

'Yes.' Not really. This time I lay huddled in bed, unable to move and not just due to the hangover. Sirens kept me pinned beneath the duvet. So many sirens. They never stopped, and they were all coming for me. By late afternoon, I knew what I had to do. My rucksack didn't take long to pack and, after double-checking I had my passport and credit cards, I left the flat. Hurrying along in the dark, I couldn't escape the sensation of being followed. Terror rose in my chest.

I fought my way onto a cramped Tube train, recoiling as strangers pressed against me. I decided to turn up at Heathrow and see what flights were available. Kuala Lumpur maybe. From there I could reach the Perhentian Islands, rent a beach hut and go diving. Forget about Dan and Stella and everything that happened back then. At Paddington, I bought a ticket for the Heathrow Express and hurried along to the platform.

'Are you experiencing an above-average level of stress at the moment?' Lucy says.

I tell her about Mum. The dementia, the process of getting her into a home and her slow deterioration.

'And you're dealing with all this on your own?' Lucy's pale blue eyes express genuine concern. 'What about other family members? Can't they help?'

'There's only me.'

'That's a lot of responsibility.'

'I suppose.'

A train to Heathrow stood at the platform. Five minutes until departure. An elderly woman and her middle-aged daughter embraced by the train doors. My heart lurched as reality asserted itself. I couldn't leave Mum. Not now.

'I'm not sleeping well either,' I say, 'can you give me something to help?'

Lucy reads over her notes. 'We'll try you on a low dose of Xanax,' she says finally. 'One tablet at night as and when you need it. It's more of a backup really.' She insists I must make time for myself – have a massage now and again, maybe take up a new hobby. 'There are plenty of carer support groups I could recommend.'

'Not really my thing.'

'Then try to build up your own support network. I'm sure people will help if you ask them.'

'Thanks.'

'You don't have to go through all this on your own.'

She gives me that look of concern again. Who does she remind me of?

Do you consider yourself a criminal, Grace?

30

THEN

Thursday 7 September, Royal Edinburgh Hospital

My first scan took place early January. The sonographer, an efficient, tight-lipped woman, smeared cold gel on my stomach before producing a white, plastic object that looked like a microphone.

'It's called a probe,' she said when I asked her about it, but she wouldn't make eye contact.

As the probe roamed the surface of my belly, I prayed for a miracle. Prayed the woman would declare my womb empty. Nothing to see here. False alarm.

I don't know what she saw in there. The scanner's screen faced away from me. When I asked if she could tell the sex yet, she gave me a disparaging look and said it was far too soon to have any idea.

Not for me. I knew it was a girl. I didn't realise I knew until after I'd shown Dan the positive pregnancy test and he was cramming his rucksack with essential possessions.

'You're really going to leave me with her?' I said.

31

CASSIE

December

My mother arrived on time. I waved at her as she entered the café, and she made her way to the two green armchairs I'd bagged at the back. I stood up when she reached me, as if receiving the queen or something.

'I got my favourite seats for us,' I said.

She glanced around her. 'Great.'

I could tell the busy Starbucks was the last place in Brentham she wanted to be on this first Saturday in December. Starbucks wouldn't have been my choice either, but I figured Emma would love the place. One day, my mother and I would linger in cafés like Aroma and discuss the subtle differences between blends of tea, but for now Starbucks would have to do.

'You look nice, Emma,' she said, as she wriggled out of her coat.

'Thanks.' Even though my mother's recent abandonment of me still hurt, I'd taken ages getting ready in the staff toilet at Birch Grove before meeting her. Clean skinny jeans, a new pink polo neck and I'd tarted myself up with blue eyeshadow and pink lip gloss in true Emma style. My mother had made an effort too – red lipstick, eyelashes thick with mascara and musky perfume clouding around her.

'I'll get us some drinks,' she said.

'No, let me.' I gestured for her to sit down. 'Green tea?' Only when she looked at me with surprise did I realise my error. 'Isn't that what they drink in Singapore and places like that?' I added.

She smiled. 'It is indeed. You have done your research.' She insisted on paying for the drinks and gave me a twenty-pound note to go up and order with. I enjoyed asking the lanky boy behind the counter for a green tea for my mother. I didn't enjoy ordering Emma's caramel latte with an extra shot of syrup, but I had to keep in character.

'This is perfect,' I said once we got settled with our drinks. 'Much easier to get stuff done here than in Birch Grove.'

My mother nodded. 'I couldn't concentrate there. Not with Mum feeling so rough. I hate seeing her like that.'

My grandmother's cough had developed into a slight chest infection requiring antibiotics. However, her recent revelation had left me fuming with her, and I'd found it hard to summon much sympathy.

'I'm afraid I've got to leave at four on the dot,' my mother said, removing a blue cardboard folder from her backpack. 'I need to be in London by five.'

'No probs,' I said, but her desire for a punctual getaway annoyed me. I was being pretty patient with her, all things considered.

Grace killed her baby.

She didn't succeed, I'd told my grandmother. *I'm here.*

I'm here.

'Do you want one of these?' I offered up the packet of three mince pies I'd purchased with the drinks.

'No, thanks,' said my mother, but she looked in need of something to eat. She'd lost weight recently; I could see it in her face.

She opened up the folder and we got down to business. It touched me, the effort she'd made. Exercise sheets to explain and test basic aspects of grammar, stuff I'd done as a kid, but Emma treated each simple rule as a revelation.

'Wow,' I said after a ten-minute session on the difference between too and to, 'I didn't even know what a proposition was.'

'Preposition,' my mother corrected.

I sighed. 'You must think I'm well thick.'

My mother shook her head. 'I admire you, Emma.'

'Me?'

'You're getting out there in the world and giving it a go, and you're doing it all without the support of your parents. I think you're very brave.'

'Thanks. I never thought of it like that.' I gave her a wobbly smile. 'It's not always easy doing stuff on your own.'

'Very true.' She pointed out more of Emma's atrocious mistakes and suggested I try to rewrite the statement as a way of consolidating what we'd talked about. 'Have you got any questions?' she asked, as she handed me the folder.

I gazed at her, emptiness welling up inside me. Yes, I had questions. Why didn't you keep me? How can you live with yourself?

'Hungry yet?' I said, snatching up the mince pies from the table and tearing off the cellophane wrapping.

She laughed. 'Oh, go on then.' She picked up a pie and took a tiny bite. 'Christmas food already. It's ridiculous.'

I stirred the cold remains of my latte. 'Are you going away over the holidays?'

'No.' She brushed stray crumbs from the front of her black jumper. 'I only get a few days off from work, and I'll have to spend those with Mum.'

She sounded so sincere, so dutiful. As if she hadn't nearly ditched Grandma and I recently. Ten days ago, unsettled by my grandmother's revelation, I'd returned to London after my shift and made my way to my mother's block. I needed to see her. I even considered telling her the truth about myself so we could get everything out in the open. Then she appeared carrying a large rucksack, and I thought she might be off to visit a friend for the weekend. After a cramped journey on the Underground, we ended up at Paddington and together we scanned the departure boards. When she'd headed for the Heathrow Express platform, I'd guessed what she was up to.

'Are you working over Christmas?' my mother asked.

'Yes.' I'd signed up for the holiday shifts ages ago, hoping to enjoy the festive season with family. When Quentin heard my plans, he seemed disappointed I couldn't come to Dubai but said he understood how much my new job meant to me.

My mother washed down the mince pie with the remains of her tea. The muscles in her long neck moved up and down as she swallowed. On the platform at Paddington, she'd hesitated by the train doors. I'd almost called out, but she backed away from the train and it departed without her. Yesterday morning, I visited her flat and found her rucksack under the bed. She'd tucked her brown leather travel wallet inside it, so I took her passport away for safekeeping.

'Do you think you can manage the application now?' my mother said. So sweet, so concerned. Anger bubbled inside me, but I refused to let her see it.

'Totes, you've been so helpful. I feel like I should pay you or something.'

'Wouldn't hear of it.'

'Must be something I can do to say thanks?'

She looked at me for a moment. 'Well, if you really want—'

'I do.'

'I wouldn't mind a hand packing up Mum's house. Some stuff I can do on my own, but it's a big job.'

My anger subsided. My mother had stayed for me. That's why she didn't get on the train. She didn't know it yet but she'd chosen me. When the time came, I'd give her a chance to explain her past actions. Maybe we should talk on her birthday, which, according to her passport, would soon be upon us. I could get her something special. Meet her from work and take her for a birthday drink and finally reveal my true identity.

'Don't worry if you're too busy,' my mother said. 'I totally understand.'

'Nah, it's fine,' I said, feigning nonchalance. 'I'd be glad to help.'

My mother looked so relieved. 'That's brilliant, Emma. Thanks. Maybe next week or the week after?'

'Whatever,' I said, as if her request was no big deal. As if a new and exciting phase of our relationship had not just begun.

* * *

After she left, I went to Marks and Spencer and bought loads of goodies for my tea. Kegs had put me on an early the next day, meaning I'd have to stay in Emma's grotty bedsit, but at least I'd have something decent to eat. At the checkout, I camouflaged my purchases with an Aldi bag so I didn't give myself away.

I strolled through the precinct, the sky already inky blue. All the shop windows had succumbed to decorations now – snowflakes sprayed on, coloured lights blinking. Despite the efforts of the Harringtons to make each Christmas special, I'd always found the festive period difficult. A family holiday that reminded me I had no family. This year would be different. This year I had my mother and my grandmother. Infected with festive spirit and buoyed by my success with my mother, I took out my phone and texted Ryan.

Sorry about the other night… I miss you xxxxxx

I did miss him. Sort of.

Too excited to return to the bedsit, I decided to go to my grandmother's house. I'd walked past it before, but now I needed a closer look to prepare for my upcoming visit. How lovely of my mother to ask me. Even Emma couldn't mask the connection between us. My mother felt it; I knew she did.

Grace killed her baby.

Hurrying away from the town centre, shopping bag swinging at my side, I thought again about my grandmother's words. She must have known what my mother tried to do to me, but she had no idea I'd survived. She'd obviously never approved of my mother's actions, hence them falling out. I realised taking my anger out on Grandma wasn't fair. She'd had to keep a terrible secret all these years in order to protect her daughter, as any good mother would. She'd suffered almost as much as I had.

When I reached my grandmother's estate, I wandered around for a while, bewildered by the identical streets with their identical homes.

Finally locating the right house, I opened the tall wooden gate to the right of the front door and followed the narrow path that led to the back garden. Rotting brown leaves smothered the lawn and the withered remains of plants choked the blue ceramic pots on the patio. Removing my phone from my jacket pocket, I captured a couple of shots of the house before skirting the small conservatory and sidling up to the nearest window. Through the darkness I could just make out the bulk of a table and the shiny curve of a kitchen tap.

A burst of brightness as the light came on. I crouched down, heart thudding, eyes still peeking into the room. My mother stood naked with her back to me. Didn't she say she had to return to London? Why would she lie? Maybe she just wanted to get started with the packing. Naked packing?

She opened the fridge door, pulled out a bottle of white wine and examined the label. The harsh overhead light showed up everything – the dimples of cellulite on her upper thighs, the freckle on her right buttock, the red scratch marks on her back. I could even see the networks of veins behind her knees – the blue highways of her blood. I snapped away with my phone, taking advantage of the unexpected photo opportunity.

Another figure appeared in the kitchen doorway. I caught a glimpse of his face before ducking to the ground.

John Palethorpe.

I heard laughter and the slam of the fridge door, followed by a loud moan from my mother. Fingertips on the window ledge, I hauled myself up for another look.

John had my mother backed against the fridge. Her eyes were closed, her mouth slack. He'd gained possession of the wine bottle and, as I watched, he pushed it between her legs, teasing her with it. Then he brought it to her lips and made her lick it. I couldn't tear my eyes away, despite my fear of being caught.

He placed the wine bottle on top of the fridge and carried my mother over to the table, his muscled arms bulging. He had dark hair across his chest and at the base of his spine. He laid her on her back amid piles of tea towels, scattering some of them to the floor. I felt like a time traveller, voyaging back to the moment I was made. He plunged in and screwed her hard, his hands at her throat. I nearly shouted at him to get off, but the pleasure on my mother's face stopped me. She wrapped her legs around him, trapping him in the vice of her thighs. She cried out for more. She begged him not to stop.

32

THEN

Thursday 7 September, Royal Edinburgh Hospital

I thought I saw a sign. A message from her. I was looking out of one of the barred windows in the day room when I noticed a nest of pigeons on a narrow ledge below me. The nest appeared to be made of melted grey candlewax, but after staring at it for some time I realised it consisted of pigeon shit. Layer upon layer of it.

A baby bird snuggled at the centre, all beak and fluff. The mother hovered over it and retched up something for her little one. When the baby stuck its beak down the mother's throat, I had to look away.

33

GRACE

December

Someone keeps calling me. On Saturday, after I got back from Brentham, my mobile rang. The screen declared the caller unknown, but I answered anyway.

'Hello,' I said. A crackling, static silence, followed by the dead tone. Call centre, I assumed. Someone trying to sell me payment protection or inviting me to complete another market research survey. An identical call came thirty minutes later, and another one thirty minutes after that. Computer glitch? Call centre systems dialled hundreds of numbers at a time, didn't they?

Last night, the calls followed a similar pattern. One every half hour from seven o'clock onwards. No caller ID. I was either caught up in some automatic dialling error or the victim of a very persistent telemarketing company. I switched my phone off at eleven and didn't turn it on again until arriving at work this morning.

Now it's 8.15 a.m. and Linda, Barney, Max, Theresa and I are having a meeting in one of the classrooms. Linda wants to discuss ideas for our staff Christmas get-together and the end-of-term celebration for the students.

'Let's get the students done first. Any suggestions?' she says.

'Get them to bring in food related to a cultural celebration from their own country,' Barney proposes, 'do a sort of potluck lunch.'

'Christ no,' Linda says. 'We want them out of here by lunchtime so we can go and get pissed.'

I laugh along with the others, but my mind is on my phone. When I switched it on again before the meeting, I found not only a string of missed calls but also a voicemail message left at four this morning. I haven't had a chance to listen to it yet.

'Tea, mince pies and karaoke Christmas carols,' Max says. 'That worked well last year.'

'Perfect,' says Linda, 'I'll get Mandy to organise the equipment for us.'

'You up for karaoke, Grace?' Theresa asks. 'Bet you did plenty of that in Singapore?'

'Yes,' I reply, 'it was fun.'

'The students love it when we make fools of ourselves,' says Barney, who looks glum at the prospect.

'So, karaoke carols for them, followed by cocktails for us,' Linda says. We all agree and move on to the issue of the holiday timetable.

'Grace has volunteered to cover most of the work,' Linda says, 'for which I'm very grateful.' She explains that only a handful of students have signed up for the teaching programme, so there shouldn't be much prep to do. 'You can always catch up on admin, if you find yourself at a loose end,' she tells me. I nod and give an appropriate reply but feel detached from the proceedings, as though watching them from a distance.

Who is calling me?

After the meeting, I rush to an empty classroom with my phone. Heart hammering, I ring through to voicemail. At first, there is only silence. Then I detect a faint exhalation. A delicate sound, not the heavy breathing that would signify an obscene phone call.

'Who is this?' I ask the recorded message that cannot answer back. I sense the caller was angry. The caller wanted something from me but would not ask. The silence returns and continues, weighty and expectant, until the message ends.

* * *

After finishing work at five, I stand outside the main door of the school, checking my phone for missed calls. None show up. No more messages either. Have I been letting my imagination get the better of me?

Max and Theresa appear and invite me to join them for a drink.

'Please,' says Theresa, 'I'll be stuck talking to him otherwise.'

'Cheeky bitch.' Max tugs Theresa's black beanie over her eyes. 'Seriously though, Grace, take pity on the girl.'

Tempting. A glass or two of wine might settle my nerves, but I'm trying not to drink too much, especially with taking the tablets Lucy Anderson prescribed. I only swallow half a pill each night, wary of over-medicating myself. Each dose gifts me almost six hours of restless sleep, which is better than nothing.

'Grace?' Theresa says, rearranging her hat. 'Are you coming?'

I invent an excuse about having a yoga class. After we say our goodbyes, I light a cigarette and head up Pentonville Road. There it is again. That tickle along my spine, the impression of someone close behind. Someone watching me. Since Saturday, I haven't been able to shake this sensation. As I locked up Mum's house to leave for the station, I noticed the side gate swinging back and forth, probably blown open by the wind. When I clicked it shut, a shudder ran through me and I spun round, expecting to see a figure in the driveway.

I saw nobody, but this nobody managed to hound me all the way to the station.

I look round, but see only the usual mill of rush-hour pedestrians. I pick up pace, stopping at random intervals to glance behind me, as if playing Grandmother's Footsteps. Eventually, I feel foolish and stop the game. I march on ahead without looking back, determined to beat my paranoia.

Twenty minutes later, I reach Islington. Upper Street is a strip of cheer in the dark evening, the busy shops glowing with festive lights.

Shops filled with couples and families doing their Christmas shopping. Mothers and daughters browsing together arm-in-arm. A combination of longing, envy and sadness propels me away from the bustle towards Goswell Road.

During the final stretch of my walk home, I resolve to call Birch Grove when I get in and check how Mum's doing. Last night, Kegs reported she'd rallied after the last dose of antibiotics. It seems she's beaten this mild chest infection, although Kegs warned me it would leave her body less able to recover next time.

The weaker Mum gets the more exposed I feel. As if she has cast an invisible protective shield around me all her life. One I never knew existed. A barrier against the world that is now fading.

I turn in to my estate and hurry past the floodlit Astroturf pitch. A five-a-side match between two teams of kids is in progress. The accompanying screams and whistles have an unnerving urgency. I speed up, keen to reach the safety of home.

At the door of my block, I punch in the entry code. 'Grace.' A familiar voice behind me. Before I can push open the door, strong fingers latch on to my arm. 'We need to talk,' Dan says.

* * *

We stand at the entrance to the park. In the distance, the dope-smoking teenagers haunt their usual bench, too far away to be of assistance or to witness what might unfold.

'What do you want?' I say.

'The truth.' He looks older than he did in Brighton. I can see the lines on his forehead now, the grey in his eyebrows.

'How did you find me?' I ask, stalling.

'How do you think?'

The school website. He was waiting for me tonight. Following me all the way.

'Why did you track me down after all this time?' he asks. 'It doesn't make sense.'

'I didn't track you down.'

'Don't tell me our meeting was just a coincidence.'

I shrug.

He steps towards me. 'There must have been a reason? Something you wanted to tell me?'

I needed to work out what was real and what was not, but I cannot tell him that.

'I was curious about what had happened to you, that's all,' I say. 'When I read about you and Stella and your kids, it hurt. All those old feelings came back to me.'

'I don't believe you.'

'It's true.' I glance away. 'Things aren't great for me at the moment. My mum's in a home with dementia and I... I have a lot on my plate. Everything just got to me, I guess.'

I wait for him to commiserate, to tell me he understands. 'Did you come to find me because you had something to confess?' he asks.

'No.'

'So you took care of it?'

It. The fault line shifts and strains. A sharp bolt of pain in my guts.

'Yes,' I say.

'You didn't change your mind?'

'No.' I fold my arms across my chest. 'I don't want to talk about the past.'

He gives me a long, steady look. 'I've got my family to think about. I can't have a kid turning up out of the blue.'

'Don't worry, your perfect life won't be disturbed.' I hope he might contradict me and admit his life is far from perfect, but he doesn't.

He edges closer. 'So you had the abortion?' he says.

I am in a green hospital gown on a narrow hospital bed. Is it time? My hands grip the side of the bed. Is it time?

'Grace.' He grabs my shoulders. 'Did you go through with it?'

I consider saying no, just to see the look on his face.

'Did you go through with it?' he repeats, and I know he will not leave until I answer his question.

'Yes, Dan,' I say, 'I went through with it.'

34

THEN

Friday 8 September, Royal Edinburgh Hospital

Simon is trying to prise me open. In a nice way. Today, he asked if I'd ever had hallucinations before. If I'd ever seen stuff and heard stuff like I did during my episode.

I wanted to appear cooperative without giving too much away, so I told him about the nightmares that had started seven months ago. He asked what had happened around that time, and I told him I'd fallen out with my mother. He wanted to know why, but I claimed it was nothing important. Usual mother–daughter stuff.

'What else was going on in your life?' he asked, and I said I didn't really remember.

I do remember though. I remember it snowed the week of my appointment. A thick white blanket settled over West Yorkshire, disrupting trains and buses and closing off roads. Mum would have declared the bad weather a sign. The Almighty trying to make me change my mind. I was terrified of not being able to reach the hospital. After everything I'd gone through – two doctor's consultations, the scan, and the brutal arguments with Mum – the thought of missing my slot had me in a panic.

I remember leaving the house at 6 a.m. and discovering that the bus from

Leeds City Centre to the infirmary was running on schedule. A good omen, I thought. I arrived at the hospital in the dark, sidling up to reception with my appointment letter and whispering my request for directions to the ward.

By 7 a.m., I was sitting up in a narrow hospital bed wearing a green gown, my hair tucked beneath a matching cap. I counted about twenty other women on the ward, all of us avoiding eye contact. An Indian woman, whose swollen belly placed her much further on than the rest of us, wouldn't stop crying. No wonder – she kept caressing her bump. I gripped the side of the bed so I didn't make the same mistake. Two hours later, nothing had happened. I called over a nurse, a young woman with a kind face and spiky blonde hair, and asked her if it was time. She told me to be patient. Not long now.

One woman a few beds down had her boyfriend with her. He sat in a chair next to the bed and held her hand. I recalled standing in the doorway of our bedroom, watching Dan pack. 'You're not going to keep it, are you?' he said, as he rammed his trainers into his rucksack.

I said no, an instinctive answer to a question I hadn't had time to consider. The right answer, confirmed by the relief surging through me. Now I wished I'd said yes. Just to see the look on Dan's face.

He said I'd made the right decision. Said he wouldn't have wanted anything to do with the kid anyway.

And I was glad no child of mine would have him as a father.

The long blast of a horn sounded outside the house. I rushed over to the bedroom window and saw Stella's white VW Beetle parked outside, engine running.

Dan hoisted his rucksack onto his back and said he'd make sure I was out when he came back for the rest of his stuff.

By 9.30 a.m., the women either side of me had been wheeled away. I badgered the nurse again, told her I needed to get it over with. She promised I'd be next and sure enough, ten minutes later, two men in blue scrubs appeared and pushed my bed out of the ward. As they steered me down a corridor, my hands sought out my stomach and covered it with tender strokes.

In a small, white room, I met the anaesthetist, another man in blue scrubs. He tried to relax me with cheery, weather-based banter as he administered the injection. He told me to count backwards, ten to one. I started counting, convinced the drugs wouldn't have any effect. I think I got to six.

When I came round, my forehead was buzzing. I propped myself up on one elbow and immediately threw up. The nurse with the blonde hair appeared and held a bowl under my chin, lifting back a stray hair so it wouldn't dangle in the regurgitated fluid.

I told her I didn't remember anything and burst into tears. I'm not sure what made me cry. Sadness? Relief? Fear? The fact I couldn't recall anything about the operation scared me. Something important had taken place, and I'd surrendered all control of it. Or perhaps I chose to focus on this loss of memory rather than my other loss. 'I don't remember anything,' I repeated.

The nurse said that was for the best and rubbed my back.

She said the worst was over and I believed her.

35

CASSIE

Yes, I called her. I was angry. She lied to me. I'd left Starbucks thrilled about us growing closer, and all the time she was itching to escape and spread her legs for John Palethorpe. I only meant to phone once but couldn't resist the sound of her voice. When she started ignoring the calls, I decided to leave a message and tell her everything. Almost did it too, but I realised that particular conversation could only take place in person.

By the time today's mid-week shift at Birch Grove rolled round, I was still furious. Good old Emma morphed into grumpy old Emma. She even snapped at Surinder while they were hanging twists of tinsel in the corridors.

'Oh my God,' Surinder said, as she balanced on the stepladder, 'I am so excited about Christmas.' She banged on and on about the traditional turkey dinner Arun would cook for them and about the presents she'd already bought for her boys.

'Shut up, Surinder,' I said, 'you're not even a Christian.'

She called me a racist and stomped off in a huff. I had to leave four cigarettes tied with tinsel in her coat pocket before she forgave me.

'I'm sorry,' I said, 'I love Christmas too, but it always makes me think about my mum. I'm not racist, honest.'

'I know, babes.' She opened her arms wide. 'Come on, hug it out.'

After lunch, Kegs asked if I'd stay on until seven to cover for someone. I said yes, not like I had anything else on. Ryan had replied right away to my text on Saturday:

Miss you too, you mad cow.

Hearts and smiley faces. Sadly, the subsequent events had put me off seeing him, and I'd yet to return any of his calls.

My grandmother did little to improve my mood. She made no comment when I said I'd forgiven her for any part she may have played in my mother's crime. To be fair, the chest infection had wiped her out. The antibiotics had seen the danger off, but now she refused to eat properly. A nibble of toast, a spoonful of yoghurt.

'You need to get your strength up,' I said to her. She asked for her daughter so I left her to it. Didn't need any more of her mad whisperings about my mother. To be honest, I thought about walking out of the care home and never going back. Of giving up on my mother completely. Fortunately for her, I persuaded myself to hang on a bit longer. Maybe her meeting with John was just a one-off? Only time would tell.

My tea round took me into Mr Reeves's old room, the one next to my grandmother's. After his death, a man called Len Daley had moved in. A cantankerous seventy-six-year-old with a tenuous grip on reality, Len had been giving Mrs Palethorpe serious competition for the title of Most Difficult Resident. The smell of cigarette smoke hit me as soon as I walked in.

'Oh, Len, not again,' I said. He grinned at me from his armchair, a white-haired ghoul with long, yellow fingernails. A quick search of the room uncovered two spent cigarette butts in a breakfast bowl beneath his bed. In accordance with procedure, I fetched Vera who gave him a major bollocking about health and safety.

'If you want a cigarette, just ask and someone will take you down to the smoking room,' she said.

'This is my house,' said Len, 'and I'll smoke where I bloody well want, you fat cow.'

'You're not allowed to smoke in your room,' Vera said, ignoring his insult. 'You're an accident waiting to happen, Len Daley.'

'Do you think it's his grandson bringing him the fags again?' I asked her.

She nodded. 'I reckon he's tapping the old man for money in exchange for a few smokes.' She revealed she'd grown up in the next street to the Daleys. 'They were always trouble,' she said. 'My sister went out with one of them years ago. Teenage sweethearts.'

That's when the idea about John came to me. Why hadn't I thought of it before?

'You all right?' Vera asked. 'You look bushed. Go and take your break.'

I dashed to the kitchen, made myself an Emma-style tea – milky with two sugars – and took it into the back yard. I lit a fag between sips and examined my new theory. What if John had grown up in Brentham too? What if he and my mother knew each other years ago? They could have been teenage sweethearts. Maybe they'd stayed together all through university, or perhaps, after graduating, my mother had returned to her home town for a holiday and had a fling with him for old times' sake.

What if John was my father?

I'd thought about my father over the years, but he'd never mattered to me like my mother had. I'd wondered if he knew about me and if he'd wanted me or not. Was he in on it or did she get rid of me without him knowing? Such thoughts always led me to the same conclusion – I was my mother's responsibility. She grew me and pushed me out into the world, and she chose not to keep me. Only she was to blame.

* * *

Still, I wanted to know. Who wouldn't? I hurried inside and headed for my grandmother's room. She was asleep, wheezing as her chest rose and fell. I borrowed the pink nail varnish from her bedside drawer and made my way upstairs. Mrs Palethorpe sat alone in a brown armchair by the window, staring out over the garden. Her smart outfit of a cream blouse with a beige skirt and cardigan suggested she might be having a good day.

'Hiya, darlin,' I said. She swivelled her head and glowered at me. 'Just popped in to see how you are.'

I examined the photograph hanging on the wall beside the bed. John and his wife and their kids – two girls with toothy smiles and springy dark curls. 'Your grandchildren are well cute,' I said. An affair with a married man; what was my mother thinking? Hardly a good example to be setting me. I lifted the photo off the wall and scrutinised the girls' faces. No resemblance between them and I.

'Are you from Brentham, Mrs Palethorpe?' I asked, replacing the picture. 'Is this where you raised your family?'

She said nothing, and the pictures on her sideboard gave little away. Her wedding photo could have been taken outside any church, and the pictures of her son were recent ones. Under her agitated gaze, I rummaged through the drawer of the bedside cabinet. Among the tubes of hand cream and packets of barley sugar, I found an address book with a red leather cover.

'Mine.' Mrs Palethorpe's expression was a shifting blend of recognition and panic.

'You're hardly using it.' I found John's address and typed it into my phone, along with his home and mobile numbers.

'Hello, John,' said Mrs Palethorpe.

'He's not here.' I dropped the address book back into the drawer. The door to the room swung open.

'Hello, Mum.'

There he was. Standing in the doorway in a navy blue suit with a red tie. Mrs Palethorpe smiled, and I marvelled at her maternal instinct. She'd sensed her son approaching. Felt him before she could see him. Why couldn't my mother be like that with me?

'Hi, Emma,' he said, as he entered the room. I didn't realise he knew my name. Some relatives didn't bother to remember. He bent down and kissed his mother's cheek. Her arms circled his neck and held him there until he eased himself free.

'How's she doing today?' he asked me.

'Good,' I said, although I had no idea really. 'Settled.'

'Hope I'm not interrupting. I like to look in if I finish work early.'

'Nah, it's fine.' I hold up the nail varnish. 'I thought your mum might like a manicure.'

'She used to like getting her nails done.' He stroked her arm. 'Didn't you?'

Mrs Palethorpe pointed at me. 'Ugly little bitch,' she said.

I gasped.

'Emma is a very lovely young girl,' John said, 'and she's doing her best to look after you.'

I liked the way he defended me. Protecting me like a father would.

Mrs Palethorpe cackled and looked out of the window.

'I'm so sorry,' John said.

'All part of the job,' I replied with a smile. He sat on the edge of the bed, looking exhausted. No wonder, carrying on with my mother like that at the weekend. My cheeks flamed up at the thought of him on his knees, face buried between my mother's legs. One of many images I couldn't wipe from my mind. The photographs I took didn't help. I shouldn't have looked at them afterwards.

'I don't think you'll be giving her a manicure today,' he said.

'No.' Up close, I could detect kindness in his cool grey eyes. Despite his dodgy morals, he clearly cared for his mother. I could have a worse man for a father. 'I try to get the women chatting about the past when I do their nails,' I said. 'It's good for them.'

'Reminiscence therapy,' John said.

'Yeah, that's it.' My blood thundered in my ears. 'Before you came in your mum was saying she's from Brentham.'

John frowned. 'She's from Folkestone.'

'Oh. You didn't grow up here then?'

John shook his head. 'My wife's from Brentham. I moved here when we got married and brought Mum to live here about eight years ago.'

'Bless her heart,' I said, 'she's well confused.'

* * *

Deflated, I made my excuses and left. It didn't take long for anger and jealousy to swamp my disappointment. Taking refuge in the empty laundry room, I sat on the floor with my back against the warm side of one of the tumble dryers. I scrolled through the pictures of John and my mother on my phone. Silly to be so envious. I'd lived right inside her once, curled up cosy to the sound of her heartbeat, consuming her from the inside. He could never get as close to her as that.

In one of the pictures, John stood with his eyes closed, my mother on her knees in front of him. Thank God he wasn't my father. I thought about deleting the photos but decided not to edit my mother's life to suit myself. To truly know her, I'd have to accept her less agreeable parts. Including the fact John might not be her only lover. I flicked through to a picture taken a couple of days later – Grace and some blond man arguing outside her block. The row sounded ugly, and at the end my mother broke down sobbing. I got a good shot of the man as he walked away. He had incredible cheekbones and distinctive green eyes. I thought about following him to find out more but couldn't leave my mother in that state, no matter how much she'd upset me.

My phone chimed, signalling the arrival of a new email to Emma's Yahoo account. My insides melted, and I nearly dropped my phone in excitement. My mother's short but beautiful message had me in tears.

> Hi Emma, hope you're well. I wondered if you're still interested in helping me clear out some of Mum's stuff? I really need to get the kitchen done. If you're free Sunday morning, that would be great.
> Best wishes, Grace

The email was a sign, telling me not to give up hope. I'd read tons of stories online about adopted children meeting their birth mothers, so I'd always known our reunion would have its challenges. I would give my mother the benefit of the doubt this time and trust that eventually she'd do the right thing as far as these men were concerned. She and I were about to get much closer, and once she had me she wouldn't need anyone else.

36

GRACE

December

I reach Mum's house just before ten and let myself into the cold hallway. After turning up the thermostat by the front door, I hang my damp trench coat on the coat stand, next to the beige rain mac my mother will never wear again.

In the kitchen, I open the fridge and place a newly purchased carton of milk next to the unopened Sauvignon Blanc. Recalling John's inventive use of the bottle fills me with an uncomfortable blend of desire and guilt.

We left the kitchen in a mess, but there's no point clearing up before the morning's work begins. Instead I sit at the table, one eye on the clock above the cooker and wait for Emma. I imagine the families in the houses either side of me having Sunday breakfast together. Noisy tables of people arguing and loving one another. What happens in Dan's house on a Sunday? Does he read the paper while Stella jots down lines of poetic genius in a journal? Are they out walking on the beach with their children? Stopping off for coffee and croissants at that seafront café?

I don't like him knowing where I live. What if he comes back? I tell myself he has no reason to. He didn't send me the cards or the mug and nothing else has arrived over the past week. No more calls to my mobile. It has all been in my head. I mustn't dwell on the past or I'll make myself ill again.

Time to move on. Time to pack it all away. At ten-thirty, the doorbell rings.

'Hiya,' Emma says when I open the door, a wide smile on her face. A dull ache ripples across my stomach.

'Hello there,' I reply. A large, pink umbrella shelters her from the rain. The white slogan printed on it tells me to keep calm, it's only raining. 'Come on in.'

I hang up her green Parka jacket and put her umbrella in the brass stand next to the telephone table. She insists on taking her ankle boots off.

'Don't want to muck up your carpets.' She pulls a pair of slippers from her backpack with a magician's flourish. 'Ta-da.'

'Very organised.' The slippers she pushes her tiny feet into are the same pink as her umbrella, each one embroidered with an instruction to keep calm and snooze. I turn and head towards the kitchen. 'If we can make a start in here, that would be fab.' When I look back she is gone. 'Emma?'

I hear the sound of doors opening and closing upstairs.

The faint pad of her footsteps.

'Just sussing the place out.' She appears at the top of the stairs. 'There's tons to do.'

'Well, getting the kitchen sorted will be a big help.'

'Sure.' She skips downstairs, oversized gold hoops swinging from her ears. 'We can do the rest another time.'

'Thanks, but that won't—'

'Can't wait to get started,' she says, squeezing past me. I follow her into the kitchen. My email did only ask for her help today, but I can put her off at a later date. Don't want to offend her.

'That's proper weird, seeing your mum's stuff like this,' she says. 'Bet she misses it all, bless her.'

'I don't think she remembers the house most of the time.'

Emma bends down and picks up the tea towels that lie scattered on the floor around the kitchen table. I smile at the memory of how they ended up there. While I fill the kettle, Emma folds the towels and places them back on the table in a neat pile. Almost exactly in their original position.

'Thanks,' I say. Her fingers trace a pattern across the surface of the table.

'No worries,' she replies. We stand in silence for a moment.

'Tea?' I ask. 'I'll make you one for a change.'

She nods.

I fill the kettle and switch it on. 'Hope this hasn't mucked up your work schedule for the weekend?'

'Nah. I've been covering loads recently so Kegs owed me a day off.' She fiddles with one of her earrings, twisting it back and forth. I ask how she's getting on with her application form. 'Great,' she says, 'that stuff you gave me was well helpful.'

'If you need me to take another look once you've finished, just ask.'

'Cheers, that'd be brill.'

I show her the dinner services in the dresser and ask her to wrap them in the old newspapers I've been collecting.

'No problemo,' she says.

After I've made the tea, we get to work – Emma on the crockery and me sorting through Mum's baking cupboard, which contains an extensive collection of equipment, including the large, round tin Mum used for my birthday cakes. My eyes fill up as I deposit it in one of the charity boxes, but I have to be ruthless. Getting rid of bad memories means losing some good ones too.

Emma has no intention of leaving the past undisturbed. She asks question after question. How long did my family live in the house? What did I like most about growing up here? Why did my mother have three dinner services?

'Bet she baked amazing cakes,' she says, nodding at the pile of loaf tins beside me on the floor. 'Did you make stuff together when you were little?'

'Sometimes.'

'That must have been fun?' Her expression is wistful.

I nod. We had some good times in this room, Mum and I. Her measuring and stirring, me in charge of licking clean the mixing bowls and wooden spoons. We had darker times too. Me, twenty years ago, sitting at the table sobbing. Begging for support. Her refusing me in the worst way possible.

Don't do it, Grace. It's a sin.

Yesterday, as soon as I entered her room, she said, 'Only trying to help.'

'You didn't help me, though,' I said. 'Did you?' Her eyes burned into me. For a moment, I feared we might finally talk, but she drifted back to the TV.

'I've finished all the plates and stuff,' Emma says, loading the last of the dinner services into a cardboard box.

'One more thing to do.' I fetch the Virgin Mary from the windowsill. 'She can go.'

'Hail Mary, full of grace,' Emma says, as I swaddle the statue in layers of newspaper. 'I don't know the rest.'

'Who cares?' I shove the Virgin Mary in a box.

Emma frowns. 'Won't your mum want that? You could take it to Birch Grove.'

'No.'

She watches as I fold the flaps of the lid shut. 'Can I have a look at the living room?' she asks.

'Sure.'

As soon as we move next door, Emma rushes across to the bookcase and homes in on the family photographs. 'Who is everyone?' She picks up a black-and-white picture of my nan in her mother-of-the-bride outfit. 'That must be Polly's mum? Oh my God, they are literally lookalikes. Tell me about her.'

I'm in no mood for reminiscing, but Emma's excited enquiries are impossible to refuse. I tell her about my nan, a hard-drinking Catholic charlady from Stockport. Emma doesn't believe me when I say she had an outside toilet.

'It's true,' I say. 'When I stayed with them I had to use a potty during the night.'

She laughs. 'That's mental.'

It's fun, sharing my family history with someone. I'm about to launch into a story about my dad's father, who fought with the Chindits in Burma during World War Two, but Emma moves on to the next shelf and my mother's menagerie of crystal animals.

'Super cute,' she says, picking up a hedgehog with glittering spikes. I understand now why I followed Emma, why I like having her around. She gives me glimpses of the life I chose not to have.

'Would you like to keep it?' I ask, aware I'm acting out what might have been. Role-playing a moment meant for someone else.

Her eyes widen. 'I couldn't.'

'Might as well. Better than it going to charity.'

'Wow. Thanks.' She holds the hedgehog in her cupped palms. 'I'll look after it.'

Her gratitude moves me. She has no one to give her gifts, and I have no one to give gifts to. We're just two people helping each other through a difficult time. What harm can it do?

* * *

I wake, fighting for air, and grope for my bedside lamp. As light floods the room, I glance at the bedroom door.

Nothing.

Touching the bony hollow between my breasts, I wipe away the sweat collecting there. Force myself to take slow, rhythmic breaths. In, hold, out.

The dream I haven't been able to remember is a nightmare. An old foe. I fell asleep to find her waiting. When I ran, she followed. Terror tied a knot around my heart. Terror drove me up a flight of stairs and into a room. I crouched in the dark belly of a wardrobe, each breath bold as a thunderstorm. I knew she would find me. She always found me.

I heard her solemn, deadly footsteps. I heard her heartbeat. Her accusatory little heartbeat, drumming just for me. The wardrobe door clicked open, and she slipped her hand inside. Her tiny, pink hand.

I woke before it could reach me.

37

THEN

Monday 11 September, Royal Edinburgh Hospital

She came back for me. Two nights ago. I don't remember waking, but Simon said I was in a bit of a state and that's why the nurses sedated me. I was out of it all day yesterday but feel better today.

He asked if it was the same nightmare I started having months ago. I said yes and, at his request, described it to him. He wanted to know what I thought the dream was about. A longing to talk came over me. To unload myself, just a little. 'I was pregnant,' I said. He asked me what happened to the baby, and I said I didn't keep it. I told him about the abortion.

His expression didn't alter, but he radiated the quiet triumph of a man who thought he'd reached the heart of the matter. He asked if the nightmare began after the termination and I said, yes, about a week afterwards.

I had no idea what the nightmare signified at the time. No clue it would lead me here.

Simon glanced at the notepad on his desk. He reminded me that when I'd arrived at the hospital, I'd insisted I was being punished. Kept saying it over and over. Did I think I was being punished for not keeping my baby? he asked.

Tears clustered in my eyes. Simon said I'd had a difficult choice to make but insisted it had been my right to make it. I said he should try telling my mother that.

He let out a knowing sigh and said he finally understood why I'd refused to let him contact Mum. I'm not under section, so he couldn't ignore my wishes. Mum thinks I'm on tour in Germany. I told her months ago I'd got a part in a musical revue and wouldn't be able to contact her very often. Yesterday, I rang her from the payphone outside the dayroom and told her I was in Frankfurt. After a few minutes of strained small talk, I said the tour had been extended for another few months.

In a cold, flat voice she said, 'Oh well, career comes first, I suppose.'

Simon asked if Mum had disagreed with the decision I made, and I said that was one way of putting it. He was adamant that none of what I'd been through was a punishment for making that choice. He pleaded with me to believe him.

I knew he was right. I longed to go back in time, to the moment I'd made my decision with confidence, never questioning my right to make it. A victory for reason over biology.

If only I'd kept the news of my disaster to myself. If only I hadn't phoned Mum.

As soon as she asked me what was wrong, I burst into tears. I explained that Dan had left me and she said, 'Honestly, all this over some boy.'

I confessed I was pregnant and told her I couldn't keep it. A long silence followed and then she begged me to come home. I asked her if she'd help me.

'Just come home, love,' she said.

38

CASSIE

December

'You seem agitated,' Dr Costello said.

'No, I'm not.' My right thumb and forefinger fiddled with the diamond stud in my right ear. An annoying habit I'd picked up from Emma.

'A bit down then?' he ventured.

'I'm not feeling suicidal, if that's what you're asking.'

'No, Cassie. That's not what I'm asking.'

My mother's upcoming birthday had me all over the place. So many decisions – what to get her, how to celebrate, whether to divulge the real me.

I shrugged. 'It's Christmas in eleven days. That's enough to make anyone feel bad.'

He raised his eyebrows. 'Can't disagree with you there.'

'Buying presents already?' I said, pointing at the Harrods bags stuffed under his desk.

'A necessary evil.'

As was this appointment. I'd considered cancelling it, but during yesterday's Skype call Quentin begged me not to neglect my therapy and hinted he'd check up on me if necessary. Couldn't risk that at this crucial stage. He'd looked in need of help himself. Unshaven with a glass of whisky in his hand, the ends of his sentences disintegrating. Pitiful, really.

'Can you describe how you've been feeling?' Dr Costello asked.

'Are those presents for your kids?'

He folded his arms. 'Are you sure it's just the season of goodwill that's getting to you?' He never liked me asking questions about his kids. Or his wife. Especially his wife. Guess he had to maintain some professional boundaries. 'Cassie?'

'Yes. I hate Christmas.' I should have been in a great mood, the best mood ever, but my conflicting feelings for my mother had left me confused as always. I'd spent nearly all Sunday with her, packing up some of my grandmother's stuff. We'd cracked up laughing when we found a whole drawer of Mills and Boon books under the coffee table. We spent ages reading out the naffest bits to each other – women with pulsating hearts and tall, dark men seething with dangerous passion. So much fun I could have wept with happiness, but then my mother gathered up the books and dumped them in a box for charity. A brutal cull. Did she get rid of me so easily? She knelt on the floor beside me, gathering up the loose pages that had fluttered from the tattered romances.

A line from my grandmother's Bible came to me: *But I am full of the wrath of the Lord; I am weary of holding it in.* I picked up a crystal swan from the bookcase. It was small but heavy and would do some damage if applied with enough force. My mother glanced up and urged me to take the swan as well as the hedgehog if I had room for it. Her voice cracked. She looked so sad I felt awful for even thinking of hurting her.

'Things going well with your boyfriend?' Dr Costello asked.

'Great.' Ryan had forgiven me for our last falling-out. He'd had no choice after I'd bought us tickets for a VIP tour of Arsenal football stadium. One of the dullest afternoons of my life, but it got him back on side.

Dr Costello smiled. 'Good. And you're still enjoying the job? It's not too much for you?'

'I feel sorry for them.'

'Who?'

'The olds. The way they just get dumped in these places.'

'It's a little more complex than that, Cassie.'

'Is it?' What about my poor grandmother? My mother had hardly seen her recently. No excuse for that.

'Sometimes,' said Dr Costello, 'the elderly aren't safe at home and need to be where they can receive better care.'

'Their families should do it.'

Costello pressed his lips together before he spoke. He always did that when I was getting to him. 'Sometimes family members aren't able to provide the right care,' he said. 'Sometimes they have to do what's best for the person they love.'

I sighed. 'You're talking about my mother, aren't you?'

'Am I?'

'You know you are.'

'Weren't you?'

'You're always making excuses for what she did.'

'I'm suggesting reasons.'

'I nearly died.'

'I believe your mother was sorry for what she did.'

'You think being sorry makes it okay?'

He sighed. 'Perhaps she was scared and alone. She may have been too young to understand what she was doing. She might not even have realised she was pregnant.'

'My mother's not stupid,' I said. 'She's got a degree.'

He lurched forward then, eyes alive with the possibility of catching me out. 'Why do you say that?'

I sat very still, working out how to evade him. 'That's how I like to think of her,' I said. 'Clever, with a university degree. Something arty.'

He relaxed back into his chair. 'Have you been thinking about her a lot recently?'

'A bit. I suppose that's because of Isobel dying?'

'Perhaps.' That's when he asked about the people at work.

Had I made any friends? If so, how old were they and what were their names? I guessed what he was getting at and made it very clear that my best friend at work, Surinder, was almost the same age as me.

'That's good then,' he said.

Before I left, he told me to make another appointment before Christmas. He said we shouldn't leave it too long at this trying time of year. 'Oh, and, Cassie,' he added, as I stood up to leave, 'bring your scrapbook with you next time.'

My scrapbook. The fragments of my early life that Costello and I had compiled when he first started helping me. I'd taken it to Emma's bedsit a few weeks ago.

'I think it would be helpful if we looked through it together,' he said.

* * *

The steamy air around me filled with the sounds of a beating heart and sloshing fluid.

'What the hell is that?' Ryan asked from his end of the bath.

'Womb music,' I said.

'Where's it coming from?'

I pointed to the speakers above the bathroom door.

'It's a bit weird,' he said.

'It's relaxing.'

He moaned as I massaged his calves beneath the foam-filled surface of the water. 'Now that's relaxing.'

'Better than dinner with Nick and Maya?'

His eyelids drooped shut. 'Yeah, you win.' I'd had to tempt him with something special to get out of the double-date nightmare he'd planned for me. What if I met his friends and they didn't like me? The longer I could put it off the better.

'I said they'd get to meet you at the Christmas party,' he murmured.

'What Christmas party?'

'The Aroma one. It'll be awesome.' He opened one eye. 'You will come?'

'Don't know. Maybe.'

His pained expression irritated me.

'Will I be seeing you at all over Christmas?' he asked.

'I'll be spending it with my gran.'

'Yeah, but we'll see each other at some point?'

Unlikely, but I couldn't face an argument now. I slid my hands up his thighs, and he groaned as I cupped his balls. It didn't take long to finish him off, and afterwards the subject of Christmas appeared forgotten.

I instructed him to do my feet and lay back amongst the bubbles as he rubbed the ball of my right foot.

'You look tired, babe,' he said.

'I am.' The effort of not screwing up in front of Costello always left me drained. The same kind of exhaustion I often felt after being Emma for the day.

I focused on the hollow heartbeat echoing round the bathroom, hoping it would take me back to my mother. To the time we were as one. Instead I remembered lying in a bath with a belly full of paracetamol, waiting to slip from this world to the next. I was seventeen and trying to get over Miss Robertson, my A-level English Literature teacher. She had blonde hair and blue eyes. She'd shown kindness towards me and I thought I could trust her. When I tried to get to know her better, she caused such a fuss. Making me move schools was a bit harsh in my opinion, but Isobel and Quentin didn't stick up for me, so I had no choice.

My suicide attempt took weeks of planning, but I hadn't counted on the bath water cooling so fast around me. The cold had dragged me back into consciousness. Back to Isobel's screams, muffled and distant. *Why, Cassie? Why?*

Ryan switched to my other foot. I sank beneath the water and bubbled the air out of my lungs. If I stayed under long enough, would I find it again? That slow, sleepy slip road that almost took me where I wanted to go.

After a while my eyes bulged and my chest strained, but I refused to break the rippling skin of the water. Ryan tugged at my foot, shouted my name. I pressed myself against the floor of the bath.

'Cassie.'

He hoisted me up to the surface, and I flopped over the side of the bath, fighting for oxygen like a fish just landed.

'What the hell are you doing?' His face was taut with alarm.

'Your turn,' I gasped, 'see if you can beat that.'

He splashed water at me. An angry gesture not a playful one. 'Crazy bitch,' he said.

39

GRACE

December

'My mother forgot my birthday today,' I tell Leo. Leo is a barman at The Old Street, a hip hotel in Shoreditch. He has intense blue eyes and black dreadlocks tied back from his angular face.

'That sucks,' he says as he places my second vodka Martini on the glass surface of the circular bar.

'She's in a care home with dementia, so I suppose I'll let her off.'

An awkward pause before Leo excuses himself to serve a waiting customer.

It does suck. Forty-three today, and I will never receive a birthday card from my mother again. I sip my cocktail – 5.30 p.m. on a Tuesday and I'm drinking vodka. Might as well admit I want to lose control and obliterate this depressing day. I woke up groggy this morning and trudged to work in the dark, my body bewildered by lack of light. In the staffroom, my equally jaded colleagues and I exchanged muted hellos. No one knew about my birthday, and I didn't mention it.

At lunchtime, I phoned Birch Grove to speak to Mum, but Kegs found her sleeping. He said she's been sleeping a lot the past few days and hardly eating anything when awake. I asked to speak to Emma instead but she had the day off. Pity. She would have found a way to cheer me up. My bar stool swivels as I cross my legs. My dress falls away from my thighs, forcing me to yank it back again. The mauve, silk wrap-around hasn't had an outing for months, and I'm regretting my decision to wear it. Draughts swirl around the spacious bar and lounge area, raising goosebumps on my arms. The sheer black stockings beneath the dress do nothing to keep me warm, and I should have worn boots, not these stupid black stilettos. Earlier, up in the hotel room – the room I booked and John will pay for – changing into my outfit gave me a thrill. Now I feel self-conscious, obvious. A woman gift-wrapped for sex.

What am I doing here? I think about leaving, but John appears. His arm around my waist, his lips on my cheek.

'Hello, gorgeous,' he says, 'happy birthday.'

* * *

An hour later, I'm halfway through my third Martini and my mood has lifted. John and I have taken over one of the grey sofas by the log fire at the back of the lounge. The place is packed, buzzing with after-work energy. Only ten days until Christmas and people are already in a party mood. A house music soundtrack sets the mood – classics like 'Voodoo Ray' and modern stuff I don't recognise but tap my foot along to anyway.

'They wind me up,' John says, concluding a rant about bearded young men on laptops. Plenty of them here, typing away in earnest at tables and in armchairs. 'I mean, what do they actually do?'

'You sound so middle-aged.' He looks different in his navy blue work suit. Smaller, more ordinary.

He laughs. 'I am middle-aged.' He picks up a prawn skewer from the sharing platter we ordered earlier but have hardly touched.

I gasp as 'Don't Fight It, Feel It' by Primal Scream comes over the speakers. 'Love this song.' I sway side to side, aware I have transitioned from tipsy to drunk. My dress shifts further up my thighs, but I don't pull it down. I notice a small red stain near the hem. Wine? When did that happen?

'Sorry,' John says, reaching into his jacket pocket and fishing out his trilling phone. He checks the screen. 'Better get this.'

I stop swaying to the music and sit stock-still in my seat. He doesn't need to say who's calling. He's supposed to be in Manchester tonight after a conference there, but he took a train back early so we could spend the night together. Not in honour of my special day – his free night just happened to be tonight. I wish I hadn't even mentioned my birthday.

'Hi.' John stands up and moves towards the main doors. He steps out into the night, phone clamped to his ear. A hole opens up between my sternum and belly button. Again I consider leaving, but the thought of my empty bed and the tiny hand waiting for me in my sleep keeps me glued to the sofa.

Opening my handbag, I take out my phone, just for something to do. An urge to email Emma comes over me. A short message, just to thank her again for her help at the weekend, but I don't want to hassle her. We got much more done at Mum's than I'd anticipated, although we did waste time messing about with the Mills and Boon books. After Emma read out a dreadful passage about a Victorian heiress pining for her soulmate, I asked her if she believed in true love. 'Of course,' she said, 'I've been waiting for someone special my whole life.'

John returns, the cold from outside clinging to him. When he sits down, I shove my phone in my bag and drag him towards me. His tongue is hot and keen in my mouth. When we separate, I see a blur of faces looking our way.

'I'm going to the bathroom,' I say, 'and when I come back you're going to take me upstairs.'

Leaving my handbag with him, I weave my way across the lobby. There is a queue in the ladies, and by the time I return, John is at reception. I watch him take a wad of notes from his briefcase. He's paying for the room now, in cash. A small detail, but a sordid one.

Deflated, I pick up my bag from the sofa. John turns and waves me over. I follow him to the lift.

* * *

As soon as we enter the room, John presses me up against the wall and lifts my dress. After unzipping himself, he wraps my legs around his waist, yanks my black lace knickers to one side and pushes into me. When we tire of the wall, we make use of the floor and the writing desk before collapsing onto the bed, slick with sweat, our clothes and underwear littering the carpet.

The king-size bed is adorned with far too many cushions. I throw a few aside and try to get comfortable. John's chest rises and falls against mine. I am suddenly sober, as if the sex has chemically reacted with all the vodka and neutralised its effects.

'Christ,' he says, 'it's not often sex actually lives up to your fantasies.'

Irritation rushes through me. We have just enacted a scene from John's imagination, and I could be anyone. I am no one. Worst of all, I cast myself in the role.

'Honestly,' he continues, 'you have no idea the pornographic stunts you get up to in my head.'

'I need some water.' I stand up, only to find my instant sobriety hasn't reached my legs. Staggering to the bathroom, I fill one of the chunky glasses next to the sink with tap water and gulp it back. When I return, John removes a parcel wrapped in black tissue paper from his briefcase and hands it to me.

'Happy birthday,' he says. Inside the paper is a lingerie set – matching bra and knickers in a sheer red fabric. He instructs me to try them on.

I obey. The underwire of the bra digs into my ribcage. The knickers are the wrong size too, the elastic cutting deep into my flesh.

'Wow,' John says, oblivious to his error, 'knockout.' This underwear isn't for me. This underwear is for the woman in John's head, the fantasy I can never fulfil. I see me and Dan fucking in our kitchen, clamped together on a chair, his arms around my waist. His mocking eyes daring me to step out of character. Daring me to fail.

'I want to make love,' I say.

John frowns. 'We just did.'

'You know what I mean.'

He hesitates just long enough to prove he does. 'What's wrong? Do you want another drink?'

'No.' I feel like old snow, soiled and slushy and no fun any more.

'Grace, come on.' He grabs my waist and draws me close.

'Please,' I whisper. That fine line glitters, and this time we cross it. He pulls me onto the bed and kisses me, stroking the tops of my legs until they part for him. Edging his way down the bed, he peels off the tight knickers and settles his head between my thighs. The tenderness of his tongue lures tears from me.

'This is only for you,' he says. 'I don't do this for anyone but you.'

As if he is giving me diamonds.

He is soon inside me, and I don't realise my eyes are closed until he tells me to look at him. I try, but too much occurs to me at once. That I have never had sex with the intent of creating a child and probably never will. That my pregnancy was no accident. I got pregnant because I lacked the confidence to protect myself, or to insist that Dan protect me, fearing that to do so would drive him away. I valued his opinion of me more than I valued my own. Valued it so much I took risks I shouldn't have.

John whispers my name in my ear. He is at my core, undoing me, and I might never be able to shut down again. I open my mouth to tell him to stop, but it is too late.

His ejaculation triggers a fizzing deep within me, tiny celebratory fireworks. My body still fooled, even though his semen will never fulfil its purpose.

After he withdraws, John kisses me on the cheek and goes to the bathroom. His redundant sperm trickles down my inner thighs.

He stays in the bathroom for a long time, and upon emerging he cannot meet my eyes. He asks if I fancy a drink now and crouches down to open the mini bar. He recites its contents to me, trying to talk himself back over the line we have crossed, back to a place where we can drink and screw, but he's too late. I don't want to go back there, which means our affair can't go on.

'We should quit while we're ahead,' I say. He feigns confusion, but I can tell the same thought has crossed his mind. 'This can't go anywhere.'

He kneels next to the bed and takes my hand. 'I didn't think that was a problem.'

'It will be.' Weariness colonises my bones. 'These things always get messy.'

His shoulders slump. 'I didn't realise you had such strong feelings for me.'

I don't but am too tired to correct him. I just want to leave and be on my own.

'You're amazing,' he says, 'but I can't risk hurting my family.' I see he has always known he would one day sacrifice this temporary pleasure for his lasting happiness.

'I'd never want you to hurt them.' I recover my clothes and get dressed under his remorseful gaze. He asks me to stay the night, but I refuse.

'We're bound to see each other at Birch Grove,' he says.

I pull on my coat and pick up my bag. 'We're adults; we'll manage.'

He rings reception and orders me a taxi. He offers me cash for it, which I don't accept.

At the door of the room, we kiss goodbye. 'I'll miss you,' he says.

* * *

When my taxi turns into Goswell Road, I begin the ritual search for my keys. It is then I discover the other present John bought me. A small black box at the bottom of my handbag. As the taxi jolts along, I open it and am stunned to find a necklace inside. Attached to the delicate chain is a solid silver heart with an inscription on it.

Happy Birthday

He must have put it in my bag when I went to the toilet. A touching gesture. I take out my phone and bring up his number, no longer sure if I've made the right decision.

I press the green call button, but he doesn't pick up. Probably for the best. I coil the necklace back into the box and bury it safe in the depths of my bag.

40

THEN

Monday 11 September, Royal Edinburgh Hospital

Three weeks after the procedure, I began smoking joints of black Moroccan hash in an attempt to get a good night's sleep. The dope helped me drift off and sometimes kept the nightmare at bay, but when I was awake, paranoia set in. I often heard a baby crying next door, pitiful wails that floated through the walls. The house next door was empty.

The hash made me hungry too. The stress of the previous month had made eating almost impossible, but now I undertook regular trips to the 24-hour garage at the end of the road to buy salted peanuts, Milky Ways and loaves of white sliced bread. I was always starving, and it didn't take me long to gain half a stone. I should have stopped there, but every time I thought about Dan and Stella I rolled another joint and induced another attack of the munchies. Dan had called me from a payphone the week after I had the termination. As soon as I heard his voice, I knew what he wanted. I told him it was done and then I hung up. At least he and Stella were back on tour so I had less chance of bumping into them.

My sluggish body with the extra pounds around the middle didn't feel like it belonged to me. I didn't go out much, preferring to stay hidden away. The manager of the pub rang to offer me shifts, but I turned them down. My former friends still drank there and would know about Dan and Stella. I couldn't face anyone gloating that they'd told me so. Nor did I want to tell anyone about the termination. That was my business.

My dole payments covered some basics, and I dipped into Dad's life insurance money to pay my rent and bills. Despite my immense relief at not being pregnant any more, I couldn't motivate myself to get my life together. Each night, I resolved to get back on the audition circuit, or at least find part-time work, but, when dawn came, I'd cosy up on the sofa with Marmite on toast, a mug of tea and my first spliff of the day.

The weeks passed. Mum rang every Sunday afternoon, as usual. Our terse exchanges never lasted long. She'd asked me to phone her after 'it' was over so she'd know I was okay. During that call, I'd mentioned feeling tired and weepy. She told me not to expect any sympathy from her. Not after what I'd done.

We never mentioned 'it' again.

I really thought she would help me. I thought she'd choose me over her beliefs, but I was wrong. She lured me back home promising support and then tried to change my mind. 'What if you only have this one chance, Grace? What if you have as much trouble conceiving in the future as I did?' She spoke in detail about her three miscarriages and revived the familiar tale of my troublesome gestation and agonising birth. The miracle of me. She laid out photo albums on the kitchen table and showed me pictures of myself in my first weeks of life. 'Look at your hands, Grace. Your tiny little hands. I'll never forget the first time you gripped my finger.'

She wouldn't accept my reasons. 'What career, Grace? You can't honestly think you'll make it as an actress? You can cope without the father, Grace. You and the baby can move in with me. You can work and I'll do the childcare.' Her desperation scared me. As if she'd do anything to fill the void left by Dad's premature departure. Or perhaps that longing for another child had never left her.

'I'm only trying to help,' she said when I refused her offers of assistance. No way would my child grow up hostage to Mum's grief and maternal longings.

'I'm having an abortion,' I said.

She warned me not to do it. She was standing by the kitchen sink, looking at the Virgin Mary statue on the windowsill.

I asked her what else I was supposed to do? Have the baby adopted? The suggestion made her furious. She said she'd never allow that. No way. No way would she let a stranger bring up her grandchild.

'She's my responsibility,' I shouted, 'not yours.' Mum got all excited about me calling the baby 'she' when I couldn't possibly know the sex yet. She said that was my instinct talking. She said she could tell I wanted to keep my child.

I insisted I didn't and said it was my choice. She gazed out into the garden and told me that choices have consequences. When I asked what she meant, she came over to the table, knelt beside my chair and placed her hands on my belly.

'Don't do it, Grace,' she said, 'it's a sin.'

'What, and I'll be punished?' I replied.

She said nothing but the pitying look she gave me said, yes, you will be punished.

41

CASSIE

December

Everyone at Birch Grove was grumpy and out of sorts. An hour-long power cut this morning meant we fell behind with the breakfasts and didn't get most residents washed and dressed until nearly lunchtime. On top of that, Kegs almost had a fight with Troy, Len Daley's grandson. He'd caught the two of them having a fag out of Len's window and had dragged the skinny boy into the corridor and thrown him out of the building.

During all the drama, I couldn't stop thinking about last night's escapade, my initial elation dissolving into dread. The deed I'd carried out in a cold rage now loomed over me. What if it backfired?

I could hear Isobel's voice in my head... *You don't think before you act, Cassie. That's your problem.*

My mother turned up at lunchtime for her Saturday visit, dark rings beneath her eyes. I scrutinised her but found no obvious signs of fallout from my actions last night.

She wasn't wearing the necklace I gave her for her birthday. I shouldn't have bothered; she didn't deserve it. Yet no matter how much she hurt me, I still wanted to please her.

When she arrived, I was in the middle of washing Grandma's face with a flannel.

'Oh, Mum,' my mother said. She put a hand over her mouth and stood there for some time.

'You okay?' I asked.

'She looks so frail.'

'Probably looks worse to you, cos you haven't seen her much recently.' A dig I couldn't resist. I knew what my mother meant though. My grandmother had withered even further. Sunken cheeks and eyes that glinted like hard black stones.

My comment didn't appear to register. My mother fetched Vera and the two of them chatted in low voices by the door while I dabbed Oil of Olay cream onto my grandmother's cheeks and forehead. They discussed something called an advanced directive. Apparently my grandmother only wanted life-sustaining treatments if they would lead to certain recovery. 'She's maybe had enough, love,' Vera said. 'They often stop eating when they're getting ready to go. It's the only control they've got left.'

My mother just nodded.

'We'll keep her fluids up,' Vera promised, giving my mother a hug, 'and we'll keep encouraging her with the food. In the end it's up to her.'

No, it's bloody not, I thought.

My mother kissed her mother's forehead and said she needed to go out for some fresh air. Once Grandma and I were alone, I put my face close to hers and made it very clear she wouldn't be going anywhere soon and that this starving herself nonsense had to stop.

She shrank back against her pillows. 'Not hungry,' she croaked.

'That's because you're not eating. It's a vicious circle.'

I took out my phone, did an online search for biblical quotes about suicide and then read the best ones aloud to her. 'Do not be too wicked or too foolish either,' I said, 'why die before you have to?'

'Ecclesiastes,' she whispered. She recognised the Corinthians quote too, the one about her being a temple of God and the spirit of God dwelling within her and how God destroys anyone who destroys God's temple.

'I don't think God would approve of you willing yourself into an early grave,' I said, 'do you?'

She shook her head. I nipped to the kitchen and brought back a strawberry yoghurt. She managed almost all of it.

'That's more like it,' I said. Within minutes she appeared more alert. She even asked me to put the TV on, which proved I must have done the right thing. Yes, I needed her around to keep my mother close, but I also didn't want her to go yet. We'd had so much time stolen from us, and I didn't want to lose any more.

* * *

I left my grandmother's room, keen to share this feeding success with my mother. I thought she'd gone for a fag in the garden, but instead I spotted her in the corridor with John. He had hold of her elbow and was pushing her along in front of him. He moved with an urgency that signalled either anger or passion. I couldn't tell which.

I waited until they disappeared down the back stairwell before following, excited and scared. Their wake reeked of sour alcohol. The door at the bottom of the stairs hit the wall with a thud when John opened it. I got there just in time to see the door to the laundry room bang shut.

I lurked outside, anxious to hear which way their conversation would go.

'Why did you do it?' John said, and I knew the repercussions had begun.

'Do what?' my mother asked. 'You're scaring me,' she said when he didn't answer.

'These,' he said. 'How could you?'

The photographs. He must have handed them to her because I heard her gasp. He asked if she'd paid someone to take them, and she insisted she'd never seen them before.

'You sent them to my wife,' he said. He sounded drunk – no volume control and his words losing their shape. 'You must have put them through the letterbox last night; the envelope was there first thing this morning.'

'That wasn't—'

'Makes me sick... you creeping round my house like that.'

'This wasn't me,' she said, her voice shrill.

'The pictures are bad enough, but the stuff you wrote on the back of them. Jesus.'

This is your husband and I on my kitchen table.

Here we are on the kitchen floor.

Here we are having a drink at The Old Street Hotel in Shoreditch before going up to our room.

I'd added dates and times for authenticity, and to give his wife a record she could check his lies against.

'These are just a few of them,' he said. 'Debbie's got the rest.'

'I didn't send them.'

'You signed them with your name.'

A mistake – I could see that now. I'd wanted her to take responsibility for her misdemeanours, but what if the Palethorpes involved the police? I'd made sure my messages didn't contain any explicit threats. My experience with Miss Robertson, my English Literature teacher, had taught me the fine line between friendly email and malicious communication.

'Your wife knows who I am?' my mother said. 'What if she comes here?'

'She won't. I told her you live in London. She thinks I met you at a work thing there and that we've only seen each other in the city.'

'Thanks.'

'I did it for my mother, not for you. I can't risk Debbie coming here and kicking off.'

'John, I—'

'She's thrown me out. She won't let me near her or the kids.'

'Why would I do this?' my mother asked. 'It was me who suggested we should break up.'

They'd already broken up? I considered the awful possibility that my efforts had been unnecessary but reasoned they both deserved some kind of punishment. No chance of them getting back together now either.

'You only wanted us to break up because I wouldn't leave my wife for you,' John said.

'What? I never wanted that. I never once asked you to do that.'

'Then why have you been calling my mobile non-stop for the past few days?'

'I haven't.'

'The calls said number withheld but I knew it was you. Was that you calling the house last night, too?'

I'd never intended to speak to John. Just to annoy him, as he'd annoyed me.

My mother denied it all. 'What if someone who knows you saw us together and followed us?' she said.

A logical explanation and I feared he might go for it, but he insisted any friend of his or his wife's would have either told her or confronted him.

'How could you do this?' he said. 'I thought we had a connection?'

'Could it be someone who doesn't like you or your wife?' she said. 'Is there anyone who'd want to hurt you for some reason?'

His laughter was harsh and frightening. 'You're actually trying to get out of this?'

'What if your wife got suspicious and hired a private detective to follow you?'

'You're actually suggesting my wife would set this up to get out of her marriage?'

'What if she—?'

He slapped her then. A sharp, cracking sound. She cried out.

'Shit. Sorry,' he said. 'Shit... That was... Sorry.'

She burst into tears. Scared he might be tempted to console her, I unlocked the door.

'I heard shouting,' I said, 'what's going on?' I looked at my mother. 'Are you okay?'

She nodded, the imprint of his fingers red and clear on her right cheek. He looked appalling – bloodshot eyes and matted hair all over the place. He bent down to pick up the photographs, which lay scattered on the floor.

'Sorry,' he mumbled, as he pushed past me.

My mother sagged against one of the tumble dryers. 'Nothing to worry about, Emma,' she said, in a failed attempt to sound calm. 'Mr Palethorpe and I had a disagreement.'

'Do you need me to get Kegs?'

'God, no. Thanks. We've... it's all sorted out now.' She cleared her throat and stood up straight. 'Thanks for your concern,' she said, all formal, trying to preserve some dignity. Bit late for that.

'S'all right,' I said. 'Do you want a fag or a cup of tea or something?'

'No, no. Don't let me keep you.'

I turned to leave. 'You know where I am, if you need me.'

'Emma,' she said, as I opened the door, 'please don't tell anyone about this.'

'Don't worry,' I replied with a wink, 'mum's the word.'

***

The Christmas lights tacked to the wall above the sofa bed flashed on and off, turning the bedsit red then orange then green. I sat on the gritty carpet, gulping back my second can of Strongbow – Emma's favourite tipple. I'd grown quite fond of it.

What a day. After finishing at three, I came straight here, filled the bath to the brim and lit the scented candles I'd bought from the pound shop. I soaked in the water for two hours. Despite being so crappy, the bedsit had a brilliant hot water system. Then I'd changed into my Keep Calm dressing gown and my Keep Calm slippers and opened my first cider.

As my second can disappeared, a blurry calm did come over me. I unpacked the Christmas tree I'd bought from Argos the previous week.

A flimsy object with silver branches, small enough to sit on the drop-leaf table by the window. The total opposite of the towering pine tree that Isobel got delivered to the house every year. She and I would decorate it together, with Isobel placing the misshaped decorations I'd made during childhood in prominent positions. None of my clumsy angels or asymmetrical snowflakes fitted in with her tasteful colour schemes, but she never seemed to mind.

For Emma's tree, I'd splashed out on a box of ten red-and-gold baubles from the pound shop. Eight found a spot on the tree's spindly branches, the other two I hung from the Virgin Mary's outstretched arms. Giving the statue away had felt wrong to me, so when my mother went to the toilet, I'd rescued it from the charity box and hid it in my backpack. My grandmother would be glad the Virgin Mary had found room at the inn with me.

The cider left me light-headed. I longed to call my mother, just to hear her voice. She'd dashed away from Birch Grove as soon as she could. Didn't even come and say goodbye. The thought of John and his wife having those photos made me uneasy. I'd covered my tracks, but dragging other people into this business with my mother was foolish. Maybe I should forget about her? Give up and walk away while I still could. Reaching under the sofa bed, I pulled out my black trolley case. As soon as I lifted the lid, my scrapbook glinted back at me, the silver cover reflecting the flashing Christmas lights.

It gave me a static shock when I touched it, a warning not to look inside.

I did anyway. A quick flick through would remind me why I'd started all this. There, stuck onto the first page, was my birth certificate. On the second, my certificate of adoption. Then came the newspaper articles, but I only skimmed them. The headline of the final piece made my stomach leap as always.

POLICE LAUNCH SEARCH FOR CASSIE'S MOTHER

42

THEN

Monday 11 September, Royal Edinburgh Hospital

The audition came out of the blue. One morning in late February, as I lay on the sofa engrossed in Good Morning Britain and wreathed in hash smoke, my telephone rang. I answered it to find Tony White, one of my former tutors from NTS, on the line.

'Hello, treacle,' he said. He'd got my number from the school office. He said he had a great opportunity for me. A former student of his had written and was about to direct a six-part TV series set in the Leeds club scene. Apparently this guy wanted to use new faces and had asked Tony to recommend a few people. Tony said he thought I should have a go.

Two days later, I found myself back in one of the workshop spaces at the Northern Theatre School, reading for the part of Mel Turton, a posh girl turned drug dealer. Jared, the intense, shaven-headed director, filmed me for thirty minutes and gave me a thumbs up at the end. He declared me perfect for the part but said it might take him a week or two to let me know for certain. He promised to be in touch as soon as he could.

I floated out of the audition room, the trials of the past month forgotten. I headed to Leeds market and bought loads of fruit and vegetables. When I got home, I threw out all the junk food and flushed my remaining dope down the toilet. No need for that now.

That night, the dream returned. I woke from it to find the tiny hand resting on my chest, the chubby fingers curling and uncurling. Then I woke for real, screaming and clawing at myself.

I made a doctor's appointment the same day. This couldn't go on. My big career break awaited, and I had to get back on track. The doctor, an uptight woman with coarse, greying hair, listened in silence as I told her about the nightmare and the lying around on the sofa all day and the non-existent, crying baby in the house next door. I also explained about my recent audition and my need to be in tip-top form.

'I've read your medical record,' she said.

I twiddled my puzzle ring round and round while she explained that the body could take time to recover after 'a procedure like that'. According to her, pregnancy hormones could linger in the body for quite a while.

I pointed out that nearly six weeks had passed, but she just shrugged and asked about my periods. I told her my most recent one lasted only two days. Spotting mostly. Tender breasts before and after it. She assured me that my body would settle down eventually.

I poured out my fears to her. What if it wasn't just hormones? What if there was something wrong with me? Mentally? The nightmares were so real.

She insisted my problems would vanish once I started working again and prescribed me a course of anti-anxiety tablets.

'Only as a precaution,' she said. 'I'm certain you've got nothing to worry about.'

43

GRACE

December

I am off axis. As if some silent tectonic shift has taken place beneath my life.

'How about "Santa Baby"?' Theresa says. 'That would work as a duet.'

I cannot get the photographs out of my head. Each shot so clear and graphic.

'Shouldn't be too hard to sing,' Theresa adds, 'do you not think?'

'Yes,' I say, 'I'll do that one with you.'

Theresa places a tick on the sheet of paper attached to her clip-board. 'Barney,' she says, 'I'm thinking you're a "Silent Night" kind of guy?'

Theresa, Max, Barney and I are in the staffroom, catching up on admin and getting ready for the Christmas karaoke session at eleven-thirty. Despite it being a Monday morning, they are in a buoyant mood, giddy at the imminent end of term and the prospect of the holidays ahead. Max and Barney wear scarves of silver tinsel and Theresa has belted her grey woollen dress with a length of plastic holly.

I have a hard knot in my stomach and a small snowman badge

pinned to my black jumper. This morning I woke just in time to escape the touch of that tiny hand.

Max and Theresa are sharing their holiday plans with Barney. Christmas with Max's family, followed by New Year on their own.

'Then early Feb, we'll do Chinese New Year with Theresa's family,' Max says. Barney launches into his festive itinerary – a chaotic Christmas Day with his parents and four siblings, followed by a long run on Boxing Day.

Who took the photographs? I considered Dan as a suspect but decided he wouldn't go to that much trouble. He made it very clear he wants nothing to do with me. Nor does John now. My cheek stings at the thought of him. Part of me is livid he hit me, and part of me feels I deserved it. An inevitable punishment.

'Will you be spending Christmas with your mum?' Barney asks. I nod. 'How's she doing by the way?'

'Bit better.' She's eating again, according to my last phone call with Vera. That's something.

The conversation turns to our afternoon drinking session, with Max insisting Barney take the Tube home instead of cycling, so he can get drunk for once.

Yesterday, I didn't leave the house. Whoever took the pictures had spied on me in London and Brentham. How could I feel safe in either location? I thought about the Mother's Day cards. I opened the cupboard next to the oven and searched inside for the 'World's Greatest Mum' mug but couldn't find it. Perhaps I threw it out at the time? The fault line stirred, but I ignored it. No point looking back. Still, I opened the front door and retrieved the fake stone from the rubber plant and brought it inside, relieved to find the key still hidden there. Not taking any chances, I called an emergency locksmith who came and fortified my door with two sturdy new locks and a hefty chain.

Trish came out of her flat just as the locksmith was leaving and inspected my new additions.

'What they for?' she asked. 'You been having some trouble?'

'I—'

'Some bloke giving you shit? I got my locks changed the minute I kicked my Brian out.'

'I'm just making the place more secure.'

'Quite right,' Trish said, 'better safe than sorry.'

* * *

'Christ,' whispers Linda, as she claps along to Waleed and Nieve's attempt at 'Jingle Bells', 'this is purgatory.'

I summon a smile. 'The students are enjoying it.'

Almost thirty of them are crammed into the common room, facing the table with the karaoke machine. Some sit on the floor, some occupy the semicircle of chairs, while others – along with the staff – stay standing. At the back of the room is another table laden with plates of mince pies and jugs of fruit punch.

'Watch your pronunciation,' Max heckles, 'it's slay not slee.' We all laugh. Nieve and Waleed collapse into giggles, but everyone joins in to help them through the final verse. The moment sweeps me along with it, the playful atmosphere releasing me from the worries of the past few days.

As the applause fades, the machine belts out the intro to 'Santa Baby'.

'Ooh,' Theresa says, 'we're up, Grace.'

The students whoop and cheer as we take the microphones. Already laughing at ourselves, Theresa and I stand back to back, like the women from Abba.

The common room door opens and Mandy, lurid in a red Christmas jumper covered with green trees, steps inside. Her eyes scan the room and settle on me. She motions me over, a harassed expression on her face. I point at myself, to check she means me. She nods before tapping Linda on the shoulder.

Theresa sings over the backing track alone. The door to the common room opens again, and a woman I've never seen before pushes past Mandy. A hard-faced woman in skintight grey jeans and a black furry gilet. A woman pointing an accusing finger at me.

'You,' she shouts over the music, 'come here.'

Theresa's voice trails away, leaving the backing track exposed.

'I asked you to please wait downstairs,' Mandy says to the woman. To Debbie, John's wife. It has to be.

'And I told you I wanted to speak to Grace Walker,' she says. The music plays on as the students glance at each other and then at me.

Linda steps in and requests that Debbie wait outside, but Debbie has other ideas.

'Know what these are, do you?' The photographs she holds up make me freeze.

'Let's discuss this in my office,' Linda says, but Debbie pushes forward to the outer rim of confused and curious students.

'No,' I say, but it's too late. Debbie throws the pictures in my direction and they land among the students sitting on the floor. I rush forward, grabbing at images of my breasts, John's thighs. A shot of me on the table, legs splayed, falls in front of Nieve. She puts her hand over her mouth and looks away. I snatch up the photo, mortified.

'You look different in real life,' Debbie says, 'or maybe I just don't recognise you without my husband's dick in your mouth.'

Everyone stares at me. I press the photographs to my chest.

'That's enough.' Linda takes Debbie's arm. 'My office now or I'll call the police.'

'Wind your neck in.' Debbie shakes her arm free. 'I'm leaving.' She waves at the students. 'Merry Christmas, everyone.' She teeters out of the room on the sliver-thin heels of her boots. Linda follows and Mandy holds the door open, waiting for me. I exit the room with my head down, hot with shame. As the door closes, the karaoke machine switches from 'Santa Baby' to 'Away in a Manger', but no one sings along.

Debbie and Linda are arguing in the hallway, Debbie insisting she has no intention of going to Linda's office.

'Oh, hello, Grace,' she says as I approach them.

'I didn't send you these photos,' I say. 'I had nothing to do with this.'

Debbie's cool blue eyes hold nothing but hate. 'I told the police you'd say that.' The police? Sweat prickles on my upper lip. 'They reckon they can't do anything at this stage,' she says, 'not enough evidence. Looks like you got away with it this time.'

'Right,' says Linda, 'you've been to the police and you've had your moment of glory here. I think you're done.'

'Is this the kind of person you want working for you?' Debbie sneers. 'Standards must be low here – that's all I can say.'

I hold the pictures out. 'I didn't do it.'

'Keep them,' she says, 'they're only copies. I've got the originals, just in case you try anything else.' She steps towards me, her heels bringing her almost to my height. On the right side of her jaw, beneath the thick layer of foundation, a muscle twitches. 'You come anywhere near my house or my family again and I'll sort you out myself.'

'I didn't—'

'You're not the first affair that prick's had,' she says, turning away and heading for the stairs, 'but you will be the last.'

* * *

After a few minutes in her office, Linda holds up her hands and begs me to stop apologising.

'I honestly didn't send them,' I say, still clutching the photographs. 'I've got no idea who took them. I'm so sorry the students had to see that.' What would they think of me? How could I face them again?

'I had an affair with a married man once,' Linda says. 'He was the husband of one of my university lecturers. When he finished it, I was gutted.' She glances down at her hands. 'I know what it feels like to be in your position. And you're under so much pressure with your mum that maybe—'

'I ended the affair, not him.'

Linda subjects me to a long, intense gaze. 'If you've got nothing to do with these pictures, then you should be worried,' she says. 'Someone followed you and took them and then tried to incriminate you.'

'I know.'

'Have you been to the police?'

'No.'

'You should, Grace. Really. Do you have any idea who might have taken them?'

I tell her my theories – John's friends, his wife. 'Although the wife doesn't seem likely now,' I add.

'Go to the police right away. Today. Now.'

I nod, any excuse not to go for a drink with the others. I couldn't deal with that, and I doubt they could either.

'And I want you to take the full holiday over Christmas,' Linda says with a tight smile. 'Two of the students have dropped out of the Christmas programme, so I was thinking of cancelling it anyway.'

'It's fine. I can manage.'

'No,' she says, 'you need a break.' Does her firm tone stem from a desire to help me or a desire to get rid of me? She could easily not renew my contract in January.

'Fine,' I say, 'you're right.' Not that I have any choice.

* * *

A wiry man with a buggy blocks the entrance to Islington Police Station. The infant inside observes me with wide brown eyes, craning her head round the side of the buggy to watch me open the main door.

Is she a sign?

Legs shaking, I step inside. Automatic glass doors slide open, leading me into a large waiting room with yellow walls. The clock opposite the door puts the time at twenty past two. The pasty, middle-aged desk sergeant behind the plastic screen is dealing with a young girl in a black leather miniskirt and thigh-high boots.

'I wouldn't lose my handbag,' she says, 'some wanker's stolen it.'

He gives her a form to fill out and sends her on her way. I step up to the screen.

'Yes,' the sergeant says, 'how can I help you?' A flash of dizziness.

'How can I help you?' he repeats.

'I need to report...' What, exactly? 'Someone's been following me, taking pictures. That sort of thing.'

He tells me to take a seat and promises someone will interview me shortly.

I sit on a grey plastic chair and wait. On my left is a set of swing doors that must lead to the heart of the station. I shut my eyes and imagine the interview rooms that exist somewhere beyond them. Small, blue rooms with no windows. Rooms that make your chest constrict as soon as you enter them.

'Grace Walker?' I open my eyes to see a young, female officer waiting by the double doors. 'Come on through.'

I stand up. In the interview room, a bald policeman will hand me a cup of tea. His breath will smell like sour rubbish. He will keep asking me questions. *When we found you in the passageway, you said someone was following you. Who was following you? You said you were being punished. Who is punishing you?*

'Grace?' the officer says, her voice spiky with impatience.

The yellow walls of the waiting room appear to move closer. My temples pound.

I have to get out of here.

'Sorry,' I say to the policewoman, 'I've made a mistake.'

44

CASSIE

December

A mild afternoon. Dark, dramatic clouds overhead, threatening to break. As Ryan and I strolled through Brunswick Square Gardens, he pointed out the daffodils encircling the famous Brunswick plane tree.

'Daffodils three days before Christmas,' he said, 'that's nuts.'

We walked hand in hand, wearing the new coats I'd bought us from The Kooples. Grey duffel for him, black cape with faux mink collar for me. Ryan's hand squeezed mine.

'I'm glad we're getting the whole day together,' he said.

'Me too.' I'd cancelled this afternoon's appointment with Dr Costello. Flu, I'd told the receptionist in a feeble voice. Terrible flu.

When we reached the other side of the gardens, I led Ryan through the gate to the front of the Foundling Museum. The building's neo-Georgian façade gave little hint of the sad stories it concealed.

'This is it,' I said, suddenly shy. My favourite place to visit in all of London. I'd never taken anyone there before. I tried to keep my introduction brief but couldn't hide my admiration for Thomas Coram, the founder of the original Foundling Hospital. What a man. Starting up the country's first ever children's charity in the eighteenth century, so that mothers not fit to be mothers had somewhere to leave their offspring. 'This building was constructed in 1930 on the site of the original Foundling Hospital,' I said. 'It used to be the headquarters of the Coram Foundation and then became a museum.'

'Looks like I've got my own private tour guide.' Ryan leaned in for a kiss.

'No time for that.' I ducked away from him. 'There's a lot to see inside.'

'Great,' Ryan enthused, but in the reception area, during my detailed rundown of the museum's layout, he kept checking his phone.

'The picture gallery on the next floor's got some incredible portraits,' I said, trying to ignore his rudeness. 'The original hospital was the country's first art gallery.' I explained that Thomas Coram had invited famous artists to exhibit at the hospital in order to attract wealthy Londoners and their patronage. 'The gallery's an exact reproduction of the original room.'

'Awesome.' Ryan glanced at his phone again. 'We need to get a move on though, babe. It's nearly half three and we need to be back at yours in time to get ready.'

'There's plenty of time,' I snapped. 'Unless you aren't interested?'

'Hey.' He shoved his phone in his coat pocket. 'Of course I'm interested. It's your number-one place.' He pointed at the entrance to the ground-floor gallery. 'Let's start here,' he said and strode off. I could tell he wanted the visit over with quickly so we didn't turn up late for the Aroma Christmas party. Cocktails at seven to start with, in some bar in Bethnal Green. Ryan had nagged me to go until I gave in. He'd looked so delighted, as if I'd agreed to move in with him or something. Apparently Nick and Maya couldn't wait to meet me. The thought of the evening ahead filled me with dread, and I knew I'd have to drink myself numb to get through it.

The gallery, a compact space with pale grey walls, was busy. The usual mix of tourists ticking another attraction off the list and sincere visitors taking time to really connect with the stories of the unwanted children. These were mostly women, often wandering the museum alone. I'd spent hours watching these lone females, observing their reactions to the exhibits and guessing what secrets might lie in their pasts. No wonder the gallery assistant, a gangly guy in a black polo neck and black cords, gave me a nod of recognition.

Ryan veered towards the tall display cabinets that housed the most moving items in the museum. Keen to save these for later, I guided him to the photographs and videos of the last surviving foundlings – older adults now – who'd grown up in the hospital before its closure. The men and women spoke of their basic living conditions and the hospital's tough regime.

'Some life,' Ryan said. At least he seemed to be paying attention.

'Can you imagine being a child and knowing your mother didn't want you?' I said.

'Be tough, that's for sure.'

Understatement. The Harringtons may have given me every material comfort, but when the people in the videos spoke of their loneliness, I understood what they meant. That particular pain of waiting for a mother who never comes. When emptiness struck, I would often come to the museum and hang out with these men and women. They made me feel like I belonged.

Now my life had changed. Soon I'd be spending Christmas with my mother for the very first time, if my rash deed with the photographs hadn't spoiled everything. What if John or his wife had reported the incident? I'd worn gloves while handling the pictures and the envelope, so the police would find no traces of me there. Surely John wouldn't embarrass himself by going to the police? His wife would probably just weep over the photographs while downing a bottle of Chardonnay.

'Nick says they'll meet us at the bar,' Ryan mumbled, eyes glued to his phone.

'You're supposed to be taking this seriously,' I hissed.

Ryan smiled and slid his phone into his pocket. 'I am. I just want tonight to be perfect, you know?'

His happiness unnerved me; I didn't know what to do with it. I ushered him along to a display case containing a diary written by one of the foundlings in 1947. He peered through the glass, marvelling at the cramped writing on the pages of the tiny notebook.

My unease about the photographs had prompted me to cover my tracks a little. Yesterday, I'd visited my mother's flat with the intention of returning the World's Greatest Mum mug, which I'd recently reclaimed while in a bad mood with her. Two shiny new locks greeted me from her front door. My key fitted neither of them, nor had she left her key safe in the plant pot as usual. I told myself not to overreact. I'd spooked her, but soon she'd know the truth and all that would be behind us.

Ryan kissed my cheek. 'It means a lot to me that you're meeting my friends.'

An elderly lady in a beige quilted coat smiled at me. Did she see us as a normal young couple? Young and in love, with a normal future ahead of us?

'Check these out,' I said. Taking his hand, I led him to the most difficult exhibits, the tiny items housed in the glass cabinets on the right-hand wall of the gallery. 'Look at the scraps of fabric. Each mother had to leave one behind as a way of identifying her child if she ever came to reclaim it.'

Ryan shook his head. 'That's so sad.'

'In case the fabric got lost, they used to leave something extra.' I showed him the coins and buttons and earrings. 'They're called tokens.'

I'd gathered my own collection of tokens from my mother. Her scarf, her white vest, a few precious strands of her hair.

'It says the kids never got to see the fabric or the tokens,' Ryan said.

'I know.'

'That must have been heartbreaking for the mothers.'

'What?'

He pointed to a scrap of faded purple fabric, embroidered with two words in yellow thread. *Forgive Me*. 'She obviously wanted her kid to know how much she loved it. They should have let the literate mothers leave a note or something.'

'A note?' My raised voice invited nosy glances from the other visitors. 'So what if they had left a note? Wouldn't have changed what they did.'

'Chill out,' Ryan said, looking bewildered. 'It's not like they had much choice.' He nodded at the information plaque. 'It says here most of the women were either poor, or widowed or had some bloke run out on them.'

'You sound like Costello.'

'Keep your voice down. Who's Costello?'

'Are you seriously suggesting it was worse for the mothers than their children?'

'I don't know,' he said, exasperated. 'Society didn't make it easy for women then.'

'Oh, come on.'

'Excuse me, guys.' The gallery assistant appeared next to us. 'It's great you're engaging with the themes of the exhibition, but could you just keep it down a bit?'

No. I could not keep it down. I told Ryan he was wrong, and he claimed he didn't get why I was so hysterical. Of course he didn't. I should have known he could never understand me. Images from my scrapbook flashed through my mind.

POLICE LAUNCH SEARCH FOR CASSIE'S MOTHER

'What could be worse than your mother not wanting you?' I said.

'Jesus, Cass. What are you on?'

I slapped him. Seconds later, the security guard appeared and escorted us out of the building.

'Don't come back,' he said.

As we stood at the bottom of the museum steps, the storm clouds above spat out their first fat drops of rain.

'What the hell was all that about?' Ryan said, nursing his cheek as if it actually hurt.

Emptiness surged through me. 'I'm adopted,' I said. 'My mother didn't want me.'

Shock flashed across his face, followed by confusion. 'Why didn't you tell me?'

'Because I knew you wouldn't understand.'

'That's totally illogical. If you'd told me I would have been a bit more sensitive.'

'At least I know what you really think.'

He showed his true colours then. Told me being adopted was no excuse for treating people badly. Called me impossible.

'If you knew the whole story, you wouldn't say that,' I told him.

'I don't want to know the whole story. I can't take this, Cass. One minute we're fine, the next I've done something to piss you off. Your moods are crazy.'

'Ryan, listen—'

'I'm done. We are officially over.' The emptiness gave way to rage.

'Good,' I said. 'I'll have that coat back then.'

'What?'

'I bought the coat. It belongs to me.'

'Fine.' He unfastened the coat's leather toggles and wrestled himself out of it. 'Have the bloody thing.' He threw it at me and turned to go.

'I always knew you'd leave me,' I yelled after him.

He did leave. Abandoned me by the steps of the museum, where I stood for quite some time, the rain soaking into my coat, until the security guard told me to move on.

45

THEN

Tuesday 12 September, Royal Edinburgh Hospital

One night, while cowering in the wardrobe as usual, terrorised by her footsteps and the drum drum drumming of her heart, I sensed something had changed. When the wardrobe door opened and her hand reached for me, I reached back.

Her hand was soft and warm, our shared blood throbbing beneath her skin. Her hand tugged at mine. Come on, come on. I realised that this time she didn't want to hurt me. Come on, come on. She wanted to help me. She wanted to show me something.

I woke crying and knew what I had to do. I got up, got dressed and walked into town. I waited outside Boots until it opened at 9 a.m., and then I ran inside to buy a pregnancy test.

46

GRACE

December

I open the door to Mum's room and find her propped up in bed with Emma leaning over her. A metal object glints in Emma's hand.

'Just tidying up your mum's fringe,' she says, stepping back and dropping a pair of nail scissors into her tunic pocket. 'Can't have you being a scruff on Christmas Day, can we, sweetheart?' The bell on her green elf hat tinkles, as she reaches across to the wastepaper bin and deposits a sprinkling of white hair.

Mum responds with a weak smile.

'She didn't sleep much last night,' Emma says. 'Bit of a cough and she's got a temperature again.'

'Hi, Mum.' I kiss her cheek. 'Merry Christmas.' She smells of lavender soap and face cream, and Emma has attempted to brighten her up with a coat of pink lipstick.

'Hello,' Mum croaks. I'll have to check with Kegs to see if Mum's cough could signal another chest infection. She looks feverish and her breathing sounds shallow.

'Sorry I'm a bit late,' I say. 'No trains running today so I had to take a coach.' As I shrug off my coat and hang it on the back of Mum's door, Emma reaches into her pocket and pulls out a card.

'Merry Christmas, Grace.'

'Oh, Emma,' I say when she hands it to me, 'I feel awful. I haven't done any cards this year.' Spreading festive joy has been the last thing on my mind.

'S'all right,' she says. 'I do them for everyone.'

'Well, thank you.' The flimsy, cheap card has a jolly Santa on the front and inside, Emma has scrawled:

Have a fabby Crimbo. Love, Ems xx

'Suppose you got one from Brenda too?' she says and we have a laugh about that. When I arrived at reception, Brenda handed me a blank Christmas card from the stack on her desk and wished me a happy Christmas on behalf of Armstrong Investments.

'Are you going to have some Christmas lunch later?' I ask Mum, who nods. The odour of boiling vegetables and roasting meat hit me as soon as I stepped into Birch Grove and it has now seeped into Mum's room.

'She's not eating much at the moment,' Emma says, 'but we're going to try a few mouthfuls, aren't we, Polly?'

'Try,' Mum says.

Emma informs me Kegs has left several bottles of sherry in the visitors' kitchen for relatives to help themselves to.

'Great.' No way will I risk a visit there, just in case John appears. Last night, I texted to warn him I'd be here today.

Better keep your wife away, for everyone's sake. Do you know she came to my work?

He replied straight away.

Don't contact me again. Ever.

Furious as I am at what's happened, it upsets me to think of the miserable Christmas he and his family must be having. Does the person who took those pictures realise what they've done?

'I'm gonna pop next door and see if Len's dressed,' Emma says, 'but I'm on till five so you'll be seeing a lot of me.' When she leaves, I deposit her card in my handbag, next to the envelope containing the photographs. The memory of the images floating down among my students makes me shudder. Thank God I don't have to face anyone for two weeks. Linda emailed to ask how my visit to the police had gone. Not much they can do at this stage, I replied, which is possibly true.

After leaving the police station, I went home and decided to take charge of the situation myself. On a piece of paper, I wrote down the dates the pictures were taken and when they must have been delivered, along with estimated dates for the arrival of the Mother's Day cards and the mug. This list I placed in the envelope with the photographs, determined to add to it any new incidents that might occur. No point going to the police without solid evidence to show them.

Now I'm back in Birch Grove, I wonder if anyone here might have known about the affair? Apart from our laundry room encounter, John and I were discreet. Only Memory saw us together that day, and even if she'd guessed our intentions, she doesn't seem the kind of person to get involved in someone else's business.

From the bedside table, the carriage clock broadcasts its loud, second-by-second reminder of lost time, making me even more aware this could be the last Christmas I will ever spend with my mother. After moving abroad, I didn't return home for five years. Then I visited every alternate Christmas, but our festivities remained sad and strained. Dad's absence still hurt, and, although we never mentioned it, the child I did not keep was always there between us, in one way or another.

Today has to count. My own problems will have to wait. I open my backpack and take out Mum's gift.

'Ooh,' she says when I hold it up. 'Is it my birthday?'

I shake my head, blinking back tears. 'No, Mum.' I unwrap the gift and show her the bottle of Opium, the perfume Dad used to buy her every year. I pull the lid from the ornate bottle and spray the inside of her left wrist. She takes a sniff.

'I miss him,' she says.

How different our relationship might have been if Dad had lived. He would have supported me over the termination, and he might even have smoothed things over between Mum and I. Maybe grief drove her to treat me the way she did? Maybe grief stopped her putting her rigid beliefs aside for my sake? Loss changes people and not always for the better. 'Tired,' Mum says, her head lolling to one side. Her small skull reminds me of a spent dandelion head, her white wisps of hair like the fluffy seeds waiting to be blown away.

She points at the TV and I switch it on, muting the sound as always. Footage of a flooded village near York appears. The obligatory shot of unopened Christmas presents swirling in dirty water.

I settle in the spare chair. Mum sighs, her eyelids closing and opening. The clock ticks, and I think of all we will never recapture. I think of us in the kitchen that day, when Mum warned me I would be punished. I shared my fears, begged her not to let me go through the procedure alone. I hoped she would choose me over her unformed, unborn grandchild, but she didn't.

Now, here we are. Myself and my mother on Christmas Day with only the ticking clock for company.

* * *

Cassie

Best. Christmas. Ever. As Emma would say. Apart from my grandmother's poor form, everything was all Ding Dong Merrily on High. Even before my mother arrived, I was enjoying myself. Everyone at Birch Grove had made a real effort to make the day special. Christmas music blared out in all the communal areas – Wham, Slade, Kylie. All the cheesy, fun tunes Isobel and Quentin thought too tacky for their house.

Us care assistants and the nurses wore elf hats, and Kegs had everyone in hysterics when he pitched up in a full Santa outfit. Even Memory donned a pair of angel wings. Surinder wasn't working today, but she popped by with her boys who were, to quote Emma, too cute. She paraded them round all the residents and made them hand out sweets and Christmas greetings.

'Call me, Grandma,' my grandmother said when she saw them. I tried not to be annoyed. She couldn't help getting confused.

By mid-morning, I'd scoffed half a box of Celebrations and whizzed along with the tea trolley in record time. Was I really about to spend Christmas with my mother? I'd often fantasised about this day but never thought it would take place in an old folks' home. Funny, how things turn out. Quentin called last night and declared himself proud of me for sacrificing my Christmas Day for others. He said Isobel would have been proud too, but I cut him off before he could get too emotional. I half expected another text from Ryan, hassling me about his phone, but none came.

After the debacle at the museum, I'd discovered his mobile in the pocket of the duffel coat. He must have changed his code because I couldn't get into it. Later, he'd texted me from Nick's phone to ask for his mobile back. I told him he'd have to wait until after Christmas to come and collect it, as well as all the other crap he'd left at my flat. He wasn't happy, but what could he do? Crazy of me to get involved with him in the first place. How could I have a relationship with anyone until I'd sorted out my relationship with my mother? With John and Ryan out of the way, my mother and I could at last focus on each other.

The morning rushed by. Most of the residents had gifts from friends and relatives to open, and I helped them tackle the tricky wrapping paper and fiddly ribbons. Len received two cartons of duty-free Rothmans, which made him happy. He threw a tantrum though when Kegs took the cigarettes to the office for safekeeping and promised to dole them out as required.

My mother looked haggard when she arrived. Never mind, I thought, Christmas would cheer her up. However, my grandmother didn't exactly inspire festive joy, bless her heart. My mother sat with her for ages, looking more and more despondent. I offered to read out some of the festive passages I'd found underlined in my grandmother's Bible.

'No, thanks,' she said.

At lunchtime, she cut up Grandma's Christmas meal into tiny pieces and persuaded her to swallow a few mouthfuls before giving up and getting Santa Claus in for a chat. Kegs assured my mother that if my grandmother didn't improve overnight he'd get the doctor out tomorrow. Ho, ho, bloody ho. 'I think I will have a sherry,' my mother said when I took the dinner tray away. A few minutes later, I peeked into the visitors' kitchen and saw her knocking back a hefty glass of the stuff. She exited the room with another full glass, and that's when she saw John.

He had his daughters with him, which meant his wife had at least permitted him access for the day. My mother stopped and he stopped, and for a moment I thought they might cause a scene. I'm not sure who gave whom the dirtiest look. Then he grabbed each girl by the hand and thundered off down the corridor.

My mother sought out the wall for support. I interpreted their stand-off as a positive sign, an indicator that both sides would get over the scandal of the photographs. None of it would matter once my mother knew the real me. I would tell her today, once I'd figured out the right time to do it. Christmas Day and we would be properly reunited. It was perfect.

After the carol singing – a raucous hour led by a local man on a portable synthesiser – I popped out the front for a fag. My mother appeared with her coat on, ready to leave.

'That you off?' I said, disappointment leaking into my voice. 'It's only two-thirty.'

She shrugged. 'I don't want to be here and I don't want to go either.' Her eyes looked swollen, as though she'd been crying. 'Mum's asleep so there's no point hanging around.'

'Are you going back to London or staying over here?' I asked. She said she couldn't decide. She sounded giddy, not quite in control of herself.

'What are you doing tonight?' she said.

'Staying in by myself. Nothing else to do.' I stared at the ground, as if the thought made me sad. In the silence that followed, I could almost hear her thinking.

'Fancy coming round to Mum's house later?' she said. 'If you're not doing anything else, we could get some more packing done.'

I looked up. 'That would be great.'

She laughed. 'Well, I don't know about great, but I'd rather keep busy.'

'Better than doing nothing.'

'Okay,' she said, 'I'll stop at the corner shop and get us a couple of pizzas and some wine. If you like wine?'

'Only really sweet white stuff,' I said, staying in character.

'A Christmas packing party. It'll be fun.'

I giggled. 'What a pair of saddos.'

She smiled. 'Aren't we just?'

47

GRACE

December

Emma and I sit on the living room floor, surrounded by packing boxes. Emma, cross-legged, reaches for another slice of Margherita from the plate in front of her.

'This is well tasty,' she says, plucking a stray lump of melted cheese from her pink jumper. She has scoffed more than half of the pizza, while I've only managed a few mouthfuls. My bottle of Shiraz, however, is vanishing fast, and Emma has almost finished one of the bottles of Lambrusco I bought her.

At least she's more relaxed now. When she first arrived, she appeared startled by the new alarm system I got fitted two days ago. She eyed the control panel beside the front door with suspicion and asked why I'd had it installed. Had I been burgled or something? I told her the house was totally secure, more to reassure myself as I'll be staying here tonight.

'She is such an amazing dancer,' says Emma, pointing at the TV. The *Strictly Come Dancing* Christmas special is on, a whirl of long legs, white teeth and sequins. I own up to not recognising the skinny blonde Emma is obsessing about. Emma rolls her eyes. 'She's in loads of stuff.'

'Oh. Right.' I take another gulp of wine. My last Christmas Day with Mum has turned out to be the worst Christmas Day of my life, and here I am, finishing it off with a care worker less than half my age. A girl I invited here because I'm lonely and scared.

'This is great.' Emma pours herself more Lambrusco. 'Much better than sitting at home on my own.' Poor girl is acting like I'm doing her the favour. At least she's enjoying herself.

I nibble the cold, stodgy tip of a pizza slice as *Strictly* comes to a close.

'Oh my God,' Emma says when the next programme is announced, 'I love *Call the Midwife*.'

I grab the remote and switch channels. The theme music for *Dad's Army* fills the room. 'This is a classic,' I say.

Emma bursts out laughing. 'That's proper old fogey TV.' She glances around the room. 'We've done loads in here. Why don't we start on upstairs now?'

'You've done enough,' I say. 'Just relax. I can put another pizza in if you're still hungry?'

She springs up, glass in one hand, bottle in the other. 'We're on a roll; we shouldn't stop now.'

The combination of wine and Emma's eagerness gets to me. 'Fine.' I haul myself up with a groan. 'Let me go to the loo first.'

The lengthy time it takes me to pee signals I'm more drunk than I thought. Afterwards, I splash my face with cold water. When I emerge from the downstairs toilet, I hear Emma thudding around overhead.

'Started without me?' I say, one foot on the bottom stair.

* * *

Cassie

My mother froze when she entered her bedroom and saw me searching through the large box of her things.

'There's tons in here,' I said. 'What are you going to do with it all?'

'I didn't want that box opened.' She surveyed the curls of masking tape littering the carpet. 'You shouldn't have opened it.'

How could I not?

'I'm so sorry,' I said, 'I didn't mean to do anything wrong.' I put on an Emma face, confused and vulnerable. My mother's face softened in response.

'It's fine. Don't worry about it. You weren't to know.' No, Emma wasn't to know. My mother had invited her here, taking advantage of her good nature and then had the cheek to berate the poor girl for not knowing which box to open. Kind, sensitive Emma needed to be more assertive sometimes.

'Wow,' I said, reaching into the box and pulling out an armful of books. 'You must have been well clever.'

My mother sat on the single bed beside me, her eyes glassy, as if hypnotised. She examined the books and read the titles on their cracked spines – *Impro, The Empty Space, An Actor Prepares*. She couldn't resist the past. Who could? Next, I pulled out a load of vinyl. The Pixies, The Smiths, The Violent Femmes. My mother reminisced about the long-gone record shops of her youth and the gigs at which she'd seen her idols live. I swigged from the bottle of disgusting Lambrusco as she talked, drawing on all my acting skills to fake liking the stuff. I'd already thrown my full glass and most of the bottle down the bathroom sink.

My mother glanced at the bottle as I drank, keeping tabs on my consumption, but I had full control of myself. She had wine-stained lips and an air of unsteadiness about her. She got so wrapped up in a long-winded account of a gig in Bradford, that she didn't notice me retrieving a large photo album with a grey cover from the box. I had it lying open on my knees before she could stop me.

'Check these out,' I said, peering at pictures from her drama school days. Images of my mother and other students in costume. Beneath each one, she'd written the name of the production and the names of the cast members. 'You look so young.'

'It was a long time ago.' She looked straight ahead at the wall, avoiding the pictures, twisting that silver ring of hers round like she did sometimes.

I turned the page and found a picture that startled me. Four students in black jeans and black shirts. My mother and three men, one of whom I recognised. A handsome, blond guy with piercing green eyes. Underneath the photo my mother had written:

Les Enfants Terrible – Me, Pete Browning, Dan Thorne, Johnny Deacon.

'I'm sure I've seen that blond guy on the telly,' I said. 'Is he famous?'

My mother glanced down at the album and flinched as I pointed to him.

'No,' she said, 'he's not.'

No, but he was the blond man I'd seen arguing with her outside her block that day. Same eyes, same bone structure. I'd have to check the picture on my phone later, just to make sure.

'I honestly recognise him,' I said. 'What's his name?'

'His name's Dan and he's not famous.'

Dan Thorne, I thought. The man's name was Dan Thorne.

My mother pulled the photo album off my lap and slammed it shut. 'Let's forget this stuff for now,' she said.

* * *

Grace

I leave Emma repacking the books and records into the box and retreat to the kitchen, desperate for a cigarette. The new pack I bought earlier should be in my handbag. Where is my handbag? I find it hanging on the back of a kitchen chair and search inside for the fags, my fingers brushing the envelope with the photographs in it. I glance at the window, reassured by the white blind I pulled down earlier. I can't see out, and no one can see in.

I slump into the chair, light a cigarette and top up my wine. Emma's tiny feet patter round above my head. I shouldn't have reprimanded her about the box; she only wanted to help. The theatre books released a rush of memories, and I had to keep talking so Emma didn't sense my anxiety. I wish she hadn't found that picture of Dan, although I can't blame her for fixating on his looks. I used to.

Scurrying overhead, thudding on the stairs, and then Emma bursts into the kitchen.

'Don't go mad,' she says, 'but I found these on a shelf in your mum's room and I know you'll definitely want to keep them.'

More photograph albums. Thick and square with blue, faux-leather covers. Emma sits at the table, opens an album up and gasps.

'Your mum was so pretty.' She pushes the album closer so I can see. My sixties mother, glamorous with her beehive and minidresses, casts sultry looks into the lens. The version of my mother that ceased to exist once I came along.

'She looked much happier before she had me,' I say, not meaning to speak aloud. The wine has caught up with me.

'Rubbish.' Emma trawls through the album until she finds a picture to prove her point. 'Look at that.'

Me in my mother's arms. Red-faced with a quiff of black hair.

'She looks well chuffed,' Emma says. I see no hint of elation in my mother's drained face. She has the harrowed look of a survivor, one yet to make sense of the ordeal she's just endured.

The fault line quivers. The last person to show me these pictures was my mother. Here, at this table.

'Didn't you ever want kids?' Emma says as she pores over the pictures. She asks in such a casual manner, as though the question is a simple one.

'No,' I say.

She looks up. 'What? Never?'

'No. Never.'

She closes the photo album. A twinge in my chest gathers strength until I blurt out, 'I was pregnant once.'

'Oh.' She pulls her chair closer to mine. 'What happened?'

'I didn't keep it.' I expect her to look shocked, but she doesn't. Instead she asks me why? Why didn't I keep it?

'Lots of reasons,' I say.

'Like what?' she demands, with the loud belligerence of someone who has crossed the line from drunk to pissed. 'Like what?'

No more questions. She is drunk and I am drunk, and this night should end now.

'It's getting late,' I say. 'Why don't I call you a taxi?'

'It's not even nine.'

A burst of light to my right. I jump up and raise the blind at the kitchen window. The new sensor light I got fitted has come on, bringing the patio to life. The back of the garden remains in shadow.

'What's wrong?' Emma asks.

'There's been someone hanging round here lately,' I say. 'Probably just local kids,' I add, not wanting to scare her.

'Have you been to the police?'

'Not yet.'

'Good. I mean, you don't want to get them involved unless you have to.' Before I can protest, Emma is up and grappling with the back door key.

'Don't,' I say, but she is soon out on the patio in her socks.

'If anyone's there, just sod off,' she yells. She spins round towards the kitchen window and gives me a thumbs up, signalling I have nothing to fear, but the vision of her looking in on me makes my scalp prickle.

She skips beyond the light's reach. I peer through the glass but cannot see her. When a knock on the window gets no response, I move to the back door.

'Emma?' I call into the darkness. She groans in response. 'Emma?'

I edge across the patio and find her on her knees by the shed. The stench of vomit hits me as soon as I lean over her.

'Sorry,' she says, 'didn't think I was this pissed.'

'It's okay.' I help her to her feet and steer her back inside.

'Better lie down for a minute,' she mumbles.

'Yes. Of course. Come on through and lie on the sofa,' I say, but once in the hallway, she lurches to the stairs.

'Need to go to bed.'

We navigate the stairs together. At one point I stumble and wonder who is helping whom. I steer her along the landing and into Mum's room. As soon as I pull back the duvet, she collapses into the bed with a sigh.

'If you feel better in a bit. I'll call you a taxi,' I say, but she has already shut her eyes. I can't send her home in this state; she'll have to stay the night. This is my fault for buying her two bottles of wine. I should at least have encouraged her to drink more slowly.

I cover her with the duvet. Beneath it, her tiny body twitches and her feet jerk as she slides into sleep. My earlier fears dissolve as I watch her face relax. She looks so peaceful now. No wonder she's exhausted after her early start and hours on her feet. All the time with a smile on her face, doing her best to make a miserable Christmas bearable for all involved.

I don't move. I listen to her breathing – heavy exhalations that verge on snoring. I dip my head towards hers and inhale a mixture of lemon-scented shampoo and cigarette smoke. It would be irresponsible to leave her alone; she might be sick again. I should stay and watch over her.

My eyelids sag, unable to bear their own weight any more. I yawn. My mother's mattress yields as I recline. I'll lie here for a minute. Just a minute.

* * *

Cassie

My mother fell asleep right away. Curled on her left side, knees bent. I snuggled into her, my spine against her belly, her legs parked snug under mine. I lay awake, replaying the moment she'd almost confessed everything to me. I never expected that. When she spoke of being pregnant, her sadness surrounded us like a fog. The same sadness I'd detected the first time I saw her. If that stupid light hadn't interrupted us, she would have spilled it all out, and I'd have said, *It's me, I'm here, Mum. I'm here.*

Instead, she'd tried to get rid of me again. Getting late, I'll call you a taxi. No chance. Making myself sick was easy enough – two fingers down the throat, hard and sharp.

My mother began to snore. Deep, nasal vibrations. Her hand sought me out and rested on my waist. Was she dreaming of me? Her hand slipped down and came to rest on the jut of my hip. She held on tight, as if finding safety in it.

* * *

Grace

I wake in a room murky with grey dawn light. The hand is there to greet me. The inescapable fact of it on my chest. I draw sharp, frantic breaths.

The hand moves. It creeps towards my throat and settles on my windpipe. Where has all the air gone?

I remember I am dreaming and wait to wake again, but this release fails to arrive. Where has all the air gone? I rip the hand away. It returns, along with another. Two hands gripping my wrists. Her voice telling me to calm down. To stop screaming.

'Grace,' she says, 'it's me.'

I free my hands and slap hers away. She cries out. Then I hear a click and a bedside lamp fills the room with a soft yellow light.

'It's me,' she says, and I realise I'm awake. I realise she is Emma. Emma with messy hair and a red crease down one side of her face. Emma looking as scared and confused as I feel.

'You were having a nightmare,' she says. 'Sorry... It felt... I thought it was real.'

She places a hand on my shoulder, but I shake it off, unable to bear the contact. Red blotches appear on her cheeks.

'Should I get you some water?' she asks.

'No.' The inappropriateness of the situation hits me. 'I didn't mean to fall asleep here,' I say. 'I was worried you might—'

'It's okay.'

'It's not okay.' The scratch marks on her hands fill me with guilt. I look away, unable to meet her eyes.

'I shouldn't have got so wasted,' she says. 'Why don't I make us a cup of tea?'

'No. Please... I'm... I'm not feeling well.' The muscles around my throat are tender. I grope my way out of bed and examine my neck in the mirror above Mum's dressing table. No marks to be seen.

Stop it, I tell myself. Nightmares aren't real. 'Do you need some paracetamol?' Emma asks.

'No.' That prickling sensation in my scalp returns. I have to get her out of the house. Get her away from me.

She throws back the covers and springs out of bed. 'We really need a cup of tea.'

'For God's sake.' My barked words paralyse her.

'What's wrong?' she asks, voice and bottom lip trembling.

She looks so young. So innocent.

'Nothing, Emma. I'm just really not feeling well. Maybe you should go.'

The red blotches on her cheeks grow and merge. Anger transforms her face; she looks like a stranger. 'You're kicking me out?' she says. 'Why? What have I done wrong?'

'Nothing.'

'You're just using her.'

'What?'

'Me. You're just using me. When your mum's dead, you won't need me and you won't even bother keeping in touch.'

'Emma—'

'I'll see myself out.' She pushes past me, slamming the door behind her.

I can't let her go. I have to let her go.

When the front door bangs shut, I make my way to the kitchen with tentative steps, flinching at the early stirrings of a headache.

Half an hour later, as the terror of the dream recedes, the extent of my appalling behaviour dawns on me. What on earth was I thinking, treating Emma that way? No wonder she was furious.

I have to get a grip. I'll lose myself again if I'm not careful. I decide to send her an email to apologise. Last thing I need is any awkwardness between us at Birch Grove. I have enough of that already with John. I lift my bag from the back of the kitchen chair and reach inside for my phone.

It is only as I'm trying to compose the first sentence of the email, that I realise what is missing. I empty the contents of my handbag onto the carpet. I even check behind the ripped lining, but the envelope containing the photographs is nowhere to be found.

48

THEN

Tuesday 12 September, Royal Edinburgh Hospital

I bought two pregnancy tests, just to be on the safe side. Desperate to find out as soon as possible, I rushed to a nearby shopping centre and took the escalator down to the toilets in the food hall.

In the end cubicle, I read the instructions for the test carefully, even though I'd used the same brand last time. One blue line for negative, two blue lines for positive. It would take four minutes. I settled myself on the toilet, the white plastic stick expectant beneath me. The heavy stream of urine I released soaked my hand as well as the stick.

I kept telling myself I was crazy. No way could I be pregnant.

By the time I'd dried my hand on a piece of toilet roll, the first blue line had appeared.

As I waited to see if another line would join it, the main door to the toilets banged open. Screams, swearing and leg slapping followed. A little boy's voice begged to return to Toys R Us, but his mother wrestled him into the cubicle next to mine.

She told him to stand still so she could undo his trousers. I could see his blue wellingtons, patterned with yellow ducks. I thought he might be an omen.

I thought if he crouched down and stuck his face into my cubicle it might mean something.

They left, I never saw his face. A minute later, the second blue line appeared.

PART III

49

CASSIE

December

ISOBEL HARRINGTON
BELOVED WIFE AND MOTHER
ALWAYS IN OUR HEARTS

Isobel's memorial stone lay embedded in the grass in the Garden of Remembrance behind Aldersham church. The Harringtons had never attended the village church, apart from to drag me to the Christmas carol concert every year, but when Isobel died, Quentin insisted on finding somewhere close to keep her.

I laid my bouquet of pink gladioli on top of the white marble slab.

'Happy birthday,' I said and then stood in silence, not sure what else we had to discuss. I remembered how Isobel loved having her birthday three days after Christmas. She said it made the festive season into one long party. I took a few pictures of the stone and the flowers with my phone to send to Quentin, as requested. Proof I'd visited Isobel, as promised.

A light drizzle began to fall. I opened up the black golf umbrella provided earlier by Stuart the chauffeur, who sat waiting for me in the silver Mercedes S-Class parked across the road.

'I had to take a driver,' I explained to Isobel, 'the past few days have been hectic.'

So much travelling – Brentham, London and then Brighton yesterday. I couldn't have coped with another train journey. I wanted to get back in the Mercedes and head for London and some much-needed sleep, but my conscience kept me standing in the rain, the heels of my boots sinking deep into the sodden grass.

'She rejected me,' I said to Isobel. 'Again.'

I told you so.

'Thought you'd say that.' I wanted to go back in time, to my mother cuddling me in bed, her hand gripping my hip. The sound of her snoring, the wine fumes on her breath. A brief interlude of contentment soon spoiled by sour memories of the half-confession she'd made only hours ago. The way she'd called me 'it'. Dan Thorne wouldn't leave me alone either, forcing me out of bed and down to the kitchen to fetch my phone. I crept upstairs and into the small bedroom, opening the box again and taking out the photo album, checking every now and then that my mother hadn't stopped snoring. Definitely him, I thought, after comparing the old image and the new.

Could he be my father? The dates matched, and my mother had acted strange when I'd asked about him earlier. A quick Google search on my phone led me straight to him. I read about his wife, Stella, and their two children.

I sat for hours on the narrow single bed, going over it all. What if he and my mother had been arguing about me that day? What if he wanted to find me but she'd kept me from him all this time?

The sky outside her window mutated from black to grey. I returned to my grandmother's bedroom and stood over my mother as she slept. Her dreaming eyes roved back and forth beneath her oily eyelids. I felt sick with fury and longed to hurt her as she had hurt me, but at that moment she reached for me again in her sleep. Her hands caressed the empty mattress and lured me in. I lay in her arms, torn between joy and anger. We fitted so well together, two lost pieces reunited. I brought my head to her ribcage, spellbound by the thump of her heartbeat. The sound that had comforted me for the first nine months of my life. I placed my hand on her chest. As she exhaled, my fingers traced the journey of her breath along her windpipe. Her throat in my hand, throbbing and live.

Then she woke, flinging me from her in disgust. When I tried to offer comfort, she recoiled, unable to hide her revulsion. She tried to act as if nothing had happened between us, as if our intimacy had meant nothing to her.

She couldn't get me out of there fast enough. Before leaving the house, I wanted to take something from her. She could at least give me the money for a taxi. I rummaged through her handbag, intending to pinch ten pounds from her purse, but instead I discovered the envelope with the photographs and her notes inside. To see my own mother had gathered evidence against me left me reeling.

I'd stolen the envelope on impulse. Only afterwards did I notice the photographs were copies. Where did she get them from? Who gave them to her? I'd probably never know but better I had them than my mother, just in case she changed her mind about going to the police.

You don't think before you act, Cassie.

'I know, Isobel,' I said to the marble stone. 'I know.'

* * *

When I could no longer bear looking at Isobel's grave, I returned to the Mercedes. Stuart closed the crime novel he was reading and stepped out of the car. He fastened his grey suit jacket over his protruding belly before opening the rear door for me.

'All done?' he asked in his Glaswegian accent.

I nodded. 'Straight back to London, please.' We drove away from the church and into the heart of the exclusive village, along the main street with its deli, organic butcher and patisserie. Temptation swelled inside me until I gave in and instructed Stuart to take a right at the end of the street, followed by a left. Soon we were parked outside the wrought-iron gates of Lake View, the house I'd grown up in.

'I'll only be a few minutes,' I told Stuart as he opened the door and helped me out. I followed the red-brick wall that bordered the garden. Once out of Stuart's sight, I clambered up and over it. I'd left my keys in London, determined not to come here.

Quentin had closed up the big white house with the thatched roof until his return. All the diamond-leaded windows had their curtains drawn. I wandered across the grass to the large pond with the weeping willow. A meander around the water's edge took me to the terraced rockery – Isobel's pride and joy and the setting for our final confrontation. Apart from a few shrubs, the rockery was bare, the soil holding its breath until spring. Whatever bulbs our gardener, Harry, had buried below would then push through. Plants and flowers Isobel would never see.

My father had a lovely front garden at his place. A quick online search had uncovered two Dan Thornes in Brighton. Before my trip there yesterday, I'd used Google street maps to help me figure out which address he lived at. The first property I looked at was a grey bungalow. I guessed he wouldn't live somewhere like that, and I was right. He had one of those coloured houses on a steep street above the city. A whole building to himself, not just an upper- or lower-floor flat. His windows looked new and eggshell blue paint coated the exterior of the house. The classiest place on the street by far. I'd feared he might be away for Christmas, but tasteful silver stars twinkled in his windows, and I only had to wait an hour before he emerged with his family.

What a beautiful unit. His elegant wife with the streak of grey in her long black hair. His blonde daughter and his younger, black-haired son. And, of course, my father. Much better-looking in real life than in his profile picture. They were perfect. I wanted to hate them, but I couldn't.

We walked into town together. My half-siblings skipped ahead while my father and Stella had a heated discussion about New Year. My father didn't seem happy that Stella's parents would be spending it with them, and Stella said she could hardly have refused, and my father got cross and said he supposed he had no say in the matter seeing as Stella's father had bought them the house, and she said that's not what she meant. But by the time we reached the seafront, they'd kissed and made-up, snogging on the promenade like a pair of teenagers.

My father did father-like things with his kids as they stumbled across the pebbled beach – chased them, hugged them, swung them round – even though both son and daughter were a bit old for such games. His obvious love for his children winded me. He looked like such a natural, a man who would have yearned after fatherhood the same way most women long to be mothers. He could never have helped my mother do what she did to me. That crime was hers alone.

I sat down on the top step of the rockery and looked out over the garden. I couldn't help thinking about that last argument with Isobel. I can't remember what started it – probably me running up a massive credit card bill again – but I remember the vitriol in her voice shocking me. Despite regular warnings that the tumour would affect her behaviour as it grew, I never thought she could be so nasty.

Things soon got out of hand. I called her a bitch and she said I'd ruined her life and I said she shouldn't have adopted me then. Her failing body shook with rage.

'I know you don't like me,' she said, 'and I know you want to be with your real mother, but you have to face facts.' She grabbed hold of my wrists. 'Your mother didn't want you,' she hissed. 'She didn't want you.'

I wrenched my hands free and slapped her. Hard across her bony cheek. She slapped me back, a belter that left my right ear numb.

'I've wanted to do that for a long, long time,' she said.

If she hadn't said that, I wouldn't have hit her again. I did though. The other cheek this time. Afterwards, I turned away and ran towards the house. She cried out my name, but I didn't look back. Once indoors, I'd rushed upstairs and taken refuge in my bedroom.

The rockery step was cold beneath me. Time to go back to the car, but I couldn't move. I shivered and reached into my coat pocket for my cigarettes. Emma smoked much more than me, a habit I needed her to stop.

Last week, while I was having a fag outside the kitchen at Birch Grove, Kegs came out to join me.

'A nasty vice,' he said, as he lit up a Benson and Hedges, 'picked it up in the army.'

'When you were a soldier,' I said, 'did you ever kill anyone?'

A deep crease appeared between his eyebrows, deep enough to hide something dark in.

'I've been responsible for the deaths of others,' he said.

'Is that different from killing someone?'

He exhaled a plume of toxic smoke. 'I used to think so, but now I'm not so sure.'

50

THEN

Tuesday 12 September, Royal Edinburgh Hospital

My GP got me an appointment at Leeds Infirmary straight away. First came another scan with the same, tight-lipped sonographer. She examined my stomach with her probe, disbelief on her face as she stared at the monitor.

The screen faced away from me again, and I didn't ask to look. I didn't need to; I knew what was in there.

'Is she okay?' I asked. 'Is she normal?'

The sonographer said the foetus appeared to be healthy but there were no guarantees.

Afterwards, I met with a consultant, Dr Taylor. A woman about Mum's age, with soft hazel eyes. She put an arm around my shoulder when I entered the room and guided me to a seat by her desk.

I could barely take in the explanation she offered me. A rare occurrence, she said, very rare indeed. A trainee surgeon had failed to complete the procedure properly. It did happen but hardly ever. No surgical procedure had a hundred per cent success rate.

As she spoke, I nodded and said, 'Oh, right,' and, 'I see.' As if we were discussing nothing out of the ordinary. As if I wasn't sixteen weeks pregnant by mistake.

She asked if I had any questions about what had happened. I shook my head, too numb to think of any. She explained I had every right to make a complaint if I wanted to.

Shame kept me silent. Sitting in that office, I felt as if I'd come to collect an inevitable punishment, one predicted by my mother. What right did I have to complain?

Dr Taylor said we had to focus on what to do next. She opened up my medical file and that's when I told her about the nightmares. She asked if I'd had any similar experiences while awake. Any hallucinations.

I told her about hearing the wailing baby. She looked very concerned. She asked if I'd struggled with my decision to have the abortion, and I said no. I knew it was the right choice. She asked how I'd felt after the operation. Relieved, I said. A bit sad but glad to have it over with.

She said I had two options. Either have another termination as soon as possible or continue with the pregnancy and have the baby.

I told her I didn't know. I didn't know what to do.

She said that in her opinion, bearing in mind what I'd told her, it could be more damaging for my mental health if I continued with the pregnancy.

'Really?' I said.

She nodded. 'Potentially, but I'm afraid the decision's up to you.'

51
GRACE

December

It's 1.12 p.m. Emma should be out soon. I've picked a waiting place halfway along the road that leads into Birch Grove. So far, the day is dry and bright. Perfect weather for hanging around the streets like a weirdo. Emma will have to walk this way to reach her part of town. Then we can bump into each other as if by accident, me on my way into the home, her on her way out.

Three days have passed since she stormed out of Mum's house on Boxing Day morning. I hoped to see her yesterday when I visited Mum, but Vera said she's had a few days off. After updating me on Mum's chest infection – no response to the antibiotics this time but no deterioration either – Vera checked the staff rota and confirmed Emma would be working until one o'clock today. 'I'd have her here twenty-four seven if I could,' Vera said. 'She's a little marvel.'

I nodded but couldn't stop thinking about the photographs. After realising they were missing, I searched everywhere. Under furniture, beneath the heaps of Mum's belongings waiting to be boxed. I even opened up the boxes we'd finished the previous night in case the envelope had fallen out of my bag and Emma had packed it away by mistake.

I retraced our movements, venturing back to my own room and the box Emma had ripped into with such glee. My hands shook as I bent back the cardboard flaps to peer inside. After conducting a minimal search, I fetched a roll of masking tape from downstairs and sealed up the lid of the box for the second time.

It was now 1.15 p.m. What if she stays on to do some extra hours? That would be just like Emma. It's hard to imagine her stealing from me, but I have to be certain. Otherwise I'll be stuck with the ridiculous notion that she might be the mystery photographer. After my fruitless search for the pictures, I remembered her gazing in at me from the floodlit patio and shivered. Could she have done it? Why though? What possible motive could she have?

I did consider emailing her. A brief apology for my erratic behaviour followed by a casual enquiry about whether she'd seen a white A4 envelope lying around the house. Had she picked it up by mistake? In the end, I decided to ask her face to face. Her reaction is bound to give her away; she blushes at the slightest thing.

At 1.22 p.m. Emma saunters out of the driveway with Surinder. A black transit van roars up and stops beside them. The two girls embrace before Surinder climbs into the passenger seat. Emma waves as the van pulls away, and the driver beeps back.

I wait for her to come towards me, but instead she turns and walks the opposite way, towards town.

The fish hook tugs at my guts again and the invisible line unwinds between us, luring me on. I should catch her up and ask what I need to ask, but I don't.

* * *

I follow her through the precinct. She ignores the shops with their gaudy sale signs plastered across the windows. As we leave the town centre, I expect her to take the street that leads to the underpass and on to her bedsit, but instead she turns right. Ten minutes later, I'm standing by the taxi rank next to Brentham train station, watching Emma at the ticket machine inside. Funny, but I've never thought of her leaving the town before. She never struck me as the kind of girl who'd want to go anywhere. I wait until she goes through the ticket barrier before entering the station. By the time I reach the barrier, she has vanished down the steps beyond it.

From here I have a good view of the platforms. She emerges on number four, where the trains for London depart from. The tannoy announces a city-bound train is approaching the station now. I ransack my bag for my ticket and then hurry through the barrier. I run along the underpass to the exit for platform four, taking my time to climb the stairs, waiting for the rumble of the approaching train to cease before stepping out.

She is boarding at the front end of the train. The first-class carriage.

The tannoy reminds all passengers that the train is for London Liverpool Street only.

I open the nearest carriage door and step inside.

52

GRACE

December

I nearly lose Emma on the Underground, after getting stuck on the escalator behind a pair of Japanese teenage boys with huge trolley cases. I arrive on the northbound Victoria line platform just as she slips onto the waiting train, and I manage to squeeze in one carriage down before the doors sigh shut. When the train curves round a bend, I glimpse her grasping one of the central metal poles. As the tannoy announces our arrival into Highbury and Islington, she adjusts her backpack and edges towards the doors.

Minutes later, we exit the station. A bus disgorges its passengers onto the pavement, blocking my view of her. When the bus pulls away, I see her crossing the road at Highbury Corner. Once she is far enough away, I do the same. She turns left into a long, sweeping terrace of Georgian houses facing Highbury Fields. Expensive cars line the street.

What is she doing here? Visiting a friend? A relative?

I hang back, worried she might notice me. In the distance, she opens the front gate of one of the houses and is soon out of sight. Crossing over to the park, I find a bench with a good view of the house she entered. A house with a panel of buzzers beside its yellow door. Must be divided into flats. Nothing to do now but sit and wait. I do up the top button of my coat. Lycra-clad joggers bounce past, headphones trailing from their ears. The sun lingers above but has no warmth to give. I can't stop shaking. I sense Emma is leading me somewhere, but do I want to go?

A bike pulls up in front of the house. The rider dismounts and removes his cycle helmet. The tall, blond figure in black skinny jeans looks familiar. Is that Ryan from Aroma? At the yellow door, he presses a buzzer. Seconds later, he pushes the door open and disappears inside.

If it is Ryan, he could be going to a different flat from the one Emma is visiting. He might even live in the building. It's hardly likely the two of them would know each other.

Five minutes later, he emerges clutching a carrier bag that appears to be stuffed with clothes. He fastens his cycle helmet and mounts his bike, balancing the carrier bag on one of the handles. Before he pedals off, he raises a middle finger to the empty windows on the first floor.

* * *

It's 4.10 p.m. Daylight fading fast. I play with my puzzle ring, working it back and forth. How long should I sit here? My only alternative is to go to the house and press all the buzzers in turn until I find her. She'll think I'm insane.

My phone sounds from the depths of my bag.

'Hi, Grace,' Kegs says when I answer. My stomach plummets in anticipation of bad news.

'What's wrong?' I ask.

'Nothing to panic about, but your mum seems worse this afternoon. She's still not responding to the antibiotics.' He promises to get the doctor in again if she grows any weaker. 'Just wanted to keep you informed,' he says.

A light comes on in one of the ground-floor windows. An elderly woman enters the elegant living room and tugs one curtain then the other across the glass.

'Do all your staff have to provide references?' I ask.

'Sorry?' Kegs says. I repeat the question. 'Of course,' he replies, defensive, 'I follow them up myself. Why?'

'I'm helping Emma apply for a college course and she's worried her references might not be good enough.' The lie slips from my mouth with disturbing ease. 'If you've checked them though, they must be fine.'

'Absolutely. She had cracking references.'

'Great. That's great.' Of course Emma has good references. She's a good worker.

'Okay, then,' Kegs says. 'Feel free to call any time if you want an update.'

My mother is fading, making slow but inevitable progress towards the finish line, and all I can do is interrogate Kegs about Emma's references. I realise the absurdity of my situation. Sitting in a park, staring at a building and waiting for a girl I barely know. I should be with my mother.

'Thanks,' I say and hang up. I think of Mum in her narrow bed and wonder if she knows where she is heading. I'll go and see her tomorrow. My stomach drops again. As if my mother is a lift cable that has kept me moving smoothly up and down all these years, out of sight and unappreciated, and now the cable has snapped, sending me hurtling.

A warning pull in my abdomen turns my attention back to the house, but Emma doesn't materialise. What am I doing? Have I fixated on Emma to avoid thinking about Mum? Possible. While certain I saw the envelope in my handbag that night, I was drunk and tired and distracted. What if I made a mistake? The photographs could have fallen out of my bag at any point on Christmas Day, and I may never know what happened to them. I need to go home and rest and leave Emma alone. It was arrogant of me to assume she'd have no life outside of Birch Grove. What does it matter that she's here? Why should it affect me?

I heave my stiff body off the bench and exit the park. After a final glance at the house with the yellow door, I set off along the terrace and only look back once.

* * *

On Upper Street, I stop at Aroma but find it closed. Cold and exhausted, I can't even be sure I saw Ryan earlier. All I'm certain about is my need to get to the flat and get warm.

Ten minutes later, I turn off Goswell Road into Lever Street. My block looms ahead of me, the windows blinking and sparkling with festive lights. When I get closer, I notice a glowing Santa hanging down from one of the first-floor balconies like a garish burglar.

At the main door, I punch in my entry code and am about to step inside when someone yanks me away from the building.

'When were you going to tell me?' Dan. His face is drawn, his eyes wild. 'When?' he says.

'What are you talking about?'

'Our daughter.' From his coat pocket, he produces a card and holds it up. The card is white with a green Christmas tree on the front. Under the tree, a three-word greeting:

HAPPY CHRISTMAS, DAD

My stomach is a solid block of fear; my heart is beating far too fast.

'Why did you lie to me?' he says.

'I didn't.'

'You told me you went through with the abortion.'

'I did.'

'That doesn't make sense.'

The fault line splits apart. A savage pain rips across my belly. I double over, fighting for air.

'Did you send the card, then?' he says. 'Is this your idea of a sick joke?' He hauls me up. Another white-hot contraction tears through me. It is her. She is coming.

'Grace,' he says, 'did you send it?'

'No,' I gasp.

His eyes harden. 'You kept a pregnancy from me?'

Not just from him, from everyone. From myself. The memory of her hidden inside my mind, the way she hid inside my body all those years ago.

'I knew you were lying.' He spits the words in my face, but they cannot touch me. As if he isn't real. As if I'm watching him on a screen. 'Jesus. Another kid... I warned you I couldn't have anything to do with it.' He shakes his head. 'This can't be happening. This is not what happened.'

He isn't angry because I lied about our child and kept her from him. He is angry because I've rewritten his history, and he doesn't like this new version.

'Read what she said.' He thrusts the card at me. 'Read it.' I open the card.

> *Dear Dad. Hope it's okay to call you that? I'm your daughter, but I don't think you know I exist. That's not your fault. I'm lucky I'm still alive after what my mother did to me!!!! Maybe we'll all laugh about it together one day. Or maybe not.*
>
> *Wishing you all the best for Christmas and the New Year. Xx*

'She put it through my front door,' he says. 'If I hadn't seen it lying there, Stella might have picked it up and read it. Or one of the kids.'

I'm lucky I'm still alive.

Another searing blast of pain and she is with me. My daughter. She is hot between my thighs, and the midwife cuts the bond between us. She asks if I want to hold what I have birthed. No, I say, although I've never wanted anything so much.

'Grace?' He tries to take the card, but I clutch it to my chest. He wrestles it from me, ranting about the trouble I've caused and the stress he is under, hiding this news from Stella. The lies he had to invent to get here today.

'You'll have to speak to the girl,' he says. 'I can't have her anywhere near me or my family.'

The midwife cradles my daughter in her arms. 'Is she normal,' I ask. 'Is she healthy?' The midwife smiles and tells me my daughter is perfect.

'Where is she?' he asks. 'Where does she live?'

I shake my head.

'London?' he says.

'I don't know.'

'You're not in touch? You must have some contact details?'

Maybe we'll all laugh about it together one day.

'I didn't keep her,' I whisper.

He grabs my coat and pulls me to him. 'What?' he says.

'You all right, darlin'?' Trish appears beside us, a red bobble hat on her head and a concerned look on her face.

'We're good thanks,' Dan snaps.

'Don't look like it,' Trish says.

Dan tightens his grip on my coat. 'We're having a private conversation.'

'Not any more,' says Trish, who has switched into vigilante mode.

My hands are sweating; my heart hammers at my chest. Biology is taking over, priming me to get away. I claw his hands from my coat.

'Is that what she's talking about in the card?' Dan says, taking hold of my wrists. 'What exactly did you do to her?'

'That's enough.' Trish's wiry arms shoot out and shove him. 'Back off.'

Caught by surprise, he lets me go and steps away. 'Don't you dare touch me,' he snarls at Trish.

Trish steps in and pushes him again. 'You shouldn't have fuckin' touched her then, should ya, mate?'

The diversion is a small one, but it gives me time to turn and run.

'Go, girl,' yells Trish.

Biology carries me away from the block and out on to Lever Street. Hurtling across the road, I dodge an oncoming cab. When I reach the other side, I sprint through a complex of two-storey apartment blocks and back onto Goswell Road.

I glance behind me. Dan is nowhere to be seen.

53

GRACE

December

I don't stop running until I reach City Road. The traffic beside me slows on the approach to the Old Street roundabout.

Chest burning, I steal deep gulps of air. I grab both ends of my coat's wide belt and pull them tight, tighter than they need to be. Tight enough to sever the connection between the top and bottom of my body.

A familiar numbness settles over me. When I realised she was still with me, this numbness helped me cope. In order to survive the remaining months of my pregnancy, I grew skilled at divorcing mind and body, drifting through most of the days on automatic.

Now I drift along the noisy street, aware the buried fault line has torn apart for good and anything could emerge. I see the midwife's face, plump and serious. She had huge round glasses and straight dark hair parted in the centre. I see the wrinkled body of my baby, smeared with blood and mucus. I see the midwife wrapping her in a green towel and carrying her out of the delivery room.

Is my daughter watching me now? She could be among the people pushing past me. She could be anywhere.

A Travelodge beckons from the opposite side of the road.

A modern, anonymous building. I cross at the next set of lights and enter through the automatic doors into the lobby. A young man with a blond crew cut and a thick neck sits behind the reception desk. His white shirt strains against his muscled arms and chest.

'I need a room,' I say.

'Let me check for availability,' he says, in an Eastern European accent I cannot place. He consults his computer screen and offers me a double. I hand over my credit card, and the transaction takes place in a blur.

The third-floor room has blue carpets, blue curtains and a blue bedspread on the small double bed. I drop my bag on the floor, unbutton my coat and let that fall too. After removing my boots, my grey jeans and my black jumper, I trail naked through to the cramped bathroom.

Stepping into the narrow shower cubicle, I turn the temperature dial as hot as it will go. Scalding water pummels the tight muscles between my shoulder blades. A small bottle of shampoo sits on the soap tray. I squeeze a globule into my hand and lather and rinse my hair. Froth slides down my skin and seethes in the plughole. I work more shampoo into my armpits and between my legs. History nibbles at my fingertips, memories of what my body has endured.

I turn off the shower and dry myself, the thin towel rough as a cat's tongue against my skin. I wrap it round me and sit on the end of the bed. My arms throb with exhaustion, as if they have been holding a heavy object at bay for some time.

How have I hidden her for so long? She feels more inevitable than shocking. It is as though she has been close by all this time but in a different room, her whereabouts temporarily forgotten.

I would describe it as knowing and not knowing at the same time.

That same doctor also told me painful memories couldn't be edited out, yet I have done a good job of it for twenty years. Even when some chapters of our story were dragged to the surface, she still remained submerged.

I pull on my pants and jumper and curl up on top of the bed. My thoughts assemble into some sort of order. Dan. What will he do? Wait for me again at the flat? Go to the police out of concern for his family's safety?

The day the consultant confirmed my ongoing pregnancy, I almost told Dan the truth. After leaving the hospital, I went home and opened a bottle of red wine. At that moment, I didn't care what damage I might cause my stowaway. When sufficiently drunk, I walked to Stella's house, intending to scream my misfortune in the street until Dan listened. But the dark house showed no signs of life, and I couldn't see Stella's car in the street. I climbed over her fence and into the back garden and used a stone sculpture of a fish to shatter the glass panel on the back door.

Once inside the kitchen, I smashed the two matching espresso cups I found on the kitchen table and selected a Sabatier knife from the set next to the Aga. Their bedroom was on the top floor. I slashed their duvet and shredded their white linen sheet. I was just getting stuck into the pillows when they returned and caught me. Dan told Stella to wait downstairs while he sorted me out.

He ordered me to give him the knife. I obeyed him, as always.

'Stella doesn't know I was pregnant, does she?' I said.

He shook his head. 'Leave now,' he said, 'and I won't call the police.'

'I have to tell you something.' I braced myself for the big reveal, but a sudden darting movement in my belly stopped me. It came again, stronger this time. It was her, moving around inside me, trying to make her presence felt.

'I'm with Stella,' he said, 'nothing you can say will change that.'

I held a mangled pillow over my stomach, as if to protect our child from his callousness. Telling him would open me up to his judgement, whatever decision I made. This matter concerned her and I alone.

A few minutes later, thanks to Stella, the police arrived. She was fuming when Dan told them the situation was in hand. After they left, he escorted me downstairs while Stella shouted something at me in French.

'Leave us alone,' he said, before shutting the front door. 'It's over.'

Not for me. That night, I crawled into bed with my daughter fluttering inside me, and I knew the second termination would never take place. Her survival didn't reveal to me an innate longing to be a mother. I didn't see her presence as a miracle, a sign from God, as my own mother would have. I continued with the pregnancy because we had battled, my daughter and I, and she had won. My freedom the spoils of her victory. Most of all, I continued with the pregnancy because I was scared and ashamed. My mother's prophecy had come true, and I had been punished. I thought worse would happen if I tried the same again.

Now she has come back for me. Perhaps I always knew she would.

I'm lucky I'm still alive.

There's no way she could have discovered the truth about her past. Could she?

I have to find her and face her. How did she find me? She must have accessed her original birth certificate and traced me from my name. I shiver as a realisation hits me. Dan's name is not on her birth certificate; I claimed not to know the identity of my baby's father.

How did she know about him?

She must have seen us together. She must have been following me for some time, existing in the shadows of my life as she did once before. I think of the cards and the mug, and it all makes sense. Did she take the photographs of John and I too? A form of revenge?

The fish hook niggles deep inside. I remember Emma with my photo album, fixated on the picture of Dan. *I'm sure I've seen that blond guy on the telly.*

An idea comes to me. An idea so absurd I have to put my hand over my mouth to trap the laughter. An idea I now realise has been with me for some time.

Emma is my daughter.

54

THEN

Wednesday 13 September, Royal Edinburgh Hospital

I'm leaving the day after tomorrow. I'm no longer classed as a danger to myself or others and am free to return to my life. Our story is almost over. It is not a story I want to read again, so I'll destroy this diary as soon as I get out. Writing it has helped me though. My head feels emptier already, as though what I've put on the page might stay on the page. It has to be this way if I don't want to end up here again. Bits of the episode are returning to me now. That lost day resurrecting itself. The thought of being so out of control again terrifies me.

Earlier, Simon said that while the possibility of a relapse did exist, he felt confident I'd experienced an isolated psychotic episode triggered by guilt about the abortion.

He thinks he has established a narrative of events. I prefer his version. It cuts out the difficult part. It cuts out her.

It is a narrative I can just about live with.

55

CASSIE

December

Not even 9 a.m. and Birch Grove was already in chaos. Mrs Palethorpe died in her sleep last night, a heart attack Vera said, although no one had confirmed that yet. Everyone agreed it was a good death. Best way to go. She wouldn't have known a thing. She could have timed it better though. It was the day before New Year's Eve, and our low staff levels meant I had to run around like a nutter trying to do the morning tea trolley and get the residents up and dressed. Kegs had rung yesterday evening and begged me to cover again, so I'd travelled back from London last night to start at seven this morning.

'Morning, Len,' I said, as I entered his room, cup of milky instant coffee in hand. 'Did you sleep well?'

'Slept like shit,' he whined from the bathroom. 'This dump is noisy at night.'

Emma would have giggled and hit back with a cheery retort, but I was getting tired of Emma. Tired of stinky old people and their moaning and illness and death.

The room reeked of urine and cigarettes.

'Have you been smoking out of your window again?' I asked.

'Stop nagging,' he said, 'you're worse than my bloody wife, God rest her soul.'

I placed his coffee on the bedside table, almost tripping over the pile of old newspapers on the floor by his bed. Kit-Kat wrappers peeked out from under his pillow. Not even Memory could keep up with his mess.

'You really are revolting,' I said.

'What?' he shouted. Through the open bathroom door, I saw him standing in front of the toilet, pyjama bottoms round his ankles. His arse was a sack of droopy skin, his veiny legs almost translucent. Emma would have displayed compassion for Len and stoicism about the fate that awaits us all, but I just felt like throwing up.

He shuffled out of the bathroom. 'Pull my keks up for us.' I held my breath as I bent down and hoisted his pyjama bottoms over his rancid, withered cock. 'It won't hurt ya,' he said. 'Bloody thing's useless now.'

He insisted on putting on his dressing gown and asked me to pass him his walking frame.

'I'm going down the TV room,' he said. 'You can bring my coffee there.'

'Go fuck yourself, Len.'

He threw back his head and cackled. 'That's the spirit, girl,' he said, as he shuffled out of the room.

* * *

The stupid tea trolley squeaked as I pushed it along the corridor. I hated it now. This morning, I'd scalded my right hand while filling the coffee flask. I hated the stupid enamel cups too, and I hated laying them out on the trolley – saucer, cup, saucer, cup, saucer, cup – so boring.

Vera bustled towards me with the medicine trolley. 'Coming through,' she said, forcing me to pull over.

As she passed, I informed her Len had been smoking in his room again.

She groaned. 'I'll deal with him later. I'm chasing my tail this morning.'

Whatever.

I put my irritation with the tea duties aside as I prepared my grandmother's morning cuppa. She deserved the best. Dash of milk, half a sugar.

'Hi, Grandma,' I said, slipping into her still, quiet room.

My arrival brought a faint smile to her face.

'Hello,' she said in a raspy voice. Each time she inhaled, I detected a faint, gurgling sound. Kegs told me he doubted she'd pull through this time, although he didn't know how long she might cling on for.

'It's me, Grandma.' I propped her up and lifted the cup to her lips, but she refused to drink. After fetching a straw from the trolley I had more success, encouraging her to take several quick sips before she gave up. 'Good girl,' I said.

Two coarse, white whiskers poked out of her chin. Chiskers, as Surinder called them. I took my scissors from my tunic pocket and snipped the hairs off. Couldn't have my grandmother looking undignified, no matter how poor her health.

I kissed her cheek. 'We might not have long together, you and I.'

'Grace,' she said.

'I haven't heard from her since Boxing Day.' I'd expected an email at least. An apology for her behaviour but then again, she and Emma hadn't parted on the best of terms. By now she would know the photos were missing from her bag. What if she suspected Emma of stealing them? And what if she'd found out about me contacting my father? She'd be furious. I'd have to come clean soon and explain everything. Perhaps Emma should get her back on side before I revealed myself? Might make her a bit more receptive.

'Sorry,' my grandmother whispered. The depth of sadness in her eyes startled me.

'Bless your heart,' I said, 'you've got nothing to apologise for.' A single tear ran down the side of her face. 'Don't cry,' I said, 'please don't cry.'

'Grace,' she said, 'sorry.'

'Quite right. She's the one who should be sorry.' She should too, but my feelings for her changed by the hour. Hate to love and back again. It was so confusing.

'Only trying to help,' said my grandmother before a coughing fit took over.

'You are a great help,' I said. 'What would I do without you?'

* * *

With the tea round almost done, I tried to bypass the TV room, but Len called out for coffee when he saw me. I almost told him to get stuffed, but Memory was in there, wiping down vacant chairs so I had to go in.

Afterwards, as I wheeled the trolley through reception, the undertakers arrived – two lean men in grey suits with their temporary coffin. Kegs escorted them along the corridor to the staircase.

It was almost 9.30 a.m. In the kitchen, I decided to dump the trolley and clean it up later. Unsure if my grandmother had eaten much breakfast, I pinched her a strawberry yoghurt and stuck it in my tunic pocket, intending to pop back to her room and see if I could tempt her.

'Do you have an appointment?' Brenda asked me, as I walked past her desk.

'Yes,' I said, with a mock air of mystery, 'an appointment with destiny.'

'You're not on the list,' she said.

The main door opened, and John Palethorpe marched in with his wife by his side. True, she looked pretty sour, no comforting arm around her husband in his hour of need, but at least she was there. A good sign, surely? Adversity bringing them closer. I'd have to tell my mother. One less thing for us to worry about.

Leaving them to their grief, I sauntered back to my grandmother's room. Her corridor was deserted, the few available staff no doubt fussing round the Palethorpes and paying their respects to the coffin as it left the building.

I noticed the smell as soon as I reached her door. The scent of Bonfire Night, tinged with something more acrid and synthetic. I followed the smell to Len's room and watched as a lick of smoke shimmied out of the gap beneath his door.

56

GRACE

December

I wake fully clothed on top of a hard bed. Where am I? The open curtains reveal a blank, white sky. Stiff and cold, I sit up and pull the blue bedspread around me. As I orientate myself, the previous day's events filter through my groggy head.

Snatching up my phone from the bedside table, I check the time – 10.15 a.m. already. Thoughts of Emma kept me awake for hours last night. I convinced myself sleep would never come, but I must have crashed out around four this morning. I check my emails, hoping to hear back from Dan. At around 2 a.m., I sent a brief message to his work address.

I'm dealing with it. I'll be in touch.

No reply as yet, but hopefully he'll see the message soon and it will keep him at bay for a while.

I think of Emma again, hoping sleep might have given me a fresh perspective. Last night, I considered my theory about her from all angles. She told me she never knew her mother and she made efforts to befriend me and get close to me. Or was it the other way round? None of it makes any sense, but I can't deny my attraction to her. Have I imagined the closeness that has developed between us? Have I used her as a substitute for the daughter I couldn't bear to remember?

I call Birch Grove, to check on my mother and also to see if I can get more information about Emma from Kegs. He must know something about her background. Some fact that might eliminate her from my enquiries.

No one picks up. I try again, with the same result. I leave a message for Kegs, asking him to call me back.

If only I had someone to talk to about this.

Fiona Braithwaite. Her name comes first and then I picture her. A small woman in her late thirties with red hair and a silver nose stud. Could I contact her?

I look her up online, aware she might have retired by now or moved jobs or left the country. The first page of search results brings numerous Fiona Braithwaites, none of them relevant. Halfway through the second page, I see a listing that makes my stomach turn.

Fiona Braithwaite appointed Chief Officer for Child Protection Services

The accompanying photograph confirms that this Fiona Braithwaite is the social worker assigned to me twenty years ago. Her profile contains a link to her council office's contact details. I try the number given. The thought of speaking to her again scares me, but I have to do it. There must be a way of tracking my daughter down, and she might be able to help me. My call goes through to a voicemail message informing me the office is closed until after New Year. A helpline number is offered for emergencies.

I hang up. What now?

* * *

Aroma is packed, a queue at the counter and every table full. Ryan is nowhere to be seen. I stop one of the self-important waitresses as she weaves her way around the tables, holding aloft a plate of sourdough toast.

'He's here somewhere,' she says, when I ask if Ryan is working today. 'Check at the counter.'

I join the back of the queue but can only see another young guy with a dark beard manning the coffee machines.

'Two lattes, one flat white,' he calls and the queue edges forward. I take my phone from my coat pocket and check the screen in case I've missed a call from Birch Grove. Nothing so far.

Ryan strides through the door next to the coffee machines, a bulky hessian sack on his shoulder.

'Ryan.' I push my way to the counter, ignoring the tuts and sullen glances that come my way.

'Hey, Grace.' He dumps the sack on the floor.

'I need to talk to you.'

'Mate, I really need that coffee done,' insists the bearded barista.

'It's urgent,' I say.

'Hang on a second, Grace.' Ryan opens the sack and scoops coffee beans into a machine that emits a deafening crunching sound when he switches it on. 'Won't be long, mate,' he promises his flustered colleague, as he slips out from behind the counter.

'Do you know a girl called Emma?' I ask.

He shrugs. 'I know a few girls called Emma. Why?'

'Does one of them live on Highbury Terrace?'

He frowns.

'I think I saw you there yesterday,' I add.

'Yeah. I went over there in the afternoon.'

'What were you doing there?'

'Visiting my girlfriend.' He grimaces. 'Ex-girlfriend.'

My heart thumps. 'Emma?'

'Cassie.' He rolls his eyes. 'Or psycho-bitch, as my mates call her.'

'Are you sure that's her name?'

'Course I'm sure.'

'Do you have any photos of her?'

He glances back at the counter and the static queue. 'What's this about?'

'Please, Ryan. It's important.'

'I've deleted most of them.' He takes his phone from the back pocket of his jeans. 'Hang on.' He scrolls through the images on the screen. 'That's a fairly recent one.'

A close-up of Emma's face looks out at me. Her eyes are blue, not brown, yet I'm sure it's her.

'I know this girl,' I say. 'She's a care worker at an old people's home in Brentham.'

'Her gran lives in Brentham,' he says. 'Cass has been down there a couple of days a week to look after her, but she's not a care worker.'

'She's employed at a nursing home called Birch Grove.'

Ryan laughs. 'I doubt Cass has ever done a day's work in her life. She's a rich, spoiled girl with a ton of issues.'

'Has she ever mentioned her mother?'

'Her mother's dead.'

That ties in with what Emma told me.

'Not her real mother,' Ryan adds. 'I thought she meant her real mother but then she goes and tells me she's adopted.' He sighs. 'To be honest, I don't know how much of what she told me was true.'

I feel faint. The chatter of the café swims around me.

'She's pissed at her real mother, that's for sure,' Ryan says. 'Weird how someone so bright can be so nuts.'

My hands reach out to steady myself on the counter.

'Hey?' Ryan's hand is on my arm. 'You okay?'

I nod. Cassie. Is she my daughter?

'Grace.' Ryan gives my arm a gentle shake. 'Your phone's ringing.'

So it is. Chirping away in my coat pocket. I pull it out and see the Birch Grove number on the screen.

'Grace,' Kegs says when I answer.

'You got my message?' I say. 'Thanks for calling back.'

'No. Sorry.' He sounds hassled. 'Listen, we've had a bit of an incident here.' His next words get lost amidst the hissing of the coffee machine and manic laughter from the table behind me.

'Hang on, Kegs.' I leave the café and stand on the pavement next to the steamed-up window. 'What were you saying?'

'We've had a fire,' he says, 'a small one. The fire brigade have been and it's all contained but we've moved your mum to hospital, just to—'

'Is she hurt?'

'She inhaled a tiny amount of smoke while Emma was getting her out of there. She's in a stable condition, but the smoke hasn't helped her breathing.'

'Emma?'

'Luckily she was nearby when the alarm went off. She put your mum into a wheelchair and got her out of harm's way before going back to help the other residents.'

That sounds like the kind of heroic thing Emma would do.

But Emma isn't Emma.

'I don't think she's who she claims to be,' I say.

'Sorry?'

'Emma. I think she's someone else.'

'You're not making sense.'

'Is she still there?'

'Yep. The paramedics are checking her out.'

'She lied about her identity,' I tell him. 'Her name's Cassie.'

'Emma's middle name is Cassie,' he says, not bothering to mask his impatience. 'That must be where you're getting mixed up.'

In the background, a deep male voice interrupts us.

'Just a minute.' Kegs proceeds to talk to the man, their conversation muffled, as if Kegs has his hand over the receiver. 'Listen,' he says when he returns, 'I'm up to my eyes in it here. Can we talk later?'

'But I'm not sure if Emma and Cassie are the same person. I mean, they are, but—'

'Sorry, Grace,' he says, 'I've got to go.'

57

CASSIE

December

The charred taste of smoke lay heavy on my tongue and my chest hurt each time I took a breath. The paramedic, an efficient woman with icy hands, removed the arm cuff from my right bicep and packed away her blood pressure gauge.

'Does your throat feel burned?' she asked. I shook my head. 'Tried not to inhale,' I said, my voice hoarse. She pressed two fingers against my wrist and took my pulse. 'Do you feel dizzy?'

'No.' My eyes wouldn't stop stinging though. I longed to take my contact lenses out but couldn't risk anyone seeing me with blue eyes. My arms and back ached already from the strain of getting Grandma into a wheelchair.

When I swallowed, my pungent saliva almost made me gag. I imagined particles of Len's mattress swirling round in the smoke. Atoms of his skin and urine.

Brenda hurtled into reception, stopping short when she saw me occupying the chair behind her desk.

'Do you have an appointment?' she screeched. The fire and the ensuing drama had left her more hyper than usual.

'I'm only borrowing your chair,' I explained, but she'd shifted her attention to the firemen swaggering through the main door. With all the people coming and going, poor Brenda couldn't keep up. Once the immediate danger had passed, we'd herded most of the residents back inside to the TV and activity rooms. No one seemed to know what was happening. Could the residents go back to their rooms? Would all ground-floor residents be moved to other care homes until the fire damage had been repaired?

'You should come to A&E with us for a proper check-up,' the paramedic said.

I declined the offer, despite wanting to be near my grandmother, who'd left in an ambulance earlier. Best to stick around and find out what the fire brigade had to say about the blaze. I wondered where Len had left his smouldering cigarette butt this time – under his bed, behind the curtains, next to that stack of old newspapers?

'Here she is.' Kegs appeared beside me with one of the firemen. 'Our hero.'

'Indeed.' The fireman settled his bulk on the edge of the desk and removed his helmet. 'You showed some quick thinking.'

'It was nothing,' I said.

He introduced himself as Olly and said he had a few questions for me. 'Seeing as you discovered the fire.'

Vera scurried up and asked the paramedic to come and take a look at Len.

'Probably just stress,' Vera said, 'but he's complaining of shooting pains in his arm.' She avoided my gaze. No wonder. If she'd followed up on my information earlier, none of this would have happened.

'He should be bloody stressed,' Kegs muttered. Vera and the paramedic headed for the TV room. Kegs excused himself, saying he had to start phoning the relatives. 'I'll ring Grace first,' he said, 'let her know Polly's in hospital.'

I swivelled my chair round to get a view of him through the open office door.

'Tell me what happened,' Olly said, running a hand through his thinning ginger hair.

'It was all so fast,' I replied. Kegs had the phone to his ear and was chatting away. Fingers crossed he'd tell my mother everything I'd done.

Olly nodded. 'These things get out of control so easily.'

Memory lumbered into reception from the direction of the TV room and glared at me.

'There was so much smoke,' I said.

Memory sidled closer, eavesdropping as I described the smoke billowing out of the room when I'd pushed Len's door open.

'It was everywhere.'

Memory shook her head. 'In fire training, they tell you don't open the door if you think there is fire behind it,' she said. 'Everybody knows that.'

'I thought Len was in there. What was I supposed to do? Leave him to burn to death?'

'It's okay, Emma,' Olly said. 'The real thing is nothing like training. Everyone panics.'

'You'd just given Len coffee in the TV lounge,' Memory continued. 'How could he have walked all the way back to his room so quick?'

'I was trying to save the residents,' I said. 'I got Mrs Walker out as soon as I could.'

'I know,' said Olly, 'you did a great job.'

Memory snorted with disbelief and shuffled off, but I had other problems to contend with. Kegs still had the phone to his ear but was gazing at me with a perplexed expression. Perplexed and irritated. Or was I just imagining that?

'Excuse me.' The fireman hauled himself off the desk and strode over to speak to one of his colleagues who'd just emerged from my grandmother's corridor. The two of them interrupted Kegs, who hung up on my mother to confer with them.

'What did Grace say?' I asked Kegs as he and the two firemen walked past.

'Later, Emma,' he said, as he hurried away. What had my mother told him?

The paramedic reappeared, pushing Len in a wheelchair.

'Don't you blame me,' Len shouted. 'It's not my bloody fault.'

I had to get away. As the paramedic approached, I bent over coughing. 'I'm having trouble breathing,' I gasped.

'Come with me,' she said.

* * *

Casualties of all sorts filled the emergency ward at Brentham General. A young boy with a sling on his right arm and a fat man with bandaged eyes and a spider's web tattooed on his neck. A teenage girl vomited into one of those grey cardboard bedpans while her mother gave her a loud, overdue lecture on the dangers of recreational drugs.

At least the oxygen mask over my nose and mouth kept the odours of the ward away, and the cool air pushing into my lungs was not unpleasant. I couldn't stay long though. Not after the way Kegs had looked at me. What if he turned up here asking questions I didn't want to answer?

My backpack lay on the chair beside my bed. I'd managed to grab it from the office along with my coat before getting into the ambulance. Taking out my phone, I checked the time – 12.43 p.m. I sat up and removed the mask.

'Where do you think you're going?' A nurse with hair that matched the blue of her uniform ordered me back into bed.

'What happened to Polly Walker?' I asked when she handed me back the mask. 'The old lady in the care home fire. She's one of my favourites.'

'Put your mask on and I'll see what I can find out,' the nurse said. I obeyed and she returned five minutes later to inform me Mrs Walker now occupied a side room in the stroke ward. 'That's all we had free for her,' she said.

The man with the bandaged eyes shouted for assistance and the nurse hurried over to him. As soon as she had her back to me, I pulled off the mask, picked up my coat and bag, and crept out of the ward.

I set off down a long corridor, the overhead signs with their blue arrows guiding me to the main stairwell. The ward directory next to the lifts instructed me to go to the second floor for the stroke ward. Once there, I attempted to enter unnoticed, but the officious nurse behind the reception desk stopped me.

'Can I help?' he asked.

'I'm here to visit Polly Walker.'

'Family only at this time,' he said. I longed to tell him of my relationship to Polly Walker but decided against it.

'I'm the person who saved her life,' I said.

'Sorry.' He tucked a pen into the breast pocket of his white tunic. 'Her daughter rang and said no visitors.'

Typical of my mother. Ruining everything. I couldn't shake the fear she was closing in on me. Surely she should be grateful for all I'd done?

In the toilets near the ward, I removed my contact lenses and dumped them in a bin. I needed to get out of the hospital. I needed to walk in the fresh air and think. On my way to the building's main entrance, I spotted a sign that enticed me to take a detour. Obeying another set of blue arrows, I ended up at the hospital's neonatal unit.

The entry doors were sealed, both for security and to prevent infections from harming the newborns. A buzzer sounded from inside and the doors opened outwards. A nurse strode out of the ward, cheery in her pink smock and trousers. Just before the doors swung shut, I caught a glimpse of the world beyond them. The long glass that shielded the hissing, beeping incubators. Inside those machines, puny bodies would be swithering between life and death. A waiting game. Waiting to see which babies were too damaged to survive and which would emerge as miracles.

58

GRACE

December

I arrive at Brentham station just before one-thirty, half an hour late thanks to signal works outside Stratford. Throughout the delay, I stood by the carriage door, heart and nerves jumping, willing the train to start moving again.

Outside the station, I head for the taxi rank and clamber into the car at the head of the line.

'Priory Road,' I say, 'anywhere near the bus station will do.' The glum driver pulls away without speaking. As we surge onto the roundabout at the station exit, I almost change my mind and ask him to go to Brentham General. When I phoned the hospital from the train, a nurse from Mum's ward assured me she is stable and safe, but I still need to see her.

The taxi takes the second turn-off towards town, and I decide to stick with my plan. Before visiting Mum, I need to find out the truth about Emma. Cassie. Whoever she is.

We skirt the town centre on the ring road and are soon on Priory Road. The driver lurches to a stop.

He grunts the fare at me. I hand him a note and jump out without waiting for the change. A short walk past the bus station brings me to the street with the sex shop on the corner. Emma's street.

As soon as I see her tall, white building, a hot ball of panic lodges in my chest. If she's back from Birch Grove, I'll confront her. If not, this might be my chance to find out the truth. In the litter-strewn passageway at the side of the house, the hot ball of panic sends out a flare and coats my palms with sweat.

I press the buzzer on the bottom left of the panel. No reply. 'Yeah, what?' barks a man's voice when I hit the buzzer on the right.

'Got a delivery. Can you—'

He buzzes me in without a word.

A hallway with three doors and a narrow staircase. Grimy beige carpet beneath my feet as I ascend to the first floor. A rank smell emanates from an overflowing rubbish bag outside one of the flats. Carcass bones poke out of the black plastic, and the torn skins of Christmas crackers have spilled to the ground.

Ryan said Cassie was angry with her mother. She must be if she's willing to live here. I remind myself her anger is my fault. She's my responsibility. I hurry up to Emma's floor. Cassie's floor. Comparing this place to the grandeur of Highbury, it seems impossible that Emma and Cassie could be the same person.

A lone door greets me. Scuffed white plywood in a splintered frame. Heart struggling against my ribs, I rap on it three times. No answer. I listen for signs of her presence but hear nothing. My right hand curls around the doorknob.

With the first push, splinters of wood flake away from the frame, confirming the door's flimsiness. I place my shoulder against it and heave. The door shifts, but the lock holds fast. Another heave, and the door yields a little more. After one final push it gives way, but a door chain stops it opening. I wriggle my hand around the door but cannot slide the chain free. Frustrated, I yank it downwards. It comes away from the door with a loud cracking sound.

The door refuses to close again, so I leave it ajar. I take my phone from my coat pocket and switch it to vibrate.

'Emma?'

The cramped room offers no hiding places. I take in the messy sofa bed and the small pair of pink slippers askew beside it. The galley kitchen is a disaster – dirty plates and plastic tumblers spread across the work surface. The door next to the kitchen leads to a bathroom so small that the side of the toilet touches the narrow bath. Bargain-size bottles of cheap shampoo and body wash cluster on the shelf above the taps. Pink, purple and white candles in decorative tins line the side of the bath. I shiver. The bathroom is freezing, just like the other room, but the smell of damp is stronger here. Black spots of mould pattern the grouting between the grubby white tiles.

How awful that she lives in such a dump. Only she doesn't live here, not all the time. In the cabinet above the sink, I find a box of New You contact lenses. Dark brown, according to the label. The molten panic in my chest stirs. If Cassie is pretending to be Emma, she has method-acted the part to perfection. What kind of person would go to such lengths? Yet I've seen her with Mum and know the kindness she is capable of. According to Kegs, she risked her own safety to help Mum only hours ago.

Back in the living room, I lift a pillow from the sofa bed and inhale the scent of Emma's lemony shampoo. A piece of red material sticking out from beneath her duvet distracts me. Dropping the pillow, I reach under the bed covers and pull out my missing cashmere scarf. Identifiable by the white stub of the label I cut out soon after buying it.

Other items come to my attention. The crystal hedgehog I gave Emma sits on the floor next to the bed, along with my long-lost phone. Beside them is a framed picture of Cassie and I on a bus. Cassie's long hair is blonde, just like Dan's.

I glance around the room, searching for what else this girl has taken from me. On the table by the window, next to a miniature Christmas tree, stands the Virgin Mary. Mum's beloved statue, gold baubles dangling from her outstretched arms.

How dare Cassie steal from me! From Mum! As well as anger, I feel guilt at her need for some reminder of me.

A few hours after the birth, I crept into the room where she lay, cosy beneath a white blanket. Knowing we would soon be parted, I was desperate to leave her something but had nothing to give. I unfurled her tiny fists and planted a kiss in each hot, creased palm. A gift she could keep with her forever.

I need more information about the person who could be my daughter. Clues that reveal who she is and the life she has lived. I search the dishevelled room, unsure what I'm looking for. When I spot a black suitcase wedged under the sofa bed, my hot ball of panic mutates into something cold and tight.

I ease the suitcase out and unzip it. Inside lies an A4 exercise book with a glossy silver cover. I lift it out with caution, as though it might disintegrate into dust like some ancient manuscript. As I sit on the bed, the book falls open at the back, revealing a page of thick grey paper with a leaflet for the Museum of Childhood stapled to it. The same leaflet I received in the post and dismissed as junk mail.

Pulse racing, I work my way towards the front of the scrapbook. There are pages filled with tickets for films and art exhibitions I remember going to. I even find the ID page of my passport. On and on I go, until a faded newspaper article stops me.

MIRACLE BABY SURVIVES

Body shaking, I read on.

> The baby girl abandoned five days ago in the car park of The Rose and Crown is still alive in the Royal Infirmary's neonatal unit, despite suffering exposure. Baby Cassie, as the staff have named her, was discovered by Peter Wakely, the pub's landlord, as he put his rubbish out on Sunday night. The baby, wrapped only in a white blanket, lay next to a public bin at the entrance to the car park.

Baby Cassie. Emma Cassie Harrington?

My body slumps, overcome by terror and relief. Relief at seeing the truth written down before me. Terror at what that truth means.

I remember tucking my baby's blanket under her chin and explaining in whispers that we couldn't be together and that I hoped one day she would understand. I remember walking away and leaving her, my heart a bruised, pointless weight.

I turn the page.

POLICE LAUNCH SEARCH FOR CASSIE'S MOTHER

My phone vibrates in my pocket. I pull it out to find a Brentham number on the screen.

'Hello?' I talk in a low voice, despite being alone.

'Is this Miss Walker?' A woman introduces herself as Juliet, the staff nurse from the stroke unit. 'I'm calling about your mother.'

I cling to the scrapbook as Juliet informs me Mum's breathing is worse. An oxygen mask is keeping her going. For now.

'She's very weak,' Juliet explains, 'and her condition is deteriorating faster than we expected.' She tells me Mum asked for me earlier but is unconscious now. 'Come right away if you can,' she urges. 'Just in case.'

I tell her I'm on my way and hang up. While scrambling to my feet, I drop the scrapbook on the bed but quickly snatch it up again. I'll need it as evidence later.

'Bad news?' says a voice behind me.

I turn. There she is in the doorway, still dressed in her care worker uniform. Watching me with bright, blue eyes.

'Hello, Mother,' she says.

* * *

Cassie

My mother looked startled when I appeared. Strange, seeing as she was the one breaking into my bedsit. Emma's bedsit.

'I wasn't expecting you,' I said in my normal voice, done with Emma and her stupid accent.

'Hello, Cassie,' she replied.

'You know who I am then? How did you find out?'

'I spoke to—'

'Doesn't matter,' I said, and it didn't. After leaving the hospital, I'd walked round the town centre, thinking things through. The whole Emma charade couldn't go on. I'd resolved to come clean with my mother so we could start again, and now I had to go through with it.

'What are you doing?' she asked, as I grabbed a chair from the kitchen area and propped it under the door handle.

'Safety measure,' I explained, 'lots of break-ins round here.' I winked so she'd know I wasn't too angry with her.

She took a step forward, but retreated when I planted myself between her and the door. The cover of my scrapbook glinted in the weak sunlight filtering through the window. I should have been cross with her for snooping around, but instead I felt glad she'd had a chance to catch up on my history. Our history.

'I was going to call you later and invite you to my place in London,' I explained. 'It's much nicer than here.' My mother glanced around the room, her distaste obvious. 'It's Emma's place,' I said, 'and she's gone now.' I pulled off Emma's Parka jacket and tossed it aside. Underneath I still had on my care worker tunic and leggings. 'I wouldn't be seen dead in what she wears.'

My mother stared at me like I was mad. Not surprising, given the state of me. 'I know the whole Emma thing was a bit over the top,' I said, 'but you don't have to worry. She won't bother us again.'

'I liked Emma,' my mother said.

I rolled my eyes. 'Who didn't like Emma? Christ, even I liked her some of the time.'

'Cassie—'

'Was that the hospital on the phone?'

'Yes. I have to go there. Now.'

'How's Grandma?'

'My mum's very ill.'

I glanced away. 'She'll be fine.'

The slither of smoke beneath Len's door. The realisation of what was happening behind it. Ignoring the fire alarm on the wall in front of me. *Break Glass Here*. Walking away and entering my grandmother's room.

'She's in the best place,' I said. 'They'll be looking after her.'

Unfolding my grandmother's wheelchair and placing it next to her bed in preparation. Lowering myself into the armchair and crossing my legs. Waiting.

'Her nurse has advised me to come as soon as I can,' my mother said.

Waiting for the smoke and flames to build and for the smoke detector in Len's room to trigger the alarm. Waiting for greater danger so that my rescue of Grandma would appear more heroic and my mother would be more grateful.

'You have to let me go and see her,' she said, inching towards me, displaying none of the gratitude I'd hoped for.

Noticing for the first time the filth beneath my nails, I took my scissors from my tunic pocket. 'What?' I asked, as my mother backed away again.

'Nothing.' She pressed the scrapbook against her chest, as if to protect herself.

'I wonder if that's soot?' I slid a scissor blade beneath my thumbnail and scraped the blackness out.

My mother cleared her throat. 'Cassie, I—'

'When the alarm went off I got her out of there straight away.' Almost straight away. First I'd followed the sound of the alarm and pushed open Len's door. Monstrous plumes of smoke filled the corridor. That's when everything started to go wrong. It took me longer than predicted to lift Grandma's bony body into the wheelchair. Longer than predicted to steer her through the smoky darkness.

'You acted very bravely,' my mother said.

I did my best. Pushed the wheelchair as hard and fast as I could. Each time Grandma gasped for breath I wanted to cry.

'I had to save her,' I said. 'She's my blood.'

'Emma. Cassie—'

'I tried to see her at the hospital, but the staff didn't let me.' I slid the blade beneath the nail of my index finger.

'Please put the scissors away,' my mother pleaded. Her fearful expression reminded me of Isobel after I'd slapped her.

'Fine, if you're going to make such a fuss.' I put them back in my pocket. 'That stuck-up nurse said it was family only. How do you think that made me feel?'

'I had to be sure who you were. That's why I came here.'

I nodded at the scrapbook. 'Now you know.'

'Yes. I do.'

At last. My mother and I together with no more lies between us. Everything out in the open. 'As soon as I found you, I wanted to tell you who I was.'

'How did you find me?'

Her question irritated me. Why focus on the details when we should be thinking about the big picture?

'Then I decided it would be easier if we got to know each other first,' I explained.

'Cassie, we need to talk.'

I pointed to the sofa bed. 'Have a seat; we're not in a rush. You must have well loads to ask me, as Emma would say.'

She remained standing. Her lips twitched, as though trying to hold back the questions that jostled behind them.

'The Mother's Day cards,' she said eventually, 'you sent them?'

I nodded. 'Did you like them?'

'What about the mug?'

'Of course,' I said, exasperated. She must have known I'd come looking for her one day.

'And the necklace?'

'The silver heart?'

Her face paled. 'You did take the photographs of John and I together?'

I sighed and confessed but pointed out my good deed in getting her away from that dreadful John. 'He's back with his wife, by the way,' I said. 'I saw them together this morning.'

She opened her mouth to interrogate me further, but I got in first by admitting to sending my father a Christmas card.

'I like him,' I said. 'His family seem nice too. I'm sure we could all get on if we gave it a go.'

Her fingers tapped a nervous beat on the cover of the scrapbook. 'Dan Thorne is not your father,' she said.

'Oh.' Her words dismayed me. How could I have got it wrong? 'Who is my father then?'

'I don't know.'

'Why? Was he a stranger? Did you have a one-night stand?'

'I don't know because I'm not your mother.'

The first prick of emptiness at my core. Black and cold. 'Becoming a mother after twenty years must be a shock,' I said, 'but—'

'I'm not your mother.' She held up the scrapbook. 'This proves it.'

Hot angry blotches ignited my cheeks. 'You had a baby. You told me so.'

'Yes. I had a baby girl twenty years ago.'

'You didn't keep her. You admitted it.' She muttered something inaudible. 'What?' I said.

'I had her adopted.' Tears shimmered in her eyes. 'I had my baby adopted.'

The emptiness began to spread. 'Someone did adopt me,' I said.

'I didn't abandon my baby, Cassie.' The ease with which she lied took my breath away.

'Grandma said you killed your baby. I told her you'd almost succeeded.'

She came out with some crazy story then about having a termination and my grandmother not approving and the operation not working, and lo and behold there she was still pregnant seven weeks later. How stupid did she think I was? 'I never told Mum about the pregnancy,' she said. 'I wanted to make my own decisions about my child's future.' She told me she'd moved to Edinburgh to keep the pregnancy secret and had rented a flat and lived there using her dad's life insurance money. As if adding details like that would make her story more believable.

'It was the loneliest time of my life,' she said. 'I was five months pregnant and had to contact social services to start the adoption process.'

She broke down then. To be fair, she was quite an accomplished actress.

'Talk about denial,' I said. 'You're my mother. You gave birth, then you wrapped me in a blanket and dumped me.'

She opened the scrapbook and held up a page containing one of the newspaper articles. She pointed to the picture of me in hospital, a wrinkly, red-skinned creature with plastic tubes trailing from my nostrils.

'This is not my baby,' she said. 'This is a picture of you in Canterbury Royal Infirmary shortly after you were found in a nearby village.'

Emptiness filled me, pushed at my ribs, threatened to split me in two.

'I had my baby in mid-July,' she said, 'but you were born in the February.' She fixed a false smile to her face. 'I understand why you want to find your mum, but I'm not her.'

'Shut up.'

'I don't know why your mother left you, but I bet it was hard for her. I left my baby at the hospital with a social worker, but it still felt like I was abandoning her.'

'Shut up,' I repeated.

A buzzing noise filled the room. My mother reached into her pocket and pulled out her phone.

'That's the hospital,' she said.

'Don't you dare answer it.'

She hesitated. 'My mother is very sick. I have to go to her.'

'No.' I dived forward and knocked the phone from her hand. She screamed and backed away, stumbling as her calves met the sofa bed. Back she fell, onto the mattress, the scrapbook tumbling to the floor. 'This is our time,' I said. 'We're meant to be getting to know each other.'

'Please. We can talk later, but my mother needs me.'

Tears gathered in my eyes, threatening to embarrass me.

'I need you,' I said. 'I've always needed you.'

'That's enough.' My mother stood up. 'I'm leaving.'

'No.' I launched myself at her and we collapsed onto the bed. She had to stay. We had so much more to talk about.

'Stop it, Cassie,' she said, as I entwined myself around her. 'For your own sake.'

I only wanted to get close to her. As close as possible. My legs encircled her torso, pinning her arms to her sides. My arms hugged her neck tight.

'Don't go.' I pressed my cheek against hers, no longer able to hold back the tears. 'Don't.'

'Stop,' she wheezed, sounding all breathless. I held her tight. I'd have climbed inside her if I could.

'I wanted to get to know you,' I said, 'that's all.'

She bucked against me, writhing this way and that until I couldn't hold her in place any longer.

'Ow,' I said, as she tore my arms from around her neck, 'you're hurting me.'

She didn't care. She tossed me aside like litter before lurching off the bed.

I only wanted to talk to her, and now she was abandoning me again. Shirking her responsibilities. How could I make her listen?

My eyes fell upon the Virgin Mary. The mother of all mothers gazed at me with her serene expression, and I knew what I had to do. Dashing across to the table, I picked her up by her neck.

My mother had almost reached the door by the time I got to her.

'No,' she screamed, as I grasped her coat and dragged her backwards. Balance lost, she fell to her knees.

Before she could look up and put me off, I raised the statue high. Then came the Virgin's mighty downward swoop.

Mary, Mother of God, landed with a crack against the side of my mother's skull. Then, her work done, she shattered into pieces, falling to the floor along with my mother's body.

59

THEN

Thursday 14 September, Royal Edinburgh Hospital

Shortly after the birth, my mind and body still stretched to their limits from forcing her out of me, a familiar wailing sound filtered through the walls of my flat, keeping me awake at night. When I did sleep, I found her tiny hands waiting and soon they intruded into my waking world. A glimpse of them curled around my bedroom door. A flash of them on the arm of the sofa. Now and then I caught whispered questions. Why didn't you want me? Why did you give me away?

I'd had my long hair cut short in the hope she might fail to recognise me and leave me alone. I ate little and monitored my falling weight. I knew my body was a devious entity, capable of hiding terrible secrets and in need of constant surveillance. The day I had the episode, I woke to find her sitting on my bed. She looked about three years old. She had Dan's blonde hair and my brown eyes, and she giggled as she watched me pull on my clothes and grab my handbag.

I ran to Haymarket station and bought a ticket for Perth, but once the train had crossed the Forth Rail Bridge, I jumped off at Aberdour to fool her. Yet there she stood on the platform, a teenager this time with an accusatory expression on her face. I ran across the bridge to the opposite platform and took the next train back to Edinburgh, only to find her waiting at Waverley station. She followed me all over the city to the castle esplanade before chasing me down the Royal Mile and into one of the dark passageways that led off it.

At first, I wanted to give in. To let her hands have their way. How could I live knowing my daughter was out there in the world, growing up without me? But as she squeezed the air from my body, panic kicked in and I began to fight back. A desire to win overwhelmed me. I wanted to live, and in that instant my life mattered more than hers. My survival instinct overrode my maternal instinct, and I was powerless to stop it.

60

GRACE

December

My skull throbs. The metallic scent of blood fills my nostrils. With a groan, I open my eyes into late-afternoon gloom. On the rough carpet, centimetres from my face, rests a jagged fragment of something blue. My fingers reach for it, recoiling as they meet the sharp edges.

The Virgin Mary.

She lies scattered on the floor, her severed head facing me. A sluggish residue of fear crawls through me.

My nails. Someone has painted them sparkly red. A sloppy job, smears of dried varnish all over my fingers.

Cassie has painted them.

I lift my head. It comes away from the carpet with a sound like Velcro peeling. I touch my matted hair and discover blood, red and sticky.

The fear picks up speed. Where is she?

No sign of her; she must have gone. I come onto all fours. The chair is still propped under the doorknob and her jacket and bag are still where she dumped them.

Up onto my feet. Armies of pins and needles march beneath my skin.

I have to get out.

The bathroom door is open, but the light is off. I wait for some sound of movement or the flush of a toilet but hear only the steady drip drip drip of water.

Then I notice the smell. An overpowering combination of vanilla, rose and lavender. The white, tiled wall of the bathroom reflects a golden flicker.

I creep closer, my skull pounding with every step, ears straining for some hint of her. The echo of each drip is all I pick up.

I push open the door and see her clothes. Tunic, leggings, knickers and bra heaped on the floor by the toilet. I see a cloudy layer of condensation on the mirror. I see her, reclining in a bath full to the brim with water and bubbles. A bath surrounded by scented candles on the wane.

'Cassie?' I whisper.

Her head has rolled to one side. Water laps at the entrance of her mouth. I grope behind me, locate the cord for the overhead light and tug it on.

Islands of pink bubbles bob around her, separated by patches of crimson water. Sickly steam clogs my lungs. Where has all the air gone?

'Cassie.'

Warm water meets me when I plunge my arms into the bath. Her naked body slips one way then the other, but at last I get a firm grip under her armpits and haul her up and over the side, water sloshing with us as we land on the dirty lino.

Blood seeps from vertical slashes on her wrists. I pick up her leggings and tie a makeshift bandage around her right wrist. Then I pull off the belt of my coat and do the same to her left.

I hold my hand over her mouth. Is that a faint stream of air? Hard to tell. I rush into the living room and search the floor until I find my phone under the sofa bed.

I dial 999. The operator asks me which emergency service I require.

'Ambulance,' I say, 'soon as possible.'

61

GRACE

'Touch my finger, then touch the tip of your nose as quickly as possible,' says the weary junior doctor with the black-framed glasses.

'I'm fine. Just let me—'

'Please do as I say.'

I perform the task with ease, then glance at the curtains concealing my bed. The doctor asks me to name the months of the year in reverse and then once again asks for my name and date of birth. He nods at my answers and checks the dressing taped to my head one last time before declaring me free from serious concussion. As he pulls back the curtain, he cites a list of symptoms for me to beware of.

'All done,' he says to PC Palmer, who swaps places with him and pulls the curtains shut again.

'How's my mum?' I ask.

'PC King is finding out now.' PC Palmer's Geordie accent has the same soothing effect it did when he first arrived at Cassie's bedsit a few minutes before the ambulance. His calm voice asking questions, issuing instructions, smoothing over the bloody scene in front of him. 'We'll get you to her soon as we can.'

'What about Cassie?' They kept us apart on the way to the hospital, her in the ambulance and me in the police car.

'She's still unconscious but she'll make it,' Palmer says. 'You found her just in time.'

I nod, unsure what to say. Still unable to process what has happened. My heart quickens at the memory of Cassie's slender body smothering me. Her arms tight around my neck. 'We'll take a statement from her when she's up to it,' he says.

The curtains part, as PC King steps into the cubicle. 'Your mum's stable,' she says. 'I told the staff you'll be up once we've finished with you.' She glances at Palmer and he rewards her with a nod of approval. King is young, the rookie to Palmer's seasoned officer. She has the eagerness of someone finally putting theory into practice and takes notes as Palmer asks me once more to describe the events leading to Cassie's suicide attempt.

We go through it again, my account making more sense now my panic has subsided.

'She got a job at your mother's care home?' Palmer asks, eyebrows raised.

'Emma... Cassie was great with old people,' I say, not wanting to land Kegs in trouble. I couldn't fully blame him for not knowing; Cassie had us all fooled. 'Everyone liked her,' I add.

I still feel a need to protect the girl. To make excuses for her. 'Did she ever threaten your mother in any way?' Palmer asks.

'Not that I know of.' Guilt pricks me for leaving my mother exposed to Cassie, but as far as I know, Cassie has never hurt her. I tell him about the fire.

'You suspect she had something to do with it?' he asks.

'I don't think so.' I twist my puzzle ring back and forth. 'I'm not sure.'

'Well, we need to be.' Palmer nods at King and she puts her notebook away. 'We'll follow up on what we have and see if we can trace the girl's family.' He explains I'll have to come to the station and make a full statement. 'When you're... when you're done here,' he says.

My statement versus Cassie's. She could say anything when she wakes. What if her version of events contradicts mine? I'm sure after the police have spoken to everyone they'll know I'm telling the truth.

'Can I see her?' I ask.

'Your mother?' says King. 'Of course.'

'No. Cassie.' After all she's put me through I still want to check she's okay. Wherever my daughter is, I hope she isn't thinking of me. I hope she doesn't fixate on me the way Cassie has fixated on her mother.

King looks at Palmer, in need of guidance. 'We can't allow that,' Palmer says. 'Sorry.'

* * *

Two hours later. My mother lies motionless in a hospital bed in a side room off the stroke ward. The last space she will ever inhabit. I occupy the armchair beside her, a lukewarm cup of tea in my hand from the café in the hospital foyer.

The steady hiss coming from the oxygen tank invades the room, making me long for the intrusive tick of Mum's carriage clock. Leaning forward, I free a tuft of her hair from the elastic strap of the oxygen mask.

The door opens and Stacey, the staff nurse on duty, comes in. She's much younger than Juliet, the nurse from earlier.

'Hi there,' she says in her chirpy Essex accent. She reminds me of Emma. Part of me wishes Emma were here. She would know the right things to say and do. She would help me through what is to come. 'How we getting on?' Stacey asks.

What she means is, are you ready to let your mother die yet?

'We're okay,' I say. 'Just need a little more time.'

Stacey smiles, revealing a set of ultra-bright, perfect teeth. 'No worries, my darling.' She checks the monitors surrounding the bed. 'Looks like Mum's all comfy.' Moving closer to me, she drops her voice. 'Hearing's the last sense to go so keep talking to her,' she says. On her way out, she points to the red button on the wall behind the bed and tells me to buzz for her whenever I feel ready.

When I first arrived at the ward, a consultant took me aside and explained the situation. Mum would not recover, he said, and the advanced directive in her medical records instructed she should not be put on a ventilator if no recovery was expected. According to him, the oxygen mask would soon not be enough to sustain Mum, and so it would best to remove it and let her slip away.

'How can I make that decision?' I said.

'You're not,' he replied. 'This is the course of action your mother would want us to take.'

'She'd have been okay if it wasn't for the fire.'

The consultant shrugged. 'The smoke hasn't helped, nor did the shock of being moved,' he said, 'but your mother was already very ill. Her chest infection wasn't responding to antibiotics, so it was only a matter of time.'

With Stacey gone, the room is still again. The sound of the oxygen filling Mum's mask is deafening. The consultant didn't know how long she'd survive without it. Could be days, could be hours. Once I press that red button and summon Stacey back in, an irreversible countdown will begin. I don't have any choice, yet it still feels like I'm making one. I'm not ready yet. We need more time, my mother and I.

She looks peaceful. Younger. I swear her skin is growing smoother before my eyes, her wrinkles disappearing. In contrast, I feel I'm ageing by the second. The past couple of hours have been a blur. After speaking to the consultant, I arranged for the hospital chaplain to come and visit Mum. I waited outside while he incanted over her body. That ritual was between Mum and her God.

Her hand twitches. I clasp it. 'I'm right here,' I say.

The swelling on my head has gone from painful to tender. Despite my exhaustion, I feel strangely like myself. As if I've landed back in my body after a twenty-year absence. The confrontation with Cassie was terrifying, but at the same time I needed to speak the truth aloud. To share what I have kept hidden for twenty years, even from myself.

'I'm here,' I say again.

Time is running out. There is so much I could tell my mother. I could tell her about my decision to keep my baby. I could tell her that the day before my move to Edinburgh, the director I'd auditioned for weeks before had phoned to offer me the part in his television series, but I turned him down. I could describe the remainder of my pregnancy. Those months in Edinburgh when I lived alone in a dingy one-bedroom tenement flat. Some days, the shock of my daughter moving inside me kept me bedridden, but most of the time the two of us maintained a polite distance that enabled me to function. I was a good hostess. I provided nutritious food, and I didn't drink or smoke. I took her on educational excursions to museums and galleries and introduced her to art-house cinema. By then I'd had confirmation of her sex, not that I needed it.

I tried not to connect with her, but some days I couldn't stop myself. On such days, we would visit Mothercare and play with the garish mobiles, and I would pick up baby-grows and press the soft, towelling fabric against my cheek. Such days tempted me to phone Fiona, my social worker, and call the adoption off. Each time we met, Fiona reminded me I could do this, even up to six weeks after my child's birth. I didn't though. I stuck to what I believed was right for both of us.

All this I could tell my mother. The news might ease her passage into the next world or it might distress her. She might die resenting me even more for my past decisions.

'Sorry, Mum,' I say.

I won't tell her because the secret is mine to keep, just as the decision not to keep my daughter was mine to make. I relinquished her for so many reasons. At my initial interview, I gave Fiona the obvious explanations she expected to hear – I can't afford a child yet; I want my child to have a better life; I'm not ready for motherhood. I didn't tell her I wanted to recover the choice that was taken from me, nor could I admit I didn't want to be a mother, not unless I could do so on my own terms.

My thought process made sense to me then. I did the best I could. I'm sure even Cassie's mother had her reasons for leaving a defenceless baby by a rubbish bin.

Most mothers do what they believe is best. Even mine.

'I know you were only trying to help.' I'll never understand how she could have put her faith before me, but I do know now that she made the decision she thought was right at the time.

I stand up and press the red button on the wall. 'The nurse will be in soon,' I say.

I lean over the bed and press my ear against her fragile chest. Her faint heartbeat passes into me.

PART IV

62

CASSIE

19 February, the following year

Dear Mother,

Who knows if this letter will reach you? It's the tenth one I've written, but Dr Costello refuses to send them. All I can do is keep trying. I can't post the letter myself and when I tried to pay one of my keyworkers to do it, he reported me.

Sorry about my handwriting. The only chance I get to write to you is during art class and I'm only allowed a thick felt tip. Do you know where I am? Quentin said he told you I'm in hospital, but I bet he didn't give you any details. He wants to keep us apart. They all do.

I'm at the Sunrise Women's Unit – a place for fresh starts, new dawns. So they say. It's the red-brick bungalow in the grounds of Five Oaks private hospital. My room overlooks the garden. None of the five oaks reside there. Too much risk of one of us jumping or finding a branch sturdy enough to hang from. All of us here are under constant surveillance. Nurses note what I eat at mealtimes and shadow me so I am never alone. Drives me nuts, but I've no chance of getting out unless I go along with it.

When I see Costello, I'll explain that you must have this letter soon so you can arrange to come and visit me for my birthday. I've always hated my birthday, but this year will be different. This year I'll have you. Can you believe I'll be twenty-one? If indeed February 26th is my birthday. The doctors who treated me in the neonatal unit guessed my mother had pushed me out earlier that day, but only you can say for certain.

We have a lot to discuss, you and I. Abandoning a baby is a crime and you are technically a criminal. Don't worry, I know some crimes are more complex than others.

Dr Costello told me the coroner's inquest into Grandma's death proved it was accidental. The right verdict, in my opinion. Nothing that happened was deliberate. I believe the fire department's investigation revealed that two cigarette butts on a plate beneath Len's bed had started the blaze. Len could be difficult, but even he wouldn't have done that on purpose.

I hope you didn't feel too terrible after Grandma died. I still remember Isobel's death so clearly. By the time I came downstairs from my room and realised she'd collapsed in the rockery, she must have been lying there for over an hour. I called an ambulance right away and sat with her in the back as we sped to hospital. She'd had a brain haemorrhage, which apparently wasn't unusual for someone with a late-stage brain tumour like hers. She never woke up. I stayed with her two whole days before she died. Slept in the chair next to her bed. I was with her when her lungs shut down and she choked to death, her eyes bulging.

Are you still in touch with Kegs by any chance? I'm glad he didn't get sacked for hiring me. To be fair, I did apply for the job using my real name. Yes, my references were fake and I spoke with a fake accent and made up a fake history, but I worked hard and always helped out when they needed extra staff. I miss Emma sometimes. Now that my blonde roots are coming through, all traces of her are vanishing. Sick of her as I was by the end, she was kind and fun and she meant well. Bless her heart. Now and again, when stuck in my room here, I wish she would appear at my door and offer me a drink from the tea trolley.

Sorry for knocking you out with the Virgin Mary by the way. I was upset and confused. As soon as I hit you, something broke inside me. I waited for you to wake up, but you didn't. I sat beside you for some time, thinking of ways to fix the bond between us. I even painted your nails, remembering how much fun we'd had the last time, but it didn't work. I began to believe your lies about you not being my mother. I picked up the scrapbook and stared at the photo of me as a baby. So ugly. No wonder my real mother hadn't wanted me.

I felt desperately empty. My mother had left me outside a pub after hours in winter. She'd wanted me to die, and I was never meant to be in the world. That's when I decided to leave. I must have been quite calm this time round because I ran the bath scalding hot, determined not to repeat the mistakes of the past. However, my scissors can't have been as sharp as I'd thought and anyway, you got to me before it was too late.

When I first woke up in hospital and discovered you'd saved me, I hated you for it. I didn't want to be alive. I didn't want to have to think about everything. Then I realised what your actions meant. You'd finally come back for me. Rescued me from death, in a way you weren't able to all those years ago. You were my mother and you loved me, and one day we would be together. I understood why you'd tried to deny it. You were scared by the enormity of it. I forgive you.

My session with Dr Costello starts soon. He's very gentle with me these days, but I know what he's up to. He wants me to renounce you. He says stuff like: I know you believe Grace is your mother, but I'm not convinced. *He asks what direct evidence I have to prove my thoughts.*

I always bring up the note, the one you wrote on blue, lined paper and tucked inside my blanket before leaving me by the rubbish bin. I'm sorry. G x. *The Harringtons gave it to me so I'd have a memento of my mother. I don't have it any more. I burnt it years ago, shortly before my first attempt at departing the world.*

Whenever I mention this note, Costello brings up the other women, the false trails I have followed in pursuit of you. Gina Lockhead, William's mum from the school playground. Gayle Robertson, my English Literature teacher. Something beginning with G. He asks if I could be mistaken about you, as I was about them.

No, I tell him. You left that note so I could find you. The early newspaper articles about my abandonment say you must have wanted to be traced. Why else would you have signed the note with the first letter of your name? The police never found you though, despite months of investigation and several public appeals. In later news articles, the police suggested my mother might have used a false initial to fool them. They never realised you left that clue for me, not them.

Dr Costello wants to know how I found you. I never go into details, but I did make the mistake of telling him about our first day out together at the Museum of Childhood – how sad you looked, how I sensed the big black hole inside you – and now he insists on discussing it in every session. He has a theory he keeps asking me to consider. Is it possible, he says, that you saw Grace Walker for the very first time in the museum that day? Is it possible that she was a stranger to you? That you were feeling lost and lonely and you saw her and heard her name and decided to choose her as your mother?

Nothing I can say to that. He doesn't understand and he never will.

At the end of our sessions, we do a guided meditation. I lie on the black chaise longue by the window while Dr Costello tells me how to breathe. Inhale for four, exhale for four. He tells me to go to my safe place, the one we have been constructing together during these relaxations. A tranquil glade in a shady wood. Gurgling stream. Daisies at my feet.

I don't go there. Instead, while he murmurs instructions, I travel back to my real haven. I've often imagined the months I spent in your womb. Looked at pictures of developing babies so I could recreate them in my head as though they were memories.

There I stay, happy and snug inside you. Bathed in warm, pink light. Floating at the end of our umbilical cord, like an astronaut tethered to a space shuttle.

You are my safe place, and I will never let you go. Your loving daughter,

Cassie xxxxxxxxxxxxxx

63

THEN

Friday 15 September, Royal Edinburgh Hospital

In our final session today, Simon made it very clear I had to complete my course of medication after my release. I assured him I had every intention of doing so. No way do I want to end up in that state again.

He asked if I was looking forward to getting back to normality. I nodded, but dread crept up on me. What if I left this place only to find her waiting? For a moment, I considered telling Simon the whole story, but I feared talking about her would only make her more real.

She won't be waiting. I know that. She will be with her foster mother until her new mother can legally claim her.

Three days before my episode, I visited Fiona Braithwaite at her office near Leith Walk to sign the relinquishment papers. Now that six weeks had passed since the birth, I could officially give my permission for the adoption process to start. Despite the warm day I wore a baggy sweatshirt, conscious of the soft flesh and loose skin that dieting had not yet shifted from my middle.

Fiona talked me through the paperwork, as helpful and supportive as she had been throughout the whole adoption process. After the birth, she'd respected my wish not to visit my daughter at her foster placement. She'd understood my need for distance.

Before I signed the documents, Fiona told me a suitable couple had been found for my daughter. University-educated – the wife worked in the arts, the husband in finance. I agreed they sounded perfect.

My pen hovered over the papers. How was my daughter? I asked Fiona. Was she still healthy? Any problems? I'd asked her these questions many times and once again she reassured me my daughter was thriving.

The first time I met Fiona, I expected her to bring up my failed termination. I'd imagined we would have to discuss it and decide what to tell the adoptive parents. When she didn't mention it, I found myself unable to broach the subject. I'd assumed that at some point she would contact my consultant or midwife and ask for my medical history. Or that they would contact her. As time passed, I realised this hadn't happened and possibly never would. I made a pact with myself – if my daughter was born with any complications due to the unsuccessful termination, I would raise her myself. If she was born healthy, I would continue with the adoption and tell Fiona then.

But as I scrawled my signature in the appropriate places, I knew I wouldn't speak of it. Surely it would be better for my daughter and I to pretend it never happened? To wipe it from our pasts?

I held myself together well, but as soon as I left Fiona's office and stood on Leith Walk, I had the unsettling impression I'd entered a parallel universe. That another me had refused to sign the papers and was on her way to reclaim her daughter. A powerful feeling gripped me. A terrible certainty that this other me was the real version, whereas I was just a ghost.

64

GRACE

March

A warm spring day. Blue sky unblemished by clouds and a gentle breeze that smells like the start of something new. I make my way down Forrest Road and into the University of Edinburgh's George Square campus, past the grand domed building of McEwan Hall. I head for George Square. The garden at the centre of it appears unchanged, but modern buildings have sprung up between the Georgian terraces.

We used to come here, she and I. To wander round the square, to sit outside the library amongst the groups of chattering students. I wanted her to soak up the atmosphere of learning. How strange that this is where we will meet again.

Reaching into the back pocket of my jeans, I pull out her photograph and study it. Fascinated by the flashes of me in her dark, shoulder-length hair and her height. Her wide, green eyes display none of her father's coldness.

Her name is Anna. A name I didn't give her, and one I'm not used to yet.

After putting the picture away, I enter the gardens and pick a bench with a clear view of the three-storey modern building at 50 George

Square. Knots of students lounge on the grass around me, taking advantage of the good weather.

I remove my black leather jacket and smooth out the creases in my khaki silk shirt; don't want to turn up looking scruffy. Not much I can do with my hair though. After a few months of growth, it has reached that awkward in-between stage, forcing me to tuck it behind my ears.

I check my watch. Nearly ten-thirty. Ages yet until I see her, but I couldn't bear to wait in my hotel room. This morning, I've already walked along the Royal Mile, up the Bridges and into Southside in an effort to keep my nerves under control.

My walk took me past my old flat. It looked much the same from the outside, apart from the new windows. After getting out of hospital, I only lived there another two weeks. I was supposed to stay in Edinburgh and attend an outpatient clinic, but I wanted to escape the city as soon as possible. Too many reminders of my daughter. I moved north to Perth, making sure Fiona Braithwaite had my contact details for when the adoptive parents made their court application in two months' time. At that point, there would be more papers for me to sign, and after that, everything would be over. In Perth, I rented a cheap bedsit overlooking the River Tay and spent the next nine weeks working as a temp for Scottish Hydro. Long days filled with filing and data entry and evenings spent reading travel books about South East Asia and plotting my escape. I phoned Mum once a week, still pretending to be in Germany and promising to visit when the tour ended.

I existed in a limbo, trying not to think about my daughter and where she might be. Honing the skills of denial that would keep her from me for so long.

* * *

Half an hour passes. In my mind, I rehearse possible ways of approaching Anna. A pointless exercise. I am only here to look.

I buy a green tea from a nearby kiosk and take it back to my bench. I search the faces of the students sprawled on the grass, just in case she has skipped her tutorial. Or come out early, like she did almost two weeks before her due date, sending me rushing to hospital. During the agonising labour, I wondered if I'd caused her premature arrival? If she'd sensed my need to be free of her? Afterwards, I asked the midwife several times if my daughter would be okay. The midwife reassured me she was breathing on her own. No cause for alarm.

I can't resist taking her picture out again for another look. I'm sure there is something of Mum in her. Her nose perhaps? After Mum's funeral, I moved from London to Brentham and lived in her house while I finished packing it up. I had no desire to return to the Capital School of English. I had some savings to live off and my inheritance would pay back any debts. I suppose staying in the house was a way of being close to Mum. I hired a small storage unit on a nearby industrial estate. That way, I could still hold on to some of my past for as long as I needed to.

Sorting through Mum's possessions brought back memories not just of her but also of Emma. The boxes we'd packed together, the smears of her mascara on one of Mum's pillows. I closed all the curtains in the house at night, as if she might still be out there, spying on me.

At first, I wasn't sure what to do about Cassie. Shortly after I'd given the police my statement, PC King informed me Cassie had a history of mental health issues and obsessive behaviour. I couldn't help feeling sympathy for the girl, despite everything she'd put me through. The investigation into the fire proved she'd acted quickly and competently to protect Mum's life. I know I saw goodness in Emma, so it had to exist in Cassie too. There was still a chance for her, if she could take it. Mum would have wanted that.

When I decided not to give evidence against Cassie, PC King passed on a letter from Cassie's adoptive father, who thanked me for my understanding. He said he believed the recent death of his wife had prompted Cassie to fixate on me. He assured me Cassie would be in hospital for some time and wouldn't bother me again. That doesn't stop me looking over my shoulder when walking through town. That doesn't prevent me from waking in the middle of the night soaked in sweat.

A girl with long dark hair claims a nearby bench, and I lean forward for a closer look. She is not my daughter. I think of Cassie, watching me for all those months. I still don't know where she found me, but I have considered why she chose me. The old me might have viewed her obsession as another punishment. Retribution for the past. Now I wonder if the secret I'd hidden for so long used Cassie as a path to liberation? Maybe we'd needed each other.

* * *

It's 11.40 a.m. Not long to go. My legs jiggle with nerves. I could go for another walk but can't risk missing her. Earlier, during my visit to the Royal Mile, I passed the entrance to one of the dark passageways leading off it. An original Old Town close. I don't remember which one I ended up in when I had my episode. I only know the police found me there, screaming and tearing at myself.

I peered into the passageway but felt no compulsion to enter it. Nor did I feel any fear. That part of my past is over. My recent counselling sessions, courtesy of a therapist in Brentham called Eileen, have helped me come to terms with that day and put it in context. According to Eileen, all women possess the power both to create and destroy, a duality I couldn't comprehend at the time.

A duality my mother would never have accepted. After she died, amongst the rubble of my grief, I found an unexpected release. The shame I'd carried around with me for years began to shrink. Having forgiven my mother, I decided to forgive myself.

My stomach flutters, reminding me of the first time my daughter moved inside me, that night in Dan and Stella's bedroom. The urge for a cigarette takes hold, but I gave up a month ago. I fiddle with my puzzle ring in an attempt to distract myself. When this fails, I reach into my handbag and pull out a creased white envelope. Inside is the letter Anna sent me. No need to read it again; I know it off by heart.

After Mum's death, I couldn't stop thinking about my daughter. Wondering if my absence from her life had left her as damaged as Cassie.

With Fiona Braithwaite's help, I contacted Adoption Search Services, an agency that, for a fee, would find my daughter and act as an intermediary between us. Before the process could begin, I had to obtain a replacement birth certificate. I don't remember what happened to the original. Whether I lost it by accident or on purpose.

While waiting to hear from the agency, I tried to compose a letter for them to give to my daughter. In the numerous drafts, I asked how she was doing. Was she happy? Settled? I assured her I didn't wish to disrupt her life. Unless she wanted me to. Unless my actions had caused issues only I could resolve.

When it came to explaining why I gave her up, my writing stalled. I didn't want to tell her my reasons in a letter. Did that mean I should ask for us to meet? If she was desperate to find and meet me, surely she would have done so by now? If she had a copy of her birth certificate with my name on it, she could have traced me as I was trying to trace her. Then again, she might be too angry to initiate contact.

And what if we met and she asked about her father? Shortly after Mum's funeral, I emailed Dan and told him the truth about our daughter. I informed him of my intention to contact her and asked if he wanted to be involved, should she wish to meet her birth parents.

His swift reply made his feelings clear:

> While I'm sorry to hear what happened to you, I can't be part of this. In my mind, that child never happened, and I can't change the way I feel about it. I have the family I want and beg you to keep me out of this.

I agreed. Protecting our daughter from his lack of interest was the least I could do.

***

Just before noon, the first students stream out of 50 George Square. I exit the park and hurry towards the main doors of the building, eyes scanning the bodies scattering to my left and right. What if she did skive off her tutorial? What if she's sick or hungover? There are so many reasons why she might not be here, despite my best efforts to pinpoint a time and place. My online research identified 50 George Square as the location for the history department. I managed to access a student forum showing the timetable for her subject. Lectures Monday and Wednesday and tutorials on Thursday.

Chatter fills the air around me. More students file out, but I can't see Anna anywhere. A bad omen. I shouldn't be here. The fish hook niggles at my guts. I look up, wary it might trick me again, but there she is. My daughter. Tight black jeans encase her long legs. Her green bomber jacket is open, revealing a black T-shirt. My lips part, her name ready on my tongue, but the envelope in my hand stops me just in time. Before I could finish a satisfactory version of my letter, Sandra from the agency phoned me. My daughter had replied to their initial contact and had written me a letter that Sandra promised to send on immediately.

It arrived the next day by special delivery. Two pages of typed A4.

> Dear Grace. Thank you for contacting me. I've often wondered if you would one day. I was five years old when Mum and Dad told me I was adopted, so it's something I've known for a long time.

Mum and Dad. My tears started then and continued as I read on.

> My first name is Anna and my middle name is Lily.

Lily. The name I gave her. The one on her birth certificate. She said she'd always believed I had her best interests at heart when I gave her up.

> Mum and Dad said you must have loved me a lot to be able to go through with it.

She insisted that despite having some difficult moments, she didn't hate me or have any negative feelings towards me.

That's why I think it's best for me not to know any more about the past or for us to meet. I hope you understand. My family is wonderful and that's more than enough for me.

Relief overwhelmed me. I hadn't ruined her life. Yet I found myself fighting for breath, winded by a rejection I hadn't allowed myself to anticipate.

My breathing is shallow now as she stands near me, chatting to a group of friends. She joins them in hysterical laughter over some comment their tutor made.

Her letter gave me a few details to cling to. She was in the second year of a history degree and hoped to go into academia. She had a boyfriend. She was happy. She looked happy in the photograph she'd enclosed with the letter. Happy and healthy. That night, while not sleeping, I lay it on the pillow beside me. The next morning, I contacted Sandra and asked her to tell Anna I was grateful for her letter and would respect her wishes for no further contact.

Anna and her friends amble away. I follow them down a set of steps and onto a street of tenement buildings that house various university departments. They stop, and after a round of hugs the group splits apart, leaving Anna still talking to a girl in a green suede coat.

Her letter should have been the end of it, but once I had her name and photograph, I couldn't get her out of my head. Examining the picture for the hundredth time, I recognised the sooty stonework of the building in the background and the blue plaque attached to it. Squinting, I could just make out the white lettering of the logo for the University of Edinburgh.

My daughter might have grown up in Edinburgh, I reasoned, but that didn't mean she would be at university there. Unable to help myself, I did an Internet search:

Anna Edinburgh University Facebook.

I clicked on the first result:

Anna Edinburgh Profiles Facebook.

A long list of names accompanied by thumbnail pictures appeared. I trawled through the first page with no luck, but halfway down the second page I found her.

Anna Mackenzie, The University of Edinburgh.

I told myself to stop there, but of course I didn't. I knew her name and where she studied and what she looked like. I convinced myself I needed to see her. Just once to confirm her happiness and to check she was telling me the truth. As the days passed, I tried to convince myself she'd sent the photograph on purpose, knowing it contained a clue to her whereabouts. What if she wanted to be found?

Anna and the girl hug once more. When they part, my daughter and I continue down the street together.

* * *

She takes me to a café on South College Street. I queue behind her, noticing the scuff marks on her grey backpack and the Diesel tag on the back pocket of her jeans. She orders a skinny latte in a neutral, private school accent.

'Anything to eat?' the waitress asks.

'I'll try one of the apple muffins, please,' replies Anna.

Hardly a proper lunch, I want to say. Have something more substantial. The waitress gives her a wooden spoon painted with the number six, and Anna carries it away. I ask for a green sencha tea and take my numbered spoon to the back of the café.

A long bench runs along an exposed stone wall with individual tables in front of it. I claim the table next to Anna before anyone else can. As I sit down, she looks up from her phone and my heart stalls. What if she recognises me? If she knows my full name, she could have spent hours scrutinising numerous Grace Walkers online, myself included.

She looks away again. Only her backpack separates us on the bench. I keep very still, hardly daring to breathe, as though she is a rare animal in the wild that could bolt at any moment.

A waiter in a Ramones T-shirt brings her order over. 'Thanks,' she says, laying her phone on the table, 'that looks lovely.'

A moment later, the same waiter returns with my tea. The pot wobbles as I pour. I peek at Anna's side profile. She definitely has my mother's long, straight nose and a hint of Dan in her high cheekbones.

I want to talk to her. Nothing dangerous, just a casual exchange between strangers in a café. I could ask her what the coffee is like here and what other cafés in the city she could recommend.

She sips her latte and nibbles the outer rim of the muffin. Gazes at the wall opposite us. Is she thinking of me? Do I descend on her during quiet moments? I hope so. I hope not.

Her phone beeps. She picks it up, glances at the message on the screen and launches into a reply. I admire her long, elegant fingers, her dextrous thumbs. Maybe she plays the piano, or paints, or cooks? What talents lie in her strong, young hands? Jealousy hits me at the thought of Mrs Mackenzie witnessing each stage of their growth.

But I kissed her first. The heat of her tiny palms against my lips, the marvel of her minuscule fingernails. Her first kiss came from me, and I want to tell her that. I need to tell her that.

She tucks her hair behind her left ear, revealing a diamond stud high up in the cartilage. I could stare at her for hours. This is why I never visited her after the birth. I knew if I got too close I would have surrendered myself to her for good.

Now she's swiping through photographs. Shifting position, I glance sideways at her phone. My heart leaps at a shot of her standing beside the famous twisted tree roots in Angkor Wat. There she is again, on a beach this time, her arms around an earnest-looking, athletic young man. Her boyfriend?

An alternative future opens up. One in which my daughter and I know each other and talk about travelling, maybe even go away together. Why not? I don't have to take the assistant director of studies job recently offered to me by a school in Buenos Aires. I could stay here, and the two of us could start again.

Yet my life abroad wouldn't have happened if I'd kept her. All the countries I've lived in, the people I've met, the adventures I've had – it's impossible to imagine myself without these experiences.

I am the real woman, and the mother I might have been is the ghost.

'Would you mind keeping an eye on my bag for a minute?' she says.

I nod, too shocked at this direct contact to reply. She squeezes between our two tables, nudging my teapot as she passes.

'Sorry,' she says.

'You have nothing to be sorry for,' I whisper, but she is already on the other side of the café, opening the door to the toilets.

Get up and leave now. Before it's too late.

I pull my puzzle ring off my finger and, making sure no one is watching, I unzip Anna's bag and drop it inside.

Get up and leave. Now.

The toilet door opens again, and she is back.

'Thanks,' she says. Her phone beeps again, and she beams at the new message. The boyfriend perhaps?

I want to tell her who I am. I want to claim ownership of her. I have so much to share, so much she needs to know. She thinks she doesn't need me, but she does.

She grins as she types a reply into her phone.

If I reveal myself, she'll want to know why I gave her up. I would either have to lie and risk the truth festering between us or tell her everything and risk her hating me for her narrow escape. What if she never forgives me?

And there is another truth, one I could never share. I'm glad my daughter is alive, but I sometimes wish I hadn't continued with the pregnancy. Two contradictory ideas I may never reconcile. I can't help wondering how my life might have turned out if I'd made a different decision twenty years ago. If I'd put myself first.

Not having a child can change your life as much as having one. Nobody tells you that.

She laughs aloud at what appears on her phone.

If I drop uninvited into her world now, everything will change. This carefree girl will be saddled with the past, and she will never be the same again.

Still giggling, she slips on her jacket. I wrap my hands around my cup to stop me reaching out for her. She lifts up her backpack and manoeuvres between the tables.

This is it. She is leaving. 'Excuse me,' I say.

She looks at me – quizzical, expectant. 'The... your... your bag is undone,' I say.

'Oops. Thanks.' She closes the zip and gifts me a wide smile before walking away.

And at last, I let her go.

ACKNOWLEDGMENTS

Huge gratitude to the brilliant team at Boldwood Books for republishing *Mother's Day*. It has been a joy to put this story in such safe hands and to see it have a new life! Special thanks to my lovely editor, Rachel Faulkner-Willcocks, for helping me to see it with fresh eyes.

As always, I'm hugely grateful to my agent, Charlie Brotherstone. He championed this story and its subject matter from the start, and I am indeed lucky to have his continuing support and guidance.

More people helped with research than I have space to mention here. To those I've missed, my apologies and heartfelt thanks. To the following, thanks for your expertise: Dr Peter Copp, Dr Mark Flynn and Dr Victoria Barker. Susan Stevenson, Philip Weir and everyone at BSC Edinburgh. Laura Stephenson, Michael Brown, Stephen Grant and Andrew Palmer-Smith.

I'd also like to thank the Creative Writing lecturers at The University of Edinburgh, past and present. They played a big part in my writing journey, as did the fellow writers I studied with there. I must also mention Simon Willoughby Booth and all the DART team members for encouraging me in the early days and for letting me scribble away in my lunch hours undisturbed.

Claire Wingfield... your advice on author marketing was much appreciated. Liz Barling... your insightful readings of early drafts and your generous cheerleading were crucial. Lesley Glaister... couldn't have done it without you. Thanks for your numerous readings and for those structural light bulb moments! I am also indebted to Claire Baldwin for her editorial work along the way.

Thanks must also go to the original publisher of this novel, Legend

Press, and to my editor there, Lauren Parsons, who believed in the story and was willing to take a chance on it.

Not everyone who saw me start this book is here to read it: Anne Melville, who opened her home and heart to me whenever I needed it. Helen Lamb, my first writing mentor and good friend, who backed me from the start and whose wisdom and straight talking I will miss forever.

And of course, my beautiful mum, who didn't get to hold this book in her hands but who will be with me every time I hold it in mine.

Huge thanks to my dad, for everything, and to Susan, Charly and Billy for all the love and encouragement.

Finally, Susie and Mary. Without your love and support, this novel would not exist. Thank you for making it possible for me to write it.

ABOUT THE AUTHOR

T.J. Emerson's debut psychological thriller was published by Legend Press and received brilliant reviews. Her short stories and features have been widely published in anthologies and magazines, and she works as a literary consultant and writing tutor. She lives in Scotland.

Sign up to T J Emerson's mailing list for news, competitions and updates on future books.

Visit T.J. Emerson's Website: www.traceyemerson.com

Follow T.J. Emerson on social media here:

facebook.com/TJEmersonAuthor
x.com/TraceyJEmerson
instagram.com/tjemersonwrites

ALSO BY T.J. EMERSON

The Perfect Holiday

The Ideal Man

Mother's Day

Milton Keynes UK
Ingram Content Group UK Ltd.
UKHW040419111123
432320UK00002B/6

9 781785 136993